"Just go away ~~and forget you ever met~~ me,"

Erica said in a low, intense voice.

"Can you forget *me* that easily?" Mike challenged her. He moved closer, gazing deeply into her eyes.

"We had fun together, but it's over now," she answered miserably. "As you can see—" she gestured toward little Nicky "—I have a prior commitment."

"What does your son have to do with it?" Mike said. "Unless you also have a husband you haven't told me about...."

"She doesn't have one of those," four-year-old Nicky unexpectedly piped up. "My daddy went to heaven." He continued watching the two grown-ups with obvious fascination.

And Erica's nerves were so jangled, she could only gasp at the boy's next words.

"Would you," he asked Mike, "like to be my new daddy?"

Dear Reader,

Welcome to Silhouette **Special Edition**...welcome to romance. March has six wonderful books in store for you that are guaranteed to become some of your all-time favorites!

Our THAT SPECIAL WOMAN! title for March is *Sisters* by Penny Richards. A dramatic and emotional love story, this book about family and the special relationship between a mother and daughter is one you won't want to miss!

Also in March, it's time to meet another of the irresistible Adams men in the new series by Sherryl Woods, AND BABY MAKES THREE, which continues with *The Rancher and His Unexpected Daughter*. And continuing this month is Pamela Toth's newest miniseries, BUCKLES AND BRONCOS. In *Buchanan's Baby,* a cowboy is hearing wedding bells and the call of fatherhood. Rounding out the month are *For Love of Her Child,* a touching and emotional story from Tracy Sinclair, Diana Whitney's *The Reformer,* the next tale in her THE BLACKTHORN BROTHERHOOD series, and *Playing Daddy* by Lorraine Carroll.

These books are sure to make the month of March an exciting and unforgettable one! I hope you enjoy these books, and all the stories to come!

Sincerely,

Tara Gavin
Senior Editor

Please address questions and book requests to:
Silhouette Reader Service
U.S.: 3010 Walden Ave., P.O. Box 1325, Buffalo, NY 14269
Canadian: P.O. Box 609, Fort Erie, Ont. L2A 5X3

TRACY SINCLAIR

FOR LOVE OF HER CHILD

Published by Silhouette Books
America's Publisher of Contemporary Romance

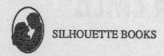 SILHOUETTE BOOKS

ISBN 0-373-24018-X

FOR LOVE OF HER CHILD

Books by Tracy Sinclair

TRACY SINCLAIR,

author of more than forty Silhouette novels, also contributes to various magazines and newspapers. An extensive traveler and a dedicated volunteer worker, this California resident has accumulated countless fascinating experiences, settings and acquaintances to draw on in plotting her romances.

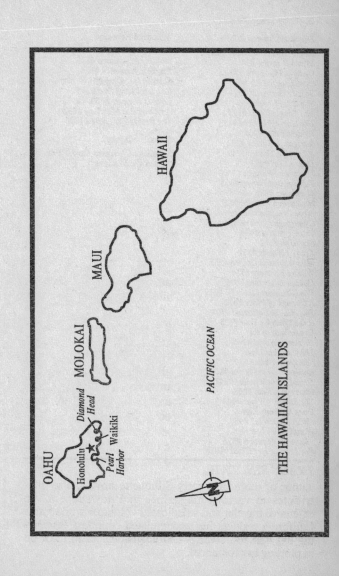

THE HAWAIIAN ISLANDS

Chapter One

Erica Barclay fell for Michael Smith on a beach in Honolulu. Actually she fell *over* him—falling in love with Mike came later.

She was taking her nightly run along the sand when the quarter moon went behind a scudding cloud. The resulting darkness turned the familiar place slightly forbidding. The only light came from the phosphorus-tipped waves that fidgeted restlessly before rushing in to foam along the shore.

Erica was looking up at the sky to gauge the possibility of a rainsquall, when she tripped over a large solid mass and fell on top of it. Panic gripped her as she realized it was a body—still warm! Her panic turned to abject terror when strong arms wrapped around her and rolled her over onto her back.

A scream was trapped in her throat at the realization that the body was not only alive, it belonged to a very powerful man. His rock solid chest was digging into her, and long muscular legs were tangled with hers.

The moon reappeared, illuminating Erica's face, but leaving his shadowed. She had only an impression of hawk-like features and high cheekbones, a rugged face to go with the powerful body that pinned her to the sand.

Erica fought back her apprehension and went on the offensive. "Let me up this instant or I'll scream my head off," she said sharply.

"I don't think anybody would hear you."

His voice was low and cultured, reassuring her somewhat—although "gentlemen" assaulted women, too. She was relieved when he rolled over onto his side, freeing her. Erica scrambled quickly to her feet, backing away as he rose from the sand, towering to over six feet of lean sinew and muscle.

"You shouldn't be on a deserted beach at this hour," he said disapprovingly. "Your travel agent should have warned you that even Paradise has a dark side."

"I'm not a tourist. I live just up the beach, and I always jog at this time of night. It isn't usually this deserted."

"It's still not a good idea." He peered in the direction she'd come from. "You live near here? There are only hotels up there."

"I live in one of them." She wasn't about to tell him which one. "What are *you* doing out here all alone?"

"Enjoying the solitude. It's hard to come by in Honolulu."

"I'm sorry I spoiled it for you."

"Don't go!" he said as she turned away. "I was getting tired of my own company." His grin was a gleam of white in the dim light. "May I buy you a drink?"

"No thanks, I have to get back."

"I'll walk you home."

"That won't be necessary."

"You never know. The next man you trip over might not let you go as easily." He fell into step beside her.

"I'm sorry about that. It got so dark all of a sudden, and of course I wasn't expecting anybody to be there. For one terrible minute I thought I'd fallen over a dead body."

"You didn't seem all that delighted when you discovered I was alive." He chuckled.

Erica had a vivid recollection of his arms closing around her and their bodies making intimate contact. It was something she hadn't experienced in a long time, but she knew this was no ordinary man—physically, anyway.

Her only previous experience had been with Jordan, who was proud of his reputation as a stud. But she suspected this man would make Jordan look like an amateur. Without even trying, he'd jolted her into an awareness of herself as a woman—a feeling she didn't welcome.

"I didn't mean to frighten you," he said, obviously not realizing that she was experiencing a quite different emotion. "I really wasn't making a pass. When you landed on top of me it was just reflex action to roll over and pin you down."

Erica was glad the darkness hid the warmth in her cheeks. "Luckily no harm was done," she said hurriedly. "It was just an unfortunate accident."

"I prefer to think we were destined to meet."

They'd reached the first of a string of hotels where the floodlit terrace illuminated the beach. His interest quickened when he got his first clear look at her exquisite face, dominated by deep blue eyes fringed with sooty lashes that matched the long black hair fluttering around her shoulders. His discreet gaze also took note of her slender figure and long, slim legs.

"After fate went to all that trouble, we really should get acquainted," he said.

"I don't believe in fate," she answered tersely.

"Okay, then call it a lucky coincidence." His smile showed even white teeth. "Whatever it was, I'm grateful."

Erica stared at him appraisingly. That deep tan, slightly shaggy hair and cutoff jeans were the mark of a typical beach bum whose only interest was surfing by day and womanizing at night. He had the physique for it, she thought cynically. That splendid body would make him good at both sports.

"Do I pass inspection?" He grinned.

She glanced away in embarrassment, as though he'd read her thoughts. "Does it matter? I don't think you're insecure enough to care, and I have to go now."

"You can't leave me dangling. I'll wonder forever after what I did to make such a bad impression."

"You're just assuming that. I didn't say you did."

"Then have a drink with me," he coaxed. "I'm really quite harmless. And even if I wasn't, there are lots of people around."

The small tables on the terrace were filled with hotel guests having a drink or a snack, and the beach was dotted with more vacationers. Still, Erica hesitated. Not because of any potential danger from him. For some inexplicable reason, she genuinely wanted to continue their innocent flirtation. *That* was the threat.

"I don't even know your name," she protested.

"That's easily rectified." He hesitated imperceptibly before saying, "It's Smith—Mike Smith."

She supplied her own name reluctantly, because to refuse would be awkward. "Erica Barclay."

He pulled out a chair for her at one of the tables, taking it for granted that she'd accepted his invitation. A waiter came scurrying over to take their orders. By then it was too late, so Erica decided to relax and enjoy herself.

"This evening has taken a definite turn for the better," Mike declared, gazing at her across the table.

She smiled. "Your problems can't be too great if they're solved simply by meeting somebody new."

"I don't really have any problems."

He didn't look as though he did. Mike seemed to have it all, looks, charm, poise. *But you never could tell about people,* she thought. "Then why were you sitting all alone on the beach?" she asked.

"I was indulging in a little intensive soul-searching."

"Because of a crisis in your life? I don't mean to pry, but sometimes it helps to talk things out with a stranger. You can be totally honest, since you know you'll never see the person again."

"I hope that isn't true in your case."

"I intend to watch where I'm going the next time I jog," she said lightly.

"You don't quite trust me, do you? I suppose that's wise. A woman as beautiful as you *should* be careful. I only hope you'll give me a chance to prove I don't usually get physical with women I've never met."

"How long do you have to know them?" she asked mischievously.

"I'm in trouble any way I answer that." He laughed.

"Not really. No one would ever mistake you for a monk."

"Appearances are deceiving. I might look entirely different in a cassock." He had unusual hazel eyes. They were more golden than green in the bright light. The eyes of a deceptively mild, stalking tiger.

"I'll bet the tourists really love that line," Erica said dryly.

His T-shirt strained over his impressive chest as he lounged in his chair and hooked one arm around the back, looking at her speculatively. "You don't seem to have a very high opinion of men. It isn't fair to judge all of us because of one bad experience."

"What makes you think I had a bad experience?"

"That's fairly obvious. He couldn't have walked out on you. What happened? Did he come on too strong?"

"We were talking about *you*," Erica said firmly. "You're the one who was wrestling with something weighty. Your conscience?"

"Nothing that interesting. I was thinking about what my mother and dad said at dinner tonight. They didn't come right out and ask when I'm going to get married, but the inference was there." He smiled wryly. "I suppose all parents want their children to settle down."

"Since you obviously don't agree, it would be foolish to rush into anything."

"It isn't that I'm opposed to marriage," he said carefully.

"As long as it's somebody else taking the plunge," she joked.

"That's not true," he protested. "I'd like to get married and have children. I love kids. I think I'd be a good father."

"You never know," Erica murmured. Long lashes hid her eyes as she stared down at her drink.

"I don't have any doubt about that. It's finding somebody I want to spend the rest of my life with that's the problem."

"I can't believe you haven't met a lot of willing women."

"You're talking about sex," he said bluntly. "I'm looking for love."

"Ah, love." Erica's voice was mocking. "If you find it exists, let me know."

His gaze wandered over her lovely face. "I'm sorry," he said gently. "You must have been hurt very badly."

"Not at all. I'm simply a bit of a skeptic. The statistics on divorce seem to prove that love is just wishful thinking."

"Or else that people give up too easily. My sister has been married for seven years, and my parents are about to celebrate one of the big anniversaries. I'm sure they had their share of arguments through the years, but they didn't split up at the first sign of trouble."

"Do your parents live in Honolulu?" Erica was glad of an opportunity to change the subject.

"Yes, my family has been here for generations. My sister and I were both born in the Islands. How about you?"

"I'm not a native. I moved here four years ago."

"Where are you from?"

"I...I'm from Philadelphia." She picked up her glass and took a big gulp. Why did the lie still fluster her after all this time?

Mike's eyes narrowed at her hesitation and subsequent nervousness, but he decided she still had reservations about him. "The climate here must be a great relief after those eastern snows. I had to go to New York once in winter. It isn't a memory I cherish."

"There are compensations, especially at Christmastime. The tree in Rockefeller Center is magical, and the ice skaters make everything seem so festive."

"You're evidently quite familiar with New York City," he remarked casually.

Erica was silent for a heartbeat. She was right to be wary of this man. He had a way of getting under her guard. "New York is only a short train ride from Philadelphia," she said. "I used to visit often to go to the theater and shop. There's no place like it."

"I suppose so. Personally, I prefer the sun."

"I can tell that by your tan. Do you spend all your time on the beach looking for a wife?"

"You persist in misjudging me. I happen to be a very hard worker."

"What do you do?"

"I'm a jobber."

"Forgive my ignorance, but I don't know what that is."

"I buy and sell job lots of sugar and pineapple, things like that," he said vaguely. "How about you?" he continued before she could question him further. "What do you do?"

"I'm the head of housekeeping at the—at one of the big hotels."

"You don't have to be afraid to tell me where you work," Mike said quietly. "I realize our meeting was unconventional, but I'm really a solid citizen. I hope you'll go out with me one night, but if the answer is no, I won't try to track you down and make a nuisance of myself."

"It isn't that," she murmured.

His gaze sharpened. "Are you married? Is that the problem?"

"No, nothing like that."

"Engaged? In a relationship?" he persisted.

"No, I'm strictly a loner." Her mouth twisted in the semblance of a smile.

"It has to be by choice," he said in a deepened voice.

"It is." She pushed her glass away. "I really have to get back."

"Don't go." He covered her hand with his, but lightly. It wasn't a restraint. "I won't ask any more personal questions."

"I don't have anything to hide," she said quickly. "I'm just a rather private person."

"Okay, we'll talk about the weather. That's a safe subject, although rather dull."

"Especially since the weather is always about the same here. If you work full-time, how did you get such a golden tan?"

"It's hard to avoid when you live in the Islands. I swim after work, and sail and water-ski when I have time. What do you like to do on the weekends, if that isn't too personal?"

Wouldn't he be surprised if he knew? "I have to work sometimes," she said evasively.

"Then you must get time off during the week. That isn't so bad. Every day is Sunday in Hawaii."

"Not for the hired help. Although, I can't complain. I have a very good job."

"I'm not sure I know what the head of housekeeping does."

"I'm the one you complain to if you don't have enough towels, or you didn't get a chocolate on your pillow. Or even if you're just annoyed because your room is so expensive." She smiled. "I have broad shoulders."

His gaze was drawn to her slim body. "Being yelled at by a bunch of clods doesn't sound like much fun."

"Actually the guests are usually quite nice. It's up to me to see that they don't have anything to complain about."

"You must have some help."

"Yes, I have a large staff of housekeepers who report to me."

Mike examined her thoughtfully. "You're quite young to have a job with so much responsibility. Did you go to one of those hotel schools?"

"No." Erica pushed back her chair and stood. "I really must get back. Thank you for the drink," she said formally.

"I stepped over the line again, didn't I?" Mike asked ruefully.

"It isn't that. Somebody is expecting me. I said I'd only be gone for half an hour." She glanced at her watch and gasped. "Where did the time go?"

"That means you weren't totally bored." He smiled engagingly. "Will you have dinner with me tomorrow night?"

"I really—"

"We can meet somewhere," he cut in. "And afterward I'll put you in a cab and send you home. How much safer can you be than that?"

She looked up into his handsome face. "I'm sure that's not your usual kind of date. Why would you want to bother with me? And don't tell me it's because I'm beautiful and you were attracted to me from the minute you saw me. Please be honest.''

"You *are* beautiful, and any man would find you desirable," he answered slowly. "That was my first impression when I got a good look at you. I still feel that way, but there's more to it. You're the first woman I can talk to without going through the usual stylized mating ritual." A grin dispelled the serious look on his face. "I don't have to wonder whether it will be your place or mine, because I know it won't be either one. Does that answer your question?''

Erica laughed. "Yes, although it isn't very flattering. You've had it for the moment with compliant women. Now all you want to do is have a quiet dinner with someone who won't expect you to perform when you take her home.''

"I could be persuaded to change my mind, but not on a first date," he joked. "How about it?''

Erica fought a brief battle with herself. Mike was a charming man, and she hadn't been out on a date in ages. It was only one dinner. What would it hurt?

"I'll let you choose the restaurant," he coaxed.

She took a deep breath. "All right, I'll meet you, but you pick the place.''

"How about The Silver Dolphin at eight? Will that give you enough time? I don't know when you get off work.''

Erica made a rapid calculation. "Eight-thirty would be better.''

"You've got it." He took both of her hands. "I'm looking forward to seeing you again.''

His anticipation couldn't compare to hers, she thought as she gazed into his golden eyes. "I won't disappoint you," she said softly.

"I doubt if you could," Mike murmured, watching her slight figure until it disappeared down the beach.

Erica was full of apologies when she rushed into the living room of her small apartment in the Haialua Hotel. "I'm so sorry, Susie!'' she told her friend. ''I had no idea it was this late.''

Susie Tarapula was a plump older woman with a broad, placid face. She was watching television and eating popcorn. ''I was getting a little worried, because you're usually back so promptly. But as long as you're okay, no problem. Where did you go?''

''It's a long story. Is Nicky all right?''

''Sleeping like a little lamb.''

''That's good. Well, I won't keep you any longer. Thanks again for sitting with Nicky.''

''Any time.'' Susie settled back on the couch with the bowl of popcorn. ''Where were you tonight? You couldn't have been jogging all this time.'' She eyed Erica's trim figure. ''You're so thin already. I don't know why you bother.''

''I don't do it to lose weight. It's the only exercise I get.''

''Are you kidding? Holding down a full-time job and running after an active four-year-old is enough exercise for three women.''

''I'm not with him that much,'' Erica said regretfully. ''Nicky is in nursery school all day. I feel guilty about that, but there's nothing I can do about it.''

''It's the best thing in the world for the boy. They take good care of him and he loves being with the other kids.''

''He does seem well-adjusted, but I worry that he's living in a bad environment. Well, not bad exactly,'' Erica corrected herself. ''Just wrong. A child shouldn't live in a hotel, even a deluxe one. He should have a backyard to play in, and friends next door.''

''Every employee here is his friend.''

''And I'm grateful to all of you, but I was referring to youngsters his own age.''

''There's a simple solution to that—get married.'' Susie eyed Erica's alluring body. ''You wouldn't have any trouble. Just be sure to pick a man who can afford to buy you a house.''

"I'm not interested in getting married again," Erica said curtly.

"Maybe not, but at least you ought to be dating. It isn't normal to sit here alone every night. A beautiful girl like you could have men begging to take you places, but you freeze them out before they can even ask. Jerry Pomeroy would kill for a date with you." He was the assistant manager at the hotel.

"He's not my type," Erica said dismissively.

"Who is? Will you kindly tell me what you're looking for?"

Unaccountably, an instant image of Mike Smith appeared in Erica's mind, the easy grace of his body, his rugged good looks. If she was looking—which she wasn't—he would be the kind of man who interested her.

"It isn't a question of what kind of man. I don't want any of them," she said flatly.

"That's unnatural," Susie stated, just as positively. "Every woman wants a man to cuddle up with at night—if you know what I mean." Her ample bosom heaved with merriment.

"Yes, I get your drift." Erica's face held only distaste.

Susie's own face sobered as Erica's expression registered. "I've heard some women don't like sex. I can't imagine it myself, but if that's your problem, I'm sorry I brought it up."

"I've always thought sex was overrated, but it's no problem."

"You just haven't met the right man."

"Possibly." Erica changed the subject. "What do you think of the new girl? I got two complaints from guests on her floor that their bath towels were taken away and not replaced."

They talked about work for a few minutes, then Susie hauled herself off the couch. "You want me to come by the same time tomorrow night?"

Erica hesitated. "Yes, but could you possibly stay a little later?"

"Sure. I have nothing else to do, and your television is bigger than mine." Susie chuckled. "Where are you going?"

"Well, I . . . uh . . . I have an appointment."

"At night? What kind of appointment?"

Erica knew Susie wouldn't give up. She'd find out the truth anyway when she came to baby-sit and saw her in a dress instead of her usual jogging outfit. "I have a sort of a date," Erica said reluctantly.

"After all that talk about not liking men?" Susie sank back onto the couch. "Where did you meet him? What does he look like? Tell me everything."

"You're making a big deal out of nothing. He's just a man I happened to meet. We're having dinner together, that's all. I'll be home right afterward."

"I'll bet! This is the first guy you've ever shown a spark of interest in."

"That doesn't mean I intend to sleep with him!"

"Well, not on the first date, anyway."

"This will be our first and last date. I don't know why I ever agreed to go out with him."

"He must be a superman. What does he look like?"

"Ordinary looking," Erica said dismissively. "He looks like one of those surfers who hang out at the beach all day."

"They're usually gorgeous."

"I guess you could say he's fairly well built," Erica said, in the understatement of the year.

"He sounds promising. I hope he's not just a tourist passing through. Is that why you don't expect to see him again?"

"No, he's a native."

Susie made a sound of exasperation. "Do I have to drag everything out of you? What does he look like?" she repeated. "And don't tell me average."

Erica sighed. "He has sort of light brown hair streaked by the sun, and I think his eyes are hazel, although they look more gold than green. Are those enough details to satisfy you?"

"It's more important that he satisfy *you*. And from what you told me, he's just the man who can do it."

"I give up!" Erica exclaimed in annoyance.

"You haven't yet, obviously." Susie laughed. "I think you've finally taken a step in the right direction."

Had she? Erica wondered after her friend left. Or was she making the biggest mistake of her life?

That question was still in her mind as Erica dressed for dinner the following night. She was as nervous as a teenager on her first date. Actually she'd dated more in her teens than she had in the last four years.

Choosing a dress wasn't difficult; she didn't have that many. Honolulu was a laid-back town, and her social life consisted of an occasional movie with women friends, or dinner at a fast-food place with Nicky. The blue silk sheath she'd bought for a co-worker's wedding would be adequate—slightly dressy, but not too much so.

Erica didn't wear much makeup as a rule, just a touch of lipstick. For this momentous occasion she'd bought eye shadow and mascara, but it had been so long since she'd worn either one that she was awkward at applying them.

"What are you doing in there?" Susie called. "You're going to be late for your date."

"I'm coming right now." Erica sprayed herself with perfume, grabbed her purse and teetered out of the bedroom on unaccustomed spike heels.

"What's a date, Mom?" Nicky had been allowed to stay up until she left. He was an adorable little boy with tousled blond curls and his mother's blue eyes.

"It's kind of like an appointment," she said.

"Like when I have to go to the doctor for my shots?"

"Something like that," she said wryly.

Susie gave her a disgusted look. "This kid will be permanently turned off of dating if he relies on you for information." She lifted the little boy onto her ample lap. "When a man and a woman have dinner in a restaurant together, it's called a date."

Erica raised one eyebrow. "You don't consider *that* misleading? How about a business dinner between colleagues, or a father taking his daughter out?"

"So I simplified it a little. It's better than having him think a date is just a little less painful than a trip to the dentist."

Nicky had lost interest. "You look pretty, Mom."

"Thank you, darling." Erica gave him a big hug, not caring that he mussed her long, shining hair.

"Your skirt could be shorter." Susie eyed her critically. "When you've got great legs you should show them off. Where is he taking you?"

"The Silver Dolphin."

"It's not top drawer, but it's nice. I guess he isn't loaded."

"How would I know?"

"You can tell about a man in a lot of little ways—the kind of clothes he wears, if he has on one of those expensive gold watches."

"He was wearing cutoffs and a T-shirt with a hole in it when we met. Judging by that, I'm lucky we're not going to the pizzeria," Erica said dryly.

"I think we'd better check this guy out. How'd you like to go down to the drugstore for a chocolate bar, Nicky?"

"Yeah!" the little boy shouted.

"Absolutely not," Erica said, not wanting Susie to see her getting into a cab alone. She left hurriedly.

Mike was waiting in front of the restaurant when Erica's taxi pulled up. He was wearing a well-cut, lightweight beige suit, and his hair had been trimmed. More than one woman passing by gave him an inviting look—with good reason. Mike was stunningly handsome. The white shirt emphasized his deep tan and the unusual, tawny color of his eyes.

They lit up when he saw her. "I was afraid you weren't coming."

"I'm sorry I'm late," she said breathlessly.

"Only a few minutes, and it was worth the wait. You look fantastic! That dress is the exact color of your eyes."

"Isn't this where I'm supposed to say—this old thing?" She laughed.

The street was crowded with tourists. When one jostled Erica, Mike put his arm around her protectively. It was only a courteous gesture, but her pulse rate sped up at the remembered contact with his splendid body.

"Let's go inside, where I hope it will be less crowded," he said.

Their table wasn't quite ready so they went into the bar first. It was filled with people, but they managed to find a small table in the corner.

"Something tells me I should have picked a less popular restaurant," Mike grumbled mildly.

"The food must be good if they're this full," Erica said.

He looked at her in surprise. "The Silver Dolphin has been in this spot for years. You've never been here?"

"No."

"I hope you'll like it. What's your favorite restaurant?"

Erica's mouth twitched in a smile she couldn't quite conceal. Her usual choices were between hamburger joints and pizza parlors. Those were what Nicky liked. "I don't really have a preference. How about you? What's your favorite?"

"I'm easy to please," he answered. "The company is more important than the food."

"Do you eat out all the time, or do you cook for yourself?"

"I'm out a great deal, but I know my way around a kitchen. Nothing fancy, although I do a mean barbecue."

"That's something I never learned how to do."

"I'd be happy to teach you, but I don't suppose you'd get much practice, living in a hotel. Do you have to take all of your meals out?"

"No, they furnish me with a small apartment."

"How convenient. You just roll out of bed in the morning and you're at work. No commuting hassles."

"It really is a bonus. The management has been very generous in other ways, too. I can use the pool and the tennis courts on my day off."

"When is that? Maybe we can have a game. I haven't played much tennis lately, but I'll try to hold up my end."

"That sounds like a classic come-on. You probably play a fantastic game."

"When are you going to trust me?" he asked reproachfully.

"When I see you floundering around the court, panting." She grinned.

"I didn't say I was a beginner, but I'm no pro, either. You can judge for yourself. How about a game Saturday morning?"

"No, I . . . I always have a lot of errands to run."

"Okay, Sunday then."

Erica was saved from having to think up another excuse when the maître d' appeared.

"Mr. Smith? Your table is ready now."

The subject was dropped while they looked at menus and listened to the waiter recite the specialties of the house.

After they'd given their orders, Mike said, "Did you have a busy day?"

"About the same as usual," Erica answered. "How about you?"

"I didn't get much work done. I kept wondering if you were going to keep our date tonight."

"I would never waste somebody's evening by not showing up—even if I'd changed my mind."

"Does that mean you did have second thoughts?"

"Wouldn't it be natural? You probably meet people that way all the time, but women have to be more cautious than men."

"You obviously haven't kept up with the sexual revolution," he said dryly. "Women can be as aggressive as men."

"I'm afraid the revolution passed me by."

"I'd be happy to help you catch up," he teased.

"I didn't expect to be propositioned until *after* dinner," she answered lightly.

"There's no point in wasting time. Will you spend the night with me?"

"No!" she gasped. "Certainly not!"

"Okay." He grinned mischievously. "Now that that's out of the way, do you think you could try to relax and enjoy your dinner?"

"I doubt it." She returned his smile ruefully. "You're a very disturbing man."

"In what way? I've tried to be on my best behavior. Where did I fail?"

"You have a knack of getting me to do things I don't want to do," she said helplessly.

"Maybe you really want to be spontaneous, but you've gotten out of the habit." Mike's face was suddenly serious. "I get the impression that you've built a wall around yourself for some reason. Perhaps subconsciously you're hoping someone will break it down."

"I'm not Sleeping Beauty waiting for her prince to come along, if that's what you're implying," she said curtly. "Fairy tales are for children."

"Not necessarily. Adults need to believe in fantasy, too. It adds spice to life."

"What happens if your fantasies are bitter instead of sweet?"

"Is that what yours turned out to be?" he asked quietly.

"No, I was just playing the devil's advocate." Erica buttered a roll with great deliberation so she wouldn't have to look at him.

Mike had a bad habit of probing all the sore spots she thought were healed. Worse yet, he goaded her into talking about them. That was a luxury she couldn't afford.

He looked at her lowered lashes, feeling an unexpected surge of tenderness. Erica was like a wary doe, ready to bolt at the first snap of a twig. Her vulnerability touched him, arousing mixed emotions. He wanted to hold her in his arms and protect her—and then make love to her all night. The combination of feelings startled him so, that he decided to back off.

"I guess our philosophies of life are different," he said lightly, as the waiter arrived with their entrées. "But I'm sure we can agree on something else."

She gave him a faint smile. "We haven't so far."

"That's not true. The only thing we've disagreed on—outside of your refusal to go to bed with me—are fairy tales. What do you like to read? I suppose we can rule out romances," he remarked ironically.

"Actually I love romantic novels. In spite of what you think, I like happy endings."

"But you don't envision one for yourself?"

"Why do you relate everything to me? I want to hear about you. What was it like growing up in the Islands? Are the schools good here?" This was an opportunity to get some information right from the horse's mouth, so to speak.

Nicky would be starting public school in the not too distant future.

"They're supposed to be excellent."

Erica gave him a puzzled look. "Didn't you go to school here?"

Mike paused for an instant. "It's been a long time since then, and I went away to college. I'm not really an authority on the current school system."

"Where did you go to college?"

"Princeton, and then Harvard."

"Both?" She grinned. "Either you had a thirst for knowledge, or you were determined to work at it until you got it right."

"Something like that."

They ate in silence for a short time. Mike's terse answers had piqued Erica's curiosity. Now that she thought about it, he asked *her* a lot of questions, but he wasn't very forthcoming about himself. She suddenly remembered how he'd seemed to hesitate last night before giving her his name. Was it really Mike Smith? That had a very anonymous sound to it—just a little more imaginative than John Doe. Did he have something to hide? Erica was scarcely in a position to criticize him for that.

The waiter arrived with dessert menus, breaking the momentary lull that had fallen between them.

"Just coffee for me," Erica said, handing the menu back to him.

"The coconut cream pie is excellent here," Mike said.

"It's one of our specialties," the waiter agreed.

"I'm really too full for dessert," she said.

"Bring us a piece and we'll share it," Mike told the waiter as the man poured their coffee.

Erica took a sip of hers and remarked, "This is wonderful coffee."

After sampling his, Mike said, "It's pure Kona coffee, that's why."

"I buy Kona coffee, but it never tastes this good."

"You probably buy a blend. Only ten percent has to be made up of Kona beans. Next time buy the real thing. It's more expensive, but it's worth it."

"Why should it cost more? Aren't the beans grown right here in Hawaii?"

"Solely on the Big Island. It has the only commercial coffee plantations in the United States. Have you seen them? They're quite impressive."

"No, I've never been to any of the other islands."

"I can hardly believe that!" Mike exclaimed. "How long did you say you've lived here?"

"Almost four years."

"But there's so much to see. Every island has something unique—the Kilauea Volcano near Hilo, the black sand beaches, skiing on Mauna Kea. And that's just on the big island of Hawaii."

"I hope to get around to all of them someday."

"What's stopping you?"

Erica didn't want to tell him it was a four-year-old boy. Nicky had been an infant when she first arrived. Even if money hadn't been scarce, it was too difficult to go sight-seeing alone with a baby. Then as the years passed, she'd settled into a rut. Her activities centered around the ones Nicky enjoyed—the beach, excursions to the playground in the park, things like that.

Mike was waiting for an answer, so she gave him a rather lame excuse. "I don't know anyone on the other islands. I wouldn't know where to go when I got there."

"We'll have to do something about that. What are your plans for the weekend? We could fly to Kauai. It's not as built-up as the other islands, but it's one of my favorites."

"I've heard it's lovely, but I'm going to be busy."

"I wasn't suggesting a passion-filled weekend—at least not on such short acquaintance." He grinned. "We can fly over in the morning, spend the day and then fly home. It won't give us time to visit places like the rain forest or the taro farms, but I'll take you to Lumaha'i. That's the beach where parts of the movie *South Pacific* were shot. We can also catch a glimpse of Niihau, the forbidden island."

Erica was about to refuse Mike's invitation again, but her interest was caught. "I never heard of Niihau. Why do they call it forbidden?"

"Because no visitors are allowed. Years ago, an influential family became alarmed that the true Hawaiian culture would die out, so they established a refuge for the few remaining pure Hawaiians. They flourished there, but less than three hundred people live on Niihau now. There's no electricity and no airport. The occasional government agent permitted on official business has to take a long helicopter ride to a remote and uninhabited part of the island."

"It sounds rather like a prison."

"Not at all. The residents can come and go as they like. The restrictions are on visitors."

"Have you been to all the islands except Niihau?"

He nodded. "At one time or another. It made learning about them in school more interesting."

Erica listened, enthralled as Mike told her stories about the islands, both mythical and modern. From Pele, the volcano goddess of ancient times, to the humpback whales that migrate to Maui each winter, singing their mysterious songs.

He finally paused, smiling ruefully. "I've probably bored the socks off you. Why didn't you stop me?"

"I didn't want to. It was fascinating. Tell me more."

"I'd rather show you. Will you let me?"

Erica was grateful to see that the waiter had brought their pie. She'd been too spellbound to notice. Seizing a fork, she hastily sampled the dessert.

"You were right, this pie is delicious," she said.

"I thought you'd like it, but that doesn't answer my question. Will you let me take you sight-seeing? It doesn't have to be this weekend," he said, forestalling her objection. "You set the date."

"I'll have to look at my calendar when I get home." The gasp she gave after glancing at her watch wasn't feigned. "Good heavens, I had no idea it was so late! I have to go."

"Even Cinderella got to stay out until midnight," he said mildly.

She didn't have a baby-sitter, Erica could have told him. "A couple of the maids are out sick," she improvised hastily. "I have a killer day tomorrow."

"Okay, check your calendar and I'll call you. Give me your phone number."

"Well, the thing is, I'd better call you. I'm rather hard to get ahold of."

"Tell me!" he remarked dryly.

"I enjoyed the dinner," she said, gathering her purse. "Thank you for a lovely evening."

"You haven't asked for *my* phone number."

"Oh . . . that's right. You'd better give it to me."

He gazed at her steadily. "We both know you have no intention of calling me—or seeing me again. Why? I thought we got on rather well."

That was true, for the most part. Except for the times when Mike questioned her too closely, Erica had enjoyed the evening immensely. Maybe too much. Since nothing could ever develop between them, it was better not to see him again. She was the one who was apt to get hurt.

"My offer to show you Kauai was quite innocent," he said. "But perhaps you need time to get to know me. Why don't we just play it by ear. How about dinner tomorrow night?"

"I can't."

The regret she felt surprised her, but she couldn't ask Susie to baby-sit again. It wasn't fair to keep her up late two nights in a row when she had to work the next day. Erica knew better than to promise herself she'd be home early. The time flew by when she was with Mike.

"Why am I so reluctant to give up?" He was looking at her with a slight frown. "This is a first for me. I usually accept no for an answer when a woman brushes me off."

"I'm sure that doesn't happen very often," Erica murmured.

"You don't have to be polite." He smiled. "I don't turn mean when I'm rejected."

"It has nothing to do with you," she assured him.

"That's hard to believe. You said you aren't involved with anyone, so I have to conclude the attraction isn't there for you. The only other possible reason for refusing to see me again would be that you're still not sure I'm trustworthy. If that's the case, tell me what I have to do to convince you."

"Listen to me, Mike. You're interested in me because you think the way we met was romantic, but it was just a fluke, not some grand design of fate." She slid out of the booth. "Take my word for it, we weren't meant to be."

Mike put some bills on the table and stood. "I'll debate that while I drive you home."

"No! Our bargain was that I come and go by myself."

His eyes narrowed. "Lady, if you're trying to intrigue me, you've sure as hell succeeded. I have to know what deep, dark secret you're hiding."

This was exactly what Erica was trying to avoid! Her pulse was racing, but she kept her voice dispassionate. "If you want to think of me as a mystery woman I can't stop you, but I'm really quite ordinary. You'd be disappointed if you knew me better."

"Then give me the chance. Let me see you again. I'll leave the time and place up to you."

Who would have thought he'd be this tenacious? Uneasiness gripped her. If she refused to go out with him again, how far would Mike go to find her? And would he stop there?

Erica took a deep breath. "All right, I'll have dinner with you here on Friday night. I'll meet you at the same time."

His pleasure was tempered by skepticism. "You wouldn't be blowing smoke in my ear?"

"No, I'll be here." She glanced despairingly at her watch. "I really have to go now."

She rushed away, ending the discussion. Mike didn't try to follow her. He remained where he was, gazing after her thoughtfully.

Chapter Two

Susie was asleep on the couch when Erica got home. She sat up, yawned and looked at her watch. "I guess I dozed off watching television."

"I'm so sorry! I didn't expect to be this late. I don't know where the time went."

"That sounds promising. It means you had a good time."

"It was all right," Erica answered with restraint.

Susie wasn't fooled. "Oh, I see. You just stayed out all this time because you'd rather be bored than hurt his feelings."

"Okay, I enjoyed the evening. No big deal. It's been a long time since I went out on a date," Erica said defensively.

"I'm glad you finally realized what you're missing. Where did you go after dinner?"

"Nowhere. Dinner lasted kind of a long time."

"I'll say! The service must have been terrible."

"Not exactly. We got to talking. Mike was telling me about the other islands. It was quite interesting."

Susie looked disappointed. "What did he tell you about himself? That's more important."

"Not much. He wanted to talk about me."

"Well, that's a good sign. How did he react when you told him about Nicky?"

"I didn't," Erica answered tersely.

"You were probably smart. No point in scaring him off before you get chummy. Some men don't want to date a woman with children. They figure she's looking for another husband."

"He has nothing to worry about. One was plenty for me," Erica said curtly.

Susie slanted a curious glance at her. "You never talk about your husband."

"It's pointless to dwell on the past." Erica's closed expression didn't invite further questions. She took some bills from her purse and handed them to the other woman. "Thanks for staying with Nicky."

"Any time. Do you think the guy will call you again?"

"Mike did ask me for dinner on Friday. I sort of accepted, but if you're busy I'll tell him I can't make it." Erica couldn't decide what she wanted Susie to answer.

"I'll be glad to baby-sit. My love life isn't what you'd call active right now." Susie grinned. "I'll have to settle for hearing about yours."

"You're due for a disappointment. It's been too long." Erica sighed. "I don't know how to act on a date."

"You must have done something right if he asked you out again."

"I really shouldn't go." Erica bit her lip and frowned. "I don't have room in my life for this sort of thing."

"Who are you kidding? Nicky is the only male in your life right now. That's not normal."

"It works for me," Erica said lightly.

"If he was really enough, you wouldn't have had such a great time. Take a look in the mirror. You're not the same woman who left here earlier. Something happened to you tonight."

"I went out to dinner with a man I barely know," Erica answered impatiently. "Stop trying to make it into the romance of the century."

"It could turn out to be. Maybe this guy will change your whole life. You never know."

"I know it's late and we both have to work in the morning," Erica said firmly.

"Okay, I can take a hint." Susie grinned good-naturedly. "But whether you like it or not, Mike got to you. Things aren't going to be the same around here."

After Susie left, Erica went into the bedroom and stood beside Nicky's bed. He looked like a small angel. Long lashes made a fan on his soft cheek, and one arm was outstretched, the fingers of his little hand slightly curled as if offering one of his precious possessions—a special seashell, or a flower he'd picked just for her.

He was so trusting, asleep or awake. All Nicky had ever known was love. No stranger could be allowed near him, or his safe world might crumble. Erica's face was sober in the dim light as she accepted the fact.

Erica bought a new dress for her dinner with Mike. It was a curious decision, since this was definitely their final date, but she found a good reason.

There were several Hawaiian holidays coming up, events celebrated by luaus that she and Nicky were invited to by her co-workers at the hotel. Erica seldom shopped for herself, so her closet was practically bare.

Susie viewed her with approval when she came to baby-sit that Friday night. "Now you're showing some sense. That outfit will have him panting like a puppy."

Erica wrinkled her nose in distaste. "Actually I bought this dress to wear to Marty and Julia's luau. I just thought I'd get a little extra wear out of it."

"Since when do we get that dressed up for a luau?"

"This isn't that fancy." The halter dress molded Erica's slim torso before flaring into a short, full skirt. It was printed with large pink and deep rose flowers on a white background. "I plan to wear it with flat sandals instead of these high heels."

"You look great, no matter who you bought it for."

Erica gave an exasperated laugh. "Why won't you believe me? You and Mike are two of a kind. You're both hopeless romantics."

"He sounds better and better all the time. I can't wait to meet him."

"I'm afraid you'll have to. He had to work late, so I told him I'd meet him at the restaurant. Help yourself to anything you want in the refrigerator. I won't be late." Erica made a hasty exit before Susie could comment or ask questions.

Mike was waiting for her in the same spot. His eyes traveled slowly from her delicate features to the long silky hair spilling over her bare shoulders. "I'd forgotten how beautiful you are," he said softly.

"In just a couple of days? You have a very short attention span," Erica joked.

"Not where you're concerned," he answered in a velvet voice.

His admiration pleased, yet disturbed her. She was so hopelessly out of practice at sexual sparring. "Well...I guess we should go inside."

"I thought we'd try a different restaurant tonight. This one is too noisy. Would you like to go to the Hibiscus Gardens? I hear the food is pretty good."

"Anywhere you choose will be fine, but I can't stay out as late this time," she warned.

"Did you get grounded for missing curfew?" he teased.

Erica smiled wistfully. "Remember when you couldn't wait to grow up so you could stay up all night? Like so many things, it didn't live up to expectations."

"That wasn't my experience. Care to give it another try?" He grinned.

She looked at him disapprovingly. "You don't waste any time, do you?"

"I don't have any to spare. You always seem poised for flight. Do I intimidate you in some way? I'm really very gentle with women."

"Next you'll be giving me a list of references," she said dryly.

"What kind of men have you known? They must be big-time losers," he said disgustedly. "A real man doesn't have to brag about his conquests to prove his virility."

Erica thought fleetingly of Jordan. "I was only joking. I told you I'm not very good at the dating game."

"I have no complaints." He took her hand and laced their fingers together. "I can't think of anyone I'd rather be with right now."

No contact between a man and a woman could be more chaste than holding hands, but a thrill shot up her arm. She laughed quickly to show she wasn't affected. "Do you expect me to believe you enjoy dates that end before midnight?"

"I'm hoping to convince you that I'm worth more of your time," he said in a silky voice.

"So you admit you have an ulterior motive. I've finally found an honest man."

As Mike's gaze shifted slightly, a young man came out of the office building they were passing. He greeted Mike with pleased surprise.

"Hey, old buddy! What are you doing over here with the working people? This isn't your regular turf." He looked at Erica curiously.

Mike's expression was unreadable. "Hi, Darren. You're working rather late tonight."

"We can't all have your kind of hours."

Since he continued to look pointedly at Erica, Mike had to introduce them. The man's full name was Darren Mackie.

"I haven't seen you around before," he said to Erica. "Are you visiting the Islands?"

"No, I live here," she answered.

"Mike has certainly been keeping you a secret."

"We just met," she said.

"I hope I'll be seeing more of you. Is he taking you to the dance at—"

"You'll have to excuse us," Mike cut in swiftly. "We're late for our dinner reservation." He took Erica's arm and hustled her down the sidewalk.

She slanted a glance at him. "You didn't have to panic. I realize you take out other women."

"Don't you want me to? Just say the word and I'm all yours," he said lightly.

"You know what I mean. You cut the poor man off in midsentence so he wouldn't tell me about a dance I'm not even interested in going to."

"Darren is a clod with minimal social graces. He holds a world record for boring small talk."

"So you were doing me a favor," Erica said dryly.

"Exactly."

After pondering for a few moments she said, "What did he mean when he asked what you were doing here with the working people?"

"It's his idea of humor. My office is in a rather nice building that overlooks the ocean. Darren likes to joke that all we do all day is look out the window at the pretty girls on the beach."

Erica had a few more questions, but they'd reached the restaurant, a long, low building set back from the sidewalk and bordered by hibiscus bushes covered with red, pink and white blossoms. Hawaiian music floated out, mixed with the sounds of voices and laughter.

The interior of the restaurant had a tropical decor. High-back, fan-shaped chairs surrounded lacquered tables centered by a vase of Vanda orchids. The walls of the room were hung with fishnets, canoe paddles and colorful flower leis.

"What a charming place." Erica glanced around at the crowds of people. "I hope you really do have a reservation. I doubt if we'll get in, otherwise."

"It's worth a try. Wait here."

She watched without much hope as Mike went to the reservation desk where a hostess presided over a large book filled with names. As Erica expected, the woman pointed to the long list and shrugged. But after Mike discreetly handed her a folded bill, her attitude changed. He beckoned to Erica.

"I'll put you at that table in the corner," the hostess said, all smiles. "It's quieter there. Follow me, please."

It must have been a large bill, Erica surmised. When they were seated at their table she said to Mike, "You didn't have to do that. We could have gone somewhere else."

"You wanted to eat here, didn't you?"

"Well, yes, but that's a terrible waste of money."

"Money is made to be spent. Now, what would you like to drink?" he asked, ending the discussion.

She glanced over at the tray a waiter was carrying. It was filled with exotic-looking drinks. "I'd like one of those things with a paper umbrella on top, I don't know what you call them."

Mike gazed at her with a raised eyebrow. "They're fairly potent, in spite of all the fruit. Are you sure that's what you want? I get the impression that you're not much of a drinker."

"Are you afraid I'll get noisy and embarrass you?" She grinned.

"I can't imagine you letting your hair down. If a Volcano Punch will get rid of your inhibitions, I'm all for it."

"Now I know your game plan. You intend to wait until I'm tipsy and take advantage of me."

"Wrong. If and when we ever make love, I want you in complete possession of your faculties."

Mike was smiling, but his smoky voice sent a little shiver up her spine. For a fleeting moment she imagined what it would be like to lie in his arms and let him bring her body to rapturous, pulsing life. There was no doubt in her mind that he would be a superb lover. She quickly banished the forbidden thought.

"A Volcano Punch for the lady, and I'll have a Scotch and soda," Mike told the waiter.

"I was hoping you'd have one of those fancy things, too," she told him after the waiter had gone to fill their order.

"Are you planning to have your way with *me?*" Mike laughed. "I'll be happy to cooperate without any added inducement."

"What I really wanted was the umbrella."

"I can ask the waiter to give us a spare. Do you collect them?"

"No, I wanted to bring them to—" Erica broke off abruptly, aggravated at herself. She'd better stop fantasizing about Mike and watch what she said. "What I meant was, a friend of mine has a little boy. I thought he might like them. Children like anything toy-size."

"Your friend is lucky. My nephew thinks bigger is better. The latest thing on his wish list is a computer."

"How old is he?"

"Scott is only four, but he'll probably get one."

"Kids learn about electronics at a remarkably early age. They're the only ones who know how to program a VCR—or open a childproof medicine bottle."

"Isn't it the truth?" Mike chuckled. "It must not be easy being a parent these days."

"I suppose you're right," Erica murmured.

"Still, it has its rewards. Or so my own parents keep telling me. They spoil Scott terribly, since he's an only grandchild."

"Grandparents can be very possessive." Erica took a sip of the drink the waiter had put in front of her.

"I wouldn't put it that way. We all have a good relationship. How about *your* family? Are they on your case all the time about getting married?"

"I haven't seen them in quite a while. They live in California."

"Surely they visit you. It's only a five-hour plane ride. A lot of Californians own condominiums here on the islands."

"I can't imagine why anyone would want to live in an apartment in Hawaii," Erica remarked. "For the same price they could buy a little house with a yard. That's what I'd do if I could afford it."

"Why would you want to be bothered when you have such a great setup?"

"I'd like a place to putter around in on the weekends, but I can tell that wouldn't appeal to you. I suppose you live in a high-rise apartment."

"Well, actually I live in a house."

"With a garden?"

"Not much of one."

"Is it in one of those new subdivisions?"

"No, it's on the beach," he said reluctantly, since she seemed determined to find out. "That's why I don't have more of a yard."

Erica's eyes widened. Oceanfront property cost a fortune! How had Mike managed to swing it?

Without giving her a chance to ask, he picked up one of the menus the waiter had left. "Shall we see what looks good?"

Mike was rather withdrawn, but Erica didn't notice. The Volcano Punch had relaxed her and for once she wasn't examining his words and behavior for hidden meanings.

The waiter appeared when he saw them scanning the menus. "May I tell you about our specialties?" He recited a list of the day's selections. "We also have broiled lobster," he finished.

"That sounds good to me," Mike said. "How about you?" he asked Erica.

She switched her attention to the menu and discovered this restaurant was a great deal more expensive than The Silver Dolphin. The price of lobster was outrageous.

When she didn't answer immediately, Mike told the waiter, "I think we need a little more time. You can bring the wine list while the lady is making up her mind."

After the man had left, Erica said, "You don't have to spend a lot of money to impress me."

Mike looked puzzled. "I don't understand. What do you think I'm doing to impress you?"

"Lobster is the most expensive thing on the menu. And we don't need wine with dinner. They overcharge terribly in restaurants."

He stared at her with a mixture of disbelief and uncertainty. "You're not serious, are you?"

"Completely," she assured him. "I happen to know what the markup is. One of my friends at the hotel works in the food and beverage department."

"Restaurants have to make a living, too."

"There are enough tourists in town. People on vacation can afford to splurge. They expect to. It's different for people like us. Honolulu can get to be quite expensive when you live here year-round.''

Mike's face was impassive. "Is this a subtle way of trying to find out how solvent I am?''

Erica stifled a sigh. Why were men so touchy? Did Mike think she was questioning his ability to pay the check? "I didn't mean to sound ungracious,'' she said quietly. "I shouldn't have brought it up.''

"I must admit I've never had a date worry about how much money I spent on her. Are you always this considerate, or am I receiving special treatment? It's quite disarming, whatever the reason.''

Erica was perplexed by the subtle change in him. There was a sardonic quality to his voice and the way he looked at her. "I was only trying to stop you from being pointlessly extravagant. I can't speak for the other women you date, but it isn't necessary with me. There are a lot of things in life more important than money.''

"You really believe that?''

"I know it for a fact, but that doesn't mean I'll convince *you*. It's something you have to discover for yourself.''

"How did your great revelation come about?'' His tone was still mocking.

"When I discovered that Oscar Wilde's observation about cynics applies to rich people as well. They both know the price of everything and the value of nothing.''

Mike stared at her searchingly for a long moment while his expression changed. "If you were trying to make me ashamed of myself, you've succeeded.''

"That wasn't my intention. I never meant to upset you.''

"I brought it on myself.'' He reached out and gripped her hand across the table. "You just reminded me of that old saying about not being able to see the forest for the trees.''

"I don't understand.''

"Never mind, let's celebrate. Is it all right if I order champagne, just this once?'' He gave her an appealing smile. "It's a special occasion, and they don't come around very often."

"What's special about tonight?"

"You are." His deepened voice held no trace of its former mockery. "I need you around to remind me that I'm not such a big deal."

"I'm sorry if you took it that way, but you must have scores of women telling you how wonderful you are."

"Only my mother, and that doesn't count. Mothers automatically think their children are perfect."

"Except for your one flaw. She wants you to get married."

"Unconditional love comes with a price." He laughed.

Erica looked at him curiously. "Your parents seem to have a happy marriage, and from what you've told me, your sister does, too. What soured *you* on the institution?"

His face sobered. "I'm not anti-marriage. I'd love to find the girl of my dreams. The trouble is, I keep waking up."

"You're one of the lucky ones," Erica said somberly.

Mike's interest quickened. "That sounds like you're speaking from experience. Did you have an unhappy marriage?"

"It doesn't have to be a personal experience," she said hastily. "Look at the statistics on divorce. I don't know how anyone is willing to take a chance nowadays."

"That's a little drastic," he protested. "My own family is living proof that marriage works."

"Perhaps for your parents' generation," she said skeptically.

"Not solely. I have a lot of friends who are happily married, and I'm sure you do, too."

Erica laughed. "If your mother could only hear you now. It would give her hope for the future."

"She'd love you. See how good you are for me? Let's drink to the start of a long and beautiful relationship." Mike beckoned the waiter over and ordered a bottle of champagne, specifying the vintage.

After the man had gone to get it, Erica said, "I wish you hadn't done that, Mike. This is just an ordinary date, not the start of a relationship."

He stared at her thoughtfully. "Why does the word spook you?"

"I just want to keep the record straight so there aren't any misunderstandings," she answered carefully.

"They're inevitable. Any man who pretends to understand a woman is only kidding himself."

"That's because you refuse to accept the truth when you hear it. I'm not your dream girl."

"You have all of the qualifications." His admiring eyes roamed over her classic features.

"Not if you knew me better."

"That's what I meant by a relationship. We'll get to know each other gradually, find out our mutual likes and dislikes. Maybe you're right and we'll discover we don't have anything in common except a powerful sexual attraction— on my part, at least. But I promise it won't become a problem."

"I wasn't worried about that," she murmured. A man like Mike didn't have to force himself on any woman.

"Good, then we'll take it slow and easy. The Film Festival opens next week. Do you like foreign films?"

"I haven't seen enough of them to form a valid opinion." Jordan hadn't liked subtitles, which meant they didn't go.

"You're in for a treat. Some of the Antonioni films are masterpieces, although the Japanese are doing very innovative things. Did you ever see *Rashoman*? That's a classic, of course."

They talked about movies and the current crop of movie stars. Erica could discuss those because she read about them in the newspaper. Her theatergoing experience was mostly limited to Disney films suitable for Nicky.

"I have tickets to the entire Festival series, but we don't have to take in all of them," Mike said. "The one on Monday sounds good, though. It's a German film and it starts early. Shall we eat afterward instead of before? I hate to eat with one eye on the clock, don't you?"

"Yes, it hardly seems worthwhile. I can't enjoy a meal I have to bolt down."

Without realizing it, Erica had accepted another date with Mike. What happened to all her good resolutions? she wondered. They didn't seem as important as they had when she made them. Everything Mike said made sense. They could be friends without getting involved. Especially since he'd accepted the situation and stopped being seductive.

The evening flew by as before. Erica was reluctant to end it, but Mike didn't press her to stay. He didn't even suggest picking her up on Monday night.

"I'll meet you in front of the Film Festival at seven o'clock," he said as he opened the taxi door for her.

"Yes, all right." She was subtly dissatisfied, which was silly. Mike was only following her rules. He couldn't have cared very much, though, if he was willing to give up that easily.

Mike stood at the curb, watching the receding taillights of the cab. The secret smile of satisfaction on his face might have made Erica wonder who was really doing the maneuvering.

The two weeks that followed were very exciting for Erica. She saw Mike often except on the weekends, which were reserved for Nicky. Mike accepted her vague excuses without trying to change her mind.

Perversely, his calm acceptance that there might be somebody else in her life didn't please Erica. She kept assuring herself that she wasn't falling in love with Mike, that it was only the stimulation of dating a very attractive man after a long time without male companionship. A woman would have to be frigid to be indifferent to him—and Erica didn't fall into that category.

The revelation came as an unwelcome surprise. After Jordan, she'd had absolutely no interest in men. But when Mike put his arm around her shoulders, or held her hand as they walked down the street, she felt a breathless kind of happiness.

His demonstrations of affection were always very casual. After a few more dates he kissed her cheek before putting her in a cab to go home, but nothing more. Erica finally accepted the fact that Mike was satisfied with the status quo and wasn't about to disturb it. Under the circumstances it seemed foolish—and expensive—not to let him pick her up. He seemed pleased, but not unduly so, when she told him.

"Good. I was always slightly uncomfortable about meeting on a street corner. It made me feel like I was dating an undercover agent." He chuckled.

"Oh, well, it just seemed easier that way," she said lamely.

"Right." Mike didn't argue the debatable point. "Would you like to give me your phone number, too? It's always bothered me that I wouldn't know how to get in touch with you in case of a last minute change in plans."

Erica couldn't go that far. Like a lot of children, Nicky loved to answer the telephone. "You can always leave a message with the hotel switchboard," she said.

Mike was silent for a long moment. "I can see I still haven't made the trusted list."

"It isn't that," she said hurriedly. "It's just that I'm difficult to get ahold of."

"That's for sure," he answered dryly.

"Having the switchboard operator take my messages is a lot more reliable. It's like having a free answering service."

He merely shrugged. "Okay, honey, if that's what you want."

Erica's happiness was tempered by an ever present sense of danger. She had so much to hide. What would Mike do if he found out he was dating a wanted criminal?

Most of the time she succeeded in burying her fears, but the chance of discovery was like a sword over her head. Even well-meaning people could trip her up by giving out information. Like Susie. Her friend and baby-sitter had a burning curiosity about Mike.

"Why doesn't he ever call for you here?" she complained.

"You know what a long wait it is for an elevator," Erica answered. "The tourists complain about it all the time. It's a lot easier for me to go down to the lobby."

"I'm dying to meet the guy. He must be something special."

"Not really," Erica said dismissively. "He's just an ordinary man."

"Is that why you're paying me a small fortune to baby-sit three or four nights a week? I could almost quit my day job and make a living off of you."

"If your conscience hurts, you might consider lowering your hourly rate." Erica grinned.

Nicky came into the living room pulling a toy fire engine by a string. His sunny smile turned to a frown when he saw his mother's pink linen suit and high heels. "I want to go with you," he stated.

"You don't even know where she's going," Susie said.

"I don't care. I wanna go, too."

Nicky was usually asleep by the time Erica went out, so she didn't feel guilty about leaving him. Now, doubts began to surface. Was she putting her own pleasure above his welfare? It distressed her to think she might be neglecting him.

As she hesitated, Susie said to the little boy, "You and I are going to have our own fun. How would you like to pop some popcorn and watch television?"

He remained unconvinced. "No... I wanna go with Mom."

"Maybe I'd better run downstairs and tell Mike I'll meet him later," Erica said to Susie in a low voice.

"Don't be such a pushover. Nicky will be fine the minute you walk out the door. Trust me." Susie turned to the child. "If you stop giving your mother a hard time I'll have a surprise for you."

"What?" he asked warily.

"It wouldn't be a surprise if I told you. Make up your mind. What do you want to do?"

"Okay, I'll stay with you. Bring me something back, Mom."

Erica looked at Susie in amazement. "You're fantastic! How do you know so much about children when you don't have any of your own?"

"You don't need to have kids to know you've got to keep the upper hand. My advice is to marry this Mike guy and give Nicky some brothers and sisters. That's what he needs." Susie didn't know she was twisting the knife.

"I'd better go," Erica murmured.

The door had barely closed before Nicky asked, "What's the surprise?"

"How would you like to go downstairs and get some ice cream from that stand on the beach?"

"Yeah!" He clapped his hands and jumped up and down.

When they reached the lobby, Susie made a detour to the gift shop. To head off Nicky's complaints, she let him play with a souvenir paperweight. Swirling snow blanketed a Hawaiian beach when he shook it.

While he was occupied, Susie scanned the lobby. She saw Mike come through the revolving front door and approach Erica.

"Wow, what a hunk!" Susie exclaimed in a spontaneous burst of admiration.

Mike had on a lightweight summer suit, since they were going to the theater. That made him stand out in the crowd of casually dressed tourists, but he would have commanded attention no matter what he was wearing. His handsome face had character, and he moved like an athlete, in complete control of his splendid body. The man also had charm. The smile he was giving Erica could melt rock candy!

"No wonder she looks like somebody lit a candle inside her," Susie remarked softly. "That guy could torch any woman's fire."

Nicky had tired of playing with the paperweight and tugged on Susie's skirt. "You said we were gonna get ice cream."

"Okay, pal, put that back on the counter first," Susie instructed.

After a quick greeting, Erica glanced away from Mike, in case her impulse to reach out and touch him was visible. Her idle glance became horrified as she noticed her son and Susie at the entrance to the gift shop. Fortunately neither one was gazing in her direction, although Susie must have come down to the lobby for the express purpose of getting a look at Mike. If Nicky ever spotted her he'd make a beeline straight to her.

Erica grabbed Mike's arm hurriedly. "We'd better hurry, we don't want to miss the curtain."

"There's plenty of time," he assured her. "I want to stop at the desk and get a stamp. I forgot to mail a letter today."

"You can get it when you bring me home." She pulled him toward the door. "It won't get picked up until morning anyway."

Mike gave her a puzzled look. "Why are you in such a rush to leave? I told you we're early."

"I don't want the parking attendant to put your car away." She glanced over her shoulder nervously. Sure enough, Susie and Nicky were leaving the gift shop. "It would take forever to have it brought around again."

"I told him to leave it in the drive, that I'd only be a few minutes. See, there it is, right where I left it."

Erica breathed a sigh of relief as they reached the outside. "Let's get in before he decides to move it."

Mike helped her into the passenger side, still perplexed. As they drove away he remarked, "You are probably the most mystifying woman I've ever known."

She was relaxed now that the danger had passed. "In what way?"

"Just when I think I'm getting to know you, I realize you're a complete enigma."

"That's not so. You know where I live, you can get in touch with me at any time." Mike had left messages for her once or twice and she'd called him back.

"I know that much about my secretary. It's the real you that eludes me. I don't know what your life is like when I'm not with you, who your friends are. You never mention anyone."

"Neither do you. The one time we met a friend of yours, you hurried me away before we could say more than a few words."

"I explained that. Darren is a bore."

"If you say so."

"I should have let you find out for yourself." Mike abruptly dropped the subject. "This play tonight should be good, it's a sellout. I had a devil of a time getting good seats."

"What row are they in?"

He put his hand in his breast pocket, then groaned. "I'm really out of it tonight. I forgot the tickets."

"Oh, Mike! What are we going to do?"

"No problem. It's a good thing I left plenty of time. We can swing by my place and pick them up."

"How far away do you live?" she asked dubiously. Even in Honolulu the freeways were crowded at this time of night.

"Don't worry, it's just a short distance from here."

Erica was faintly surprised. All ocean view property was expensive, but the houses near the hotel were in the very high-rent district. She'd just assumed that Mike lived farther out, where prices weren't as astronomical.

Diamond Head came closer, the dark bluff where a long extinct volcano had been turned into a fort in more recent times. On the lower slopes were the fabulous mansions of the superrich.

Staring at the famous landmark, Erica mused, "I wonder why they called it Diamond Head. It looks more like an elongated triangle than a diamond."

"The name has nothing to do with its shape," Mike told her. "Back in the nineteenth century some visiting sailors scooped up what appeared to be diamonds. They turned out to be calcite crystals, but maybe that's lucky. Hawaii is too beautiful to be overrun by frenzied prospectors."

"I'll bet the sailors didn't consider it lucky."

"That's what comes of wasting their time." Mike grinned. "Who ever heard of spending shore leave climbing a mountain?"

"We both know what *you* would have been doing," Erica observed dryly.

"Of course. Improving my mind at the local museum." His eyes sparkled mischievously.

The slight tension that had built between them at the hotel was completely dissipated by the time Mike pulled over to the curb and stopped the car.

"I'll be right out," he said.

"You live *here?*"

Behind a hedge of night-blooming jasmine was a long low house with a pagoda-type roof. It wasn't overly imposing, but because of the location, Erica knew it must be worth a fortune.

Mike hesitated almost imperceptibly before asking, "Would you like to come in?"

"I'd love to!"

She followed him into a wide hall that ran from the front of the house to the back, where floor-to-ceiling windows gave a glorious view of the ocean and the lights of Honolulu to the right.

The rooms were simply, yet elegantly furnished. A living room, den and library were filled with long, comfortable couches and deep armchairs in soft neutral tones, forming a quiet background for the vivid paintings on the walls. One especially lovely scene of a swimming pool looked like a David Hockney. Either a copy or an imitation of his style, Erica surmised, since an original would be worth a small fortune.

Mike disappeared briefly to get the tickets. When he returned she was examining an exquisite jade figurine, one of many precious objects that were scattered around on tables.

"This is gorgeous. Your whole place is!" she exclaimed. "I never dreamed you lived like this."

His reaction to her praise was tepid. "Does it make a difference?"

Erica barely heard him. She was too busy taking everything in, the marble floors, the gauzy drapes that would deflect the sun without obscuring the view, the lamps that were placed just right for reading. It was a luxurious home, yet comfortable at the same time.

"I'd sell my soul for a house like this." She sighed.

"Before you decide to sell something more tangible I'd better tell you, this isn't my house," Mike drawled.

"But you said—"

"I'm house-sitting for a friend."

"Oh, I see. Well, it's nice to have rich friends, anyway."

"I suppose so." He didn't return her smile. "I think it's time to leave."

Erica finally noticed the moody look on his face. "Is anything wrong, Mike?"

His mouth curved in a smile that wasn't reflected in his eyes. "No, everything is turning out pretty much as I expected."

Chapter Three

Erica could tell something was bothering Mike. He continued to be withdrawn on the ride to the theater. Since it was only a short drive and they arrived just in time to take their seats, she didn't give it much thought.

The play was a witty comedy, but it didn't improve Mike's mood. Erica puzzled over what could be bothering him. She waited until they were having a drink in a nearby cocktail lounge before taking the direct approach.

"You have something on your mind," she said quietly. "Would you like to tell me what's troubling you? Maybe I can help."

"It's nothing," he said quickly. "I'm sorry for not being more entertaining."

"I wasn't complaining. I just thought it might help to talk about whatever it is. That's what friends are for."

"Is that what you consider me?"

"Of course. Isn't that how you think of *me*?"

"I think you're a very clever lady."

Erica frowned. "That should be a compliment, but somehow it doesn't sound like one. What makes you think I'm clever?"

"You know what you want and you go after it."

"Most people do. It's called survival."

"I suppose you could look at it that way." He paused for a moment, staring at her intently. "Suppose you found out I haven't been completely honest with you. What if I told you I was having financial problems?"

"Nobody could ever tell by looking at you." Erica's eyes unconsciously shifted to his well-cut suit and the expensive gold wristwatch. Those might be part of what contributed to his money troubles.

"Appearances are deceiving," he said sardonically.

"Are you in real trouble?"

"Would it lessen my desirability if I was?"

"Be serious, Mike," she answered impatiently. "If you're truly in a bind you'll have to do something about it. We don't have to go out to dinner all the time, for one thing."

"You mean you don't want to see me anymore?" he asked impassively.

"Stop overreacting!" She hesitated uncertainly. Was Mike's confession just a ploy to break up with her? "Unless that's what *you* want."

"Don't try to make it seem as though it was my idea."

She'd hurt his pride again. Erica chose her words carefully. "Friends can speak frankly to each other. I enjoy your company and I'd miss it if we stopped seeing each other. I was merely suggesting that we could split a pizza and go to the movies for a while instead of the theater and pricey restaurants. Everybody I know is short of cash, it's nothing to be ashamed of. I could even pay my own way part of the time." A smile dimpled the corner of her mouth. "I hear that's an accepted practice nowadays, even with macho men and their dates."

Mike's face was a study in conflicting emotions. He seemed to have trouble putting them into words. After a moment he gathered both of her hands in his and held them tightly. "You've made me thoroughly ashamed of myself. I only hope you can forgive me when you find out just how stupid I've been."

"You don't have to tell me how extravagant you were. We've all been tempted to max out our credit cards at one time or another."

"I wish that's all it was," he said soberly.

Her face grew serious. "You haven't done something foolish like borrowing from the wrong kind of people?" She'd heard horror stories about loan sharks.

"This isn't about money, Erica. Or at least, not the way you think. I've used very bad judgment in not telling you more about myself. I'm sorry to say I haven't been honest and open with you."

Her gaze shifted. "Friendship means taking people on faith. We don't have to tell each other everything."

"We do if it might affect our relationship."

"In that case, I don't want to hear it," she stated firmly. "Things are fine just as they are. Why rock the boat?"

He groaned. "Erica, sweetheart, you aren't making this any easier."

"Listen to me, Mike. Anything either of us might have done in the past is irrelevant. It's over and done with. We have a good time together, that's the only thing that counts."

"You're remarkably trusting," he said wryly. "I could have committed some kind of criminal act for all you know."

"Almost everyone has." Her stomach muscles tightened, but she kept her voice light. "I read that in some state or other, it's against the law to kiss your wife on a public sidewalk. And that's just one of the laws people break every day. The same article said another state prohibits keeping livestock in the living room.''

"I could live with that one." He grinned.

"Especially in *your* elegant house—or rather, your friend's.''

Mike's face sobered. "That's part of what I want to talk to you about.''

"You have to move?"

"No, I...I can stay on indefinitely. I'd like to explain about my living arrangements, but I'll have to start at the beginning so you'll understand. At least, I hope you will,'' he muttered.

Erica had no idea what Mike wanted to confess, but she was sure it was something trivial. Perhaps the house belonged to a female friend instead of a male, as she'd assumed, and Mike was afraid she'd wonder what services he was providing in return. Erica preferred not to think about that, but she was mainly concerned that he might ask personal questions of *her* if she allowed him to bare his own soul.

"We really don't have time to go into anything weighty right now." She glanced at her watch. "I'm afraid I have to make this an early evening.''

"We haven't ordered yet.''

"I'm sleepier than I am hungry, and I have to get up really early in the morning." She improvised rapidly. "We're having a staff meeting and I have to look alert.''

Mike sighed. "There isn't any reason for you to go to bed hungry. I'll drop the subject for now.''

"That has nothing to do with it," Erica insisted. "We can talk some other time.''

"Why do I have a feeling that isn't very probable?" he asked dryly.

"You're just spoiled," she answered lightly. "You can't get your own way *all* the time.''

He put some bills on the table. "Just once would be nice," he grumbled, but good-naturedly.

Erica wasn't as relaxed with Mike after that night. His apology for holding something back reminded her that there could never be anything between them.

The sensible thing would be to stop seeing him before they got any more involved. But she shied away from that solution. Mike had filled her life with laughter and excitement, two things that were in short supply before he came along. It would be different if she was in love with him; that would make the situation impossible. But she wasn't, Erica assured herself. Mike was just a very charming companion.

As she was dressing for a date with him one night, trying to decide between white pants or a cotton dress, the switchboard put through a telephone call.

"I thought you might want to get a little more dressed up than usual," Mike said. "We're having dinner at the Catamaran Club."

It was a very exclusive and expensive club. "I thought you were going to mend your ways," Erica scolded. "How do you ever expect to get out of debt if you don't stop being so extravagant?"

"You mentioned something about paying your own way," he teased.

"I can't afford the Catamaran Club."

"Okay, honey, then be my guest." He chuckled. "Don't worry, I've solved my financial problems."

"Even so, you should be putting something aside for a rainy day."

"Our rainsqualls never last long. Get dressed, angel. I'll be there at eight."

Erica disapproved of Mike's irresponsibility, but she couldn't help looking forward to seeing the exclusive club she'd only read about. It was frequented by local society and celebrities, always dressed to the teeth.

Erica frowned at her scanty wardrobe. She'd bought a few new things when her social life heated up, but nothing really outstanding. Perhaps the jade-colored silk pants would do, paired with the matching sleeveless top.

After she belted a printed chiffon scarf around her slim waist and fastened a pair of dangling pearl earrings to her lobes, the effect wasn't too bad, she decided.

Erica was too modest. As she crossed the lobby a little later, a lot of heads turned. The women envied her flawless skin and incredible lashes, while the men showed discreet interest in her slender, curved body.

Erica was oblivious to their admiration. Mike's reaction was the only one she cared about, and it was most satisfactory.

He gently smoothed the raven-colored hair rippling over her shoulders. "How is it possible for one woman to be so beautiful?" he asked huskily.

"A lot of cosmetics. Do you think this outfit is elegant enough for the Catamaran Club?" she asked in a shameless bid for more flattery.

"It's fit for dinner at the governor's mansion."

"Too bad I don't know him." She laughed.

"Would you like to meet him? I can arrange it."

"You're just trying to get out of taking me to the Catamaran Club, but it won't work."

Mike put his arm around her shoulders as they walked out to the car. "You've certainly changed your tune. I thought you said it was too expensive."

"It is. I know we're being foolish, but I can never say no to you."

"I wish that was true."

His arm tightened and his head dipped toward hers. In the semidarkness his eyes glowed like the topaz lights bordering the driveway. Erica felt their warmth deep in her midsection. She was achingly aware of his hard body only inches away. When her lips parted unconsciously, Mike drew in his breath sharply and gathered her closer.

The parking attendant had to repeat his question before they heard him. "Sir? Would you like me to get your car?"

"What?" Mike stared at him uncomprehendingly for a moment. Then he released Erica. "No, it's right over there."

The strength and suddenness of their emotions left them somewhat shaken. They were both silent for a short time in the car, and then the conversation was a little forced.

Their brief reserve vanished when they got to the club. It was noisy and crowded with people enjoying themselves, which was infectious.

The maître d' greeted Mike by name. "We haven't seen you lately, Mr. Smith. It's nice to have you back. I have a lovely table for you."

Mike had taken Erica to increasingly expensive restaurants, but nothing like this. Everything from the plush carpeting to the huge floral arrangements in the lobby spelled luxury. Service plates on the pink linen-covered tables bore the club crest, and a phalanx of wineglasses flanked every place setting.

After they were seated, Erica said to Mike, "You must have been a regular here. The maître d' knew your name."

He shrugged. "That's their business. It's all a game."

"A pricey one." She'd seen the bill he slipped the man. "What am I going to do with you?"

"We've never been able to agree on that." He grinned as if it were a joke. "Come on, let's dance."

There were only a few people on the dance floor, but Erica wasn't aware of them. When Mike took her in his arms, everyone else ceased to exist. Her body seemed to melt into his, curving to adapt perfectly to his hard angles. She was conscious of the leashed power in his splendid frame, the clean masculine scent of his skin, everything about him.

When the music stopped and he released her, Erica moved away slowly. Mike appeared to share her reluctance. He kept possession of her hand as they left the dance floor.

On the way to their table, a woman called to him from a table in the middle of the room. She was blond and beautiful, with a golden tan that was displayed to full advantage by her white silk slip dress. The diamond-and-emerald brooch she wore was especially dramatic against the stark white gown.

Mike smiled and waved back, then continued on to their table.

When they were seated, Erica remarked casually, "She's very glamorous."

"Yes, I suppose so."

As she considered pursuing the subject, their waiter approached. "Would you care to order now, Mr. Smith?" he asked.

"Give us a couple of minutes. We haven't looked at the menu yet." After giving it a cursory glance, Mike looked questioningly at Erica. "Do you know what you want?"

"Not exactly." Everything on the menu sounded delicious, but the prices were outrageous. She was trying to figure out how to order the least expensive thing without hurting his fragile ego.

"Take all the time you need. You can call me when you've decided," the waiter said, leaving them alone.

"The mahimahi is always good here if you're in the mood for fish," Mike told her. "They also make an excellent beef Wellington. Actually everything the chef prepares is first-rate."

"You sound like a regular customer."

"That's something I want to talk to you about, but let's order first. I didn't have time for lunch today and I'm as hungry as a bear."

"What are you going to have?"

"I think I'll have the prime rib, with some fresh asparagus. And to start with, either the smoked salmon or a prawn cocktail. What appeals to you?"

"Everything looks wonderful, but I'm really not very hungry."

Mike reached out and took her menu. "If you hadn't seen the prices, what would you have?"

"That has nothing to do with it. I had a late lunch, honestly."

He sighed. "This is all my fault for pretending to be something I'm not."

"You don't have to pretend with me, Mike," she said earnestly. "I'm beginning to understand why you're overextended. You got in somehow with a crowd of people whose life-style is out of your reach. I can understand how you'd be dazzled by all the luxury they take for granted, but you have to be realistic. You can't keep living on the edge."

"These people are my friends, Erica."

It was easy to see why they'd accepted him. "If they're really your friends they'll understand why you can't keep up this pace. I honestly don't know how you manage. I guess living rent free helps, but you have to look to the future. What if your friend suddenly decides he wants his house back?"

"I'm afraid I misled you about my living arrangements," Mike began carefully.

The waiter appeared at his elbow. "Take all the time you like, Mr. Smith, but I just want to tell you we have only a few orders of mahimahi left. If you were considering it, I'll put two orders aside for you."

Mike tried to hide his annoyance at the interruption. "Thanks, Roger, but I'm going to have the prime rib, medium rare." He gave the rest of his order, then looked questioningly at Erica. "Have you decided yet, or would you like more time?"

"No, I'll have what you're having." She could tell he'd planned this evening as a special treat and she didn't want to spoil it by continuing to lecture him. He was a grown man, after all.

"Very good, sir," the waiter said. "I'll bring your first course right away."

Erica had spoken her mind and she didn't intend to belabor the point. When the waiter left, she changed the subject. "You must have been busy today if you couldn't take time for lunch. Did anything unusual happen?"

"No, just the usual controlled chaos."

"Doesn't a jobber just buy from farmers, and then sell to consumers?"

"That's the simplified version. Prices are tied to the commodity market, which can be quite volatile."

"I've never understood the stock market. Fortunately or unfortunately, I've never had to. I don't have any money to invest."

"You wouldn't want to invest in the commodity market anyway. There are safer places to put your money."

"I'll come to you for a crash course if I ever have anything left over after paying my bills. Which is unlikely." She grinned. "My only chance at wealth is to win the lottery, and I hear the odds are terrible."

"You could always marry a rich man," he remarked.

Erica's smile faded. "I can't imagine a worse reason for getting married."

"It shouldn't be the only one, but you can scarcely hold it against a guy if he's rich."

"Since I don't intend to get married, the matter is academic," she said lightly.

Mike gave her a baffled look. "You're not interested in marriage, and you don't want a relationship. That's rather strange. Do you really want to spend your entire life alone?"

Her expression softened as she thought of Nicky. The way his face lit with excitement at the pure wonder of life, the feel of his sleepy head on her shoulder when she carried him to bed.

Mike gave her a narrowed look. "Perhaps I'm being naive and there *is* a man in your life."

"No, there's no man."

He was unconvinced. "That look on your face a moment ago seemed to indicate otherwise."

"Appearances are deceiving. You said so yourself."

As Mike stared at her in dissatisfaction, the waiter arrived with their first course, smoked Scottish salmon with capers.

He offered freshly ground pepper and asked if they wanted more lemon. Then he filled their wineglasses. By the time he finished, Erica's composure was firmly in place once more.

"This is delicious," she said, sampling her salmon.

"Yes, it isn't salty like the domestic kind," Mike answered absently.

"I can't remember ever seeing it in the market."

He gave up the pretense at small talk. "I don't know why it is, but every time we start to have a serious discussion, something happens to prevent it."

"Really? I hadn't noticed."

"Now who's pretending? You're instantly on the defensive whenever I get the least bit personal."

"You're conveniently forgetting your own behavior. You get pretty evasive yourself when the spotlight is on you," she said dryly.

"Perhaps in the beginning, before we got to know each other. Lately I've been trying to discuss something with you, but you won't listen. You have to admit I—" He broke off as someone put a hand on his shoulder.

"Hi, Mike, this is a coincidence. I was going to give you a call in the morning." Darren Mackie smiled at Erica. "Hello. We met on Ala Moana Boulevard one night."

"Yes, I remember. It's nice to see you again," she said politely.

"Are you going to be in your office tomorrow?" he asked Mike.

"I'll be in and out as usual."

"Can we set up an appointment? I'd like to talk to you about something."

"Tomorrow isn't really a good day. I have a heavy schedule."

"Maybe we could have lunch together," Darren insisted. "I ran across a deal I think you might be interested in. A client of mine is looking to unload his sugar holdings. It could be a sweet deal for you—no pun intended."

"Tell him he waited too long," Mike said. "Everybody is profit taking since the market went on an upswing. Prices are starting down."

"That's why he wants to unload in a hurry. He'll take what you're willing to offer. He needs the money, and your firm is the only one with ready cash."

Erica only half listened as they discussed large sums of money. She was more impressed by Mike's crisp questions and authoritative manner. He must be very good at whatever it was he did. She'd never been very clear about it.

Finally Mike cut the conversation short. "This isn't very interesting for Erica. Have your man call me in the morning and we'll see if we can work something out."

"I'm sorry," Darren apologized to her. "I didn't mean to disrupt your dinner. Enjoy."

He was only the first in a procession of people who stopped by the table on the way to their own, or made a special trip over to say hello.

Erica tried not to show her true feelings as they talked about yacht races and parties at one or more country clubs. This was the life Mike led when he wasn't with her. He must have to walk a financial tightrope to keep up with them. Not that she disapproved of his choice of friends; they seemed like nice enough people. Nobody tried to ignore her. She simply wasn't part of their social world.

Mike tried to bring Erica into the conversation. When someone mentioned a recent party and commented on the fact that he hadn't been there, Mike said, "That was one of the nights Erica and I had tickets to the Film Festival." He smiled at her. "It was the Russian film that almost put you to sleep. We should have skipped it and gone to the party."

The other couple turned to look at her speculatively. "Have you and Mike known each other long?" the woman asked.

"Not very," Erica replied.

"Are you here on a visit?" the woman probed delicately.

"Erica lives here," Mike answered for her. "She works at the Haialua Hotel."

Erica felt a chill touch her spine. This was exactly what she didn't want, a lot of strangers finding out details of her life. Fortunately their waiter approached, wheeling a steam cart holding a large standing rib roast under a copper hood. The couple left and the waiter carved the perfectly done meat and offered horseradish sauce to go with it.

Mike picked up his knife and fork with anticipation. "They make the best prime rib in town here. All their beef comes from Molokai."

"I thought the cattle ranches were on Maui and the Big Island," Erica observed.

"The largest ones are, but there are ranches all over, even here on Oahu. The one on Molokai is something to see. Besides cattle, it has a wildlife park with antelope, giraffes and other exotic animals. Sort of a touch of Africa here in the Pacific."

"Is it open to the public?" she asked, thinking how excited Nicky would be.

"I'm not sure if you need reservations. I'll find out and we'll go some weekend, if you can get away for once."

"You're the one with the busy schedule. I had no idea you were so social." She tried not to sound judgmental, without fully succeeding.

He paused for a moment, setting down his knife and fork. "I realize now that I should have been straightforward with you from the beginning. But at the time . . . well, I just hope you understand."

"That you've been leading a double life?" she asked lightly.

"I suppose you could put it that way. I've wanted to set the record straight, but it became increasingly difficult. That's why I chose this place for dinner tonight. I wanted you to meet my friends, to see me the way—" He swore under his breath at the waiter's efficiency.

The man hovered, alert to their every need. After filling their glasses with the last of the wine, he asked, "Would you like me to bring another bottle of wine, Mr. Smith?"

"Not right now," Mike answered, when Erica shook her head. "Let's dance," he said to her abruptly. "I brought you here for a purpose, but it looks like I'm never going to get around to it. Maybe we can manage a few minutes alone on the dance floor."

But when his arms closed around her, they were both silent. Nothing else seemed to matter for the moment. Mike's embrace tightened as she curved her arm around his neck and unconsciously caressed the width of his broad shoulder. Erica never failed to respond to his strong, physical appeal.

Mike was lost in the same magic. His lips moved over her temple as they drifted slowly to the romantic music. It was infuriating when a couple dancing next to them shattered the mood.

"Are you avoiding me, Mike?" It was the blonde who'd waved to him when they first arrived. "I thought you might at least come over to say hello," she pouted.

"Hi, Adriana, Greg." Mike nodded to the man with her, then introduced them both to Erica.

Adriana acknowledged her tepidly, then turned her attention back to Mike. "I wanted to tell you I'm on the committee for the President's Day dance. Can I count on your support?"

"That depends on what it entails," he answered cautiously.

"You're safe, we're not asking for donations this year." She laughed. "This will only cost you some time."

"How much time are we talking about? I'm rather busy right now."

"Everybody is, but you won't be able to turn me down when you hear what I'm planning." She took his hand unexpectedly. "Dance with Erica, Greg. I can't wait to fill Mike in on the details."

It was done so smoothly that nobody had a chance to object. Erica found herself in Greg's arms, while Adriana danced away in Mike's.

Greg laughed at her startled expression. "Don't worry, she'll bring him back. Adriana is just a little impulsive."

"So I noticed." Erica's eyes were on the other couple. She noticed that Mike didn't look annoyed. He was listening to the blonde's vivacious chatter with an amused expression. "They seem to be good friends," she said in a small voice.

"Nothing heavy," Greg answered casually. "They've known each other since they were kids. Are you a native, too?"

"No, I moved here fairly recently," Erica said, continuing to watch the other couple.

"It doesn't matter. You're not considered a true Hawaiian unless you were born here. I've lived in Honolulu since my early teens and I'm still looked on as a newcomer." Greg smiled.

Erica barely listened as he talked about what it was like to grow up in the islands. She was gripped by a fierce pang of jealousy as she watched the intimacy between Mike and the beautiful blonde. Had they been lovers? Were they still?

The idea was so painful that Erica was forced to acknowledge what she'd rejected for so long. She was in love with Mike. It wasn't sexual attraction, or his good looks and charming personality, or any of the other reasons a woman enjoys being with a man. She was crazy, head over heels in love with him!

The admission brought only panic. How had she allowed this to happen? She couldn't afford to get involved with anyone. Erica had faced that fact when she'd taken Nicky and moved to Hawaii.

Mike returned to claim her a few minutes later. "Sorry about that," he apologized. "Adriana is hard to resist."

"Yes, I suppose so."

"I put that badly. What I meant was, she doesn't stop to think that her timing might be inconvenient."

"It's all right. Greg is charming."

"Are you trying to make me jealous?"

Erica forced a smile. "Scarcely, when you have a glamorous blonde waiting in the wings."

"I happen to prefer long black hair and big blue eyes. It's an unbeatable combination." The music stopped and he squeezed her hand and led her off the floor.

The table had been cleared and the waiter had left smaller menus. After seating her, Mike said, "Let's see what they have for dessert."

Erica didn't think she could go on pretending that nothing had changed between them. But it would be disastrous if Mike found out she was in love with him. It was painful enough that she'd found it out herself.

He looked up from the menu. "They make a fantastic Gâteau St. Honore," he commented. "Unless you prefer something chocolate. I know what an addict you are," he teased.

"I don't want any dessert. I know it's early, but would you mind taking me home?"

His face sobered. "You're angry about Adriana. I assure you she pulls stunts like that on everybody. It wasn't anything personal."

"I'm sure that's true. It has nothing to do with her. I...I don't feel very well."

He looked at her in concern. "You don't look well. You're pale. What's the matter, honey?"

"I don't know, maybe some kind of virus. I just want to go home and crawl into bed."

"Of course. I'll get the check."

Mike was very solicitous. He wanted to take her to her door, but Erica managed to talk him out of it.

"I'm worried about you, angel. I'll give you a call in the morning."

She gave him a wan smile. "I'm sure I'll be all right after a good night's sleep." If only sleep *could* cure what ailed her.

Susie was surprised to see her. "I didn't expect you for hours. What are you doing home so early?"

Erica shrugged. "We finished dinner and there wasn't anything else to do, so we decided to call it a night."

"If I had a guy like Mike, I'd think of something to do." Susie grinned.

"You're just put out because you didn't make as much money baby-sitting tonight." Erica tried for a light tone as she got out her wallet.

"That's right. I only need a few more dollars for a down payment on a limo," Susie joked. "But I'll make it up next time."

"You'll have to look for another source of income. I won't be seeing Mike anymore."

"You're kidding! What happened? Did you have a fight?"

"No, I just decided not to go out with him again."

"Why not? Nobody dumps a dreamboat like that without a darn good reason."

Erica couldn't think of one—except the truth, which had to remain secret. "Mike might be handsome, but that doesn't make up for all the negative things about him."

"Like what?"

"Well, he ... he's a very shallow person. The people he runs around with are all rich and glamorous, and Mike tries to fit in."

"That's nice work if you can get it."

"Not really. In a weak moment he admitted to me that he's in financial difficulties. Then to make up for it he took me to the Catamaran Club tonight. He even tries to impress *me!*"

"That's a private club. How did he get in?"

"Probably with a guest card. Mike uses his friends shamelessly. He even gets free rent by house-sitting for one of them."

"Who wouldn't? I think you're being too hard on the man. He's never tried to take advantage of *you*."

"I'd prefer to stop seeing him before he does."

"Well, I guess you know what you're doing, but it seems like a shame. Guys like him don't come along every day."

Erica turned away so the bleakness in her eyes wouldn't show. "Thanks for sitting with Nicky."

"Any time." Susie paused at the door. "Take my advice and give this thing some more thought before you do something you'll regret."

My whole life has been a series of bad choices, Erica thought wearily as she got undressed. Except for Nicky, her love had never been returned. Why would Mike be any different—even if she was free to find out?

Mike telephoned the next morning. "It took so long for you to answer," he said anxiously. "Are you all right?"

"I'm much better, thank you. The switchboard just had trouble locating me."

"You're working? There's such a thing as being too conscientious," he scolded. "You looked terrible last night."

"Thanks a lot!"

"You know what I mean. I worry about you, honey. Promise me you'll go to bed early tonight."

Nobody had worried about her since she was a child. "I intend to," she said, over the lump in her throat.

"Good. I'll check with you tomorrow. Do you need anything?"

"Not that I can think of." She tried to keep the irony out of her voice.

Mike phoned every day, continuing to express concern. After Erica's repeated assurances that she felt much better, he asked to see her.

"Oh . . . well, I don't think I should go out so soon," she said. "I wouldn't want to get reinfected with whatever I had."

"I doubt if it was a virus or the flu. You got over it too quickly."

"I still get terribly tired by the time I finish work. Everything is an effort," she said, overdoing it.

"I'll bet you're not eating properly—if at all. Why don't I pick up some take-out food and bring it over? I'll even clean up afterward. You won't have to lift a finger."

"Maybe some other time. I really don't feel up to it tonight."

"Okay, angel, I won't pressure you. I miss you, though. Get well soon."

Erica knew Mike wasn't going to give up, and there was a limit to how long she could continue to claim lingering symptoms. The only thing left was to duck his phone calls. He'd get the message after a while and it shouldn't take long. Adriana would lead the procession of women waiting to assure Mike that he was irresistible.

Erica left instructions with Laura at the switchboard. "If I get a call from a man named Mike, tell him you can't locate me."

"I wish *I* had men to throw away." Laura grinned. "You're a lucky gal."

"One of the really fortunate ones," Erica answered sardonically.

Mike wasn't deterred by the fact that Erica stopped taking his calls. On the contrary. When she ignored his messages to contact him, either at his home or office, he only phoned more often.

The notes were put into Erica's mailbox in the employees' locker room. At first their tone was worried, then querulous—didn't she realize he was waiting to hear from her?—and finally annoyed. She read them stoically at the end of the day, then tore them up.

Nicky was the only bright spot in a hopelessly dreary life. He was so lively and loving that it was impossible to be dejected around him. When Erica tucked him into bed at night and the long evening stretched ahead, she told herself Nicky made up for everything.

One afternoon while Erica was personally checking the luxury suites, one of the maids came to tell her she was wanted at the front desk. Erica hurried down to the lobby, hoping some guest hadn't lodged a complaint. That was the way her luck had been running!

She was totally unprepared for the sight of Mike. He was lounging against the counter, looking even more handsome than she remembered. His cream-colored silk shirt was open at the throat, and the sleeves were rolled partway up his muscular forearms. His squared jaw and the autocratic tilt to his head only made him look more virile.

Erica's heart was beating so rapidly that it left her a little light-headed. She could only stare at him wordlessly.

Mike didn't bother with preliminaries. "Why didn't you answer my phone calls?" he demanded.

"I...well, I've been busy."

"Don't hand me that," he said roughly. "You could have taken five minutes to talk to me. Or at least called me back so I'd know you were alive."

"I didn't have anything life threatening," she protested.

He stared at her with narrowed eyes. "I don't think you were ever sick at all."

"You said yourself that I didn't look well!"

"Something was bothering you that night, but I don't think it was a virus. You've been avoiding me ever since, and I want to know why."

Erica went on the offensive, since there was no other choice. "You might try being a little more understanding. I've been working every day in spite of feeling rotten, and when I get back to my apartment at night I don't feel like talking to anyone." She hoped he'd buy her excuse and leave, because she couldn't keep up this pretense of indifference much longer.

Mike frowned uncertainly. "I can sympathize with everything you've said. *I* was the one who told you to take a few days off. But that doesn't change the fact that you've been avoiding me, and I intend to find out the reason. What happened that night?"

Erica glanced aside and became aware of Jerry, the assistant manager, listening avidly. She moved away from the desk, with Mike following her. "I really can't discuss it right now. I have to get back to work."

"Okay, when do you get through? I'll come back then. Because I want some answers, Erica. What time shall I be here?"

She glanced automatically at her watch—and felt her heart lurch. Nicky would be coming home from nursery school at any minute! He would race across the lobby and throw himself into her arms delightedly.

"I'll call you," she said breathlessly.

"Sure you will!" Mike snorted derisively.

"I will, I promise!"

"I'm prepared to follow you around from room to room until I get an answer," he warned.

"All right, I'll meet you for a drink tonight."

"No. I'll pick you up here. And if you don't show up I'll come looking for you."

Erica gazed despairingly at his adamant face. She knew he was capable of it. "I'll meet you at eight o'clock," she said, barely above a whisper.

"I've had more enthusiastic acceptances in my day," he remarked mockingly. "But I'll be here—and you'd better be, too."

She watched his lithe figure walk out the front door. As Mike got into his car, the nursery school van pulled up in back of him.

Chapter Four

Susie was only too happy to baby-sit with Nicky that night, but her services came with a price. Erica's nerves wound even tighter as Susie congratulated her on coming to her senses, and predicted romantic times ahead.

Her smile changed to a frown as Erica headed for the door. "You're not going like that? Aren't you going to change?"

Erica was wearing white pants and a red-and-white striped T-shirt. The choice had been deliberate. Mike had forced her into this meeting—that's what it was, not a date. They could talk right here in the hotel and he'd realize that it would be a waste of time for them to go on seeing each other. With any luck, she'd be back in an hour.

"No, it's time he saw me the way I really am," she told Susie, cutting off any further discussion by leaving the apartment.

* * *

Mike was dressed as casually as she, almost as though he anticipated her plan. He had on tight jeans and a navy pullover, an outfit that made him look lean and mean, a change from his usual urbanity.

They greeted each other briefly and with reserve. "Shall we go?" Mike asked.

"We don't need to go out. We can have a drink right here," Erica said.

"I'd prefer someplace where we can talk without interruption." He gripped her arm firmly and started for the front door.

"The cocktail lounge here is as good as anywhere else."

"It isn't as quiet as the place I have in mind."

She continued to protest all the way to the car, but Mike kept a tight grasp on her arm. She had to go along with him, or risk making a scene.

Erica stared straight ahead as Mike drove away from the hotel, her eyes sparkling mutinously. He had no right to treat her in such a high-handed manner. That was reason enough for not seeing him again, and she intended to tell him so.

Mike didn't try to break the deep silence. When Erica stole a sidelong glance at him, his profile was remote in the darkness, as though he were alone in the car.

Why did he insist on this meeting if he wasn't going to talk to her? she wondered in exasperation. Erica was damned if she was going to ask him, though!

It was only when she noticed that they were driving away from the glittering strip of hotels that curiosity got the better of her. "Where are we going?"

"To my house," he answered tersely.

"I don't want to go to your house. Take me back immediately!"

"Relax, I have no designs on your virginal body," he drawled.

"It really bothers you, doesn't it?" she asked hotly. "The thought that any woman can resist you."

"We studs don't take rejection well."

She looked at him uncertainly. Mike seemed more amused than angry at her assessment of him. "I've never seen you like this. You're different tonight."

He smiled mirthlessly as they pulled up to his house. "Now you know how I feel about *your* chameleon act."

Mike had left the lights on and the house was welcoming when they went inside. In spite of her annoyance and apprehension, Erica couldn't help feeling pleasure at the gracious surroundings.

"What would you like to drink?" he asked, opening the bar in the den.

"Nothing, thank you." She stood stiffly, across the room from him. "I can't stay long, so let's get this over with."

"Okay." He crossed his arms over his formidable chest. "Suppose you start by telling me what the hell is going on. A man likes to know why he's being dumped."

"I realize your pride is hurt," she began carefully.

"It has nothing to do with pride," he cut in. "I don't need to reassure myself that I'm sexually attractive to women. No man appeals to every woman, but I think in your case the attraction is there. That's what puzzles me. What did I do wrong? Is it because I *didn't* make a pass? Did you get tired of waiting?"

"No!" she gasped.

"Then tell me what it is. Are you afraid of sex?" he asked more quietly. "Did you have a bad experience?"

This was even more difficult than she expected. "You're wrong about me," she said haltingly. "I like you as a friend, nothing more."

He crossed the room to stand over her. "I could prove you're wrong," he said softly.

Erica retreated until her back was against the sliding glass window. If Mike took her in his arms it would be disastrous. Every inch of her body was crying out for him.

"That would be a cheap shot," she said in a shaky voice. "You could probably make me respond, but all it would prove is that you're very experienced and I'm a normal woman."

He stared down at her, trailing his fingertips over her cheek in an almost unbearably sensuous caress. "I think it would prove a lot more than that," he said in a husky voice.

"You promised you wouldn't," she whispered.

"When did I do that, sweetheart?"

"You said you only wanted to talk to me."

"I lied." He tangled his fingers in her long hair and tilted her head back, staring down at her with a molten expression. "If I told you what I really want to do—" He jammed his hands in his pockets and turned away. "Let's go for a walk along the beach."

Erica's legs were trembling as she followed Mike outside. She was grateful for the darkness, hoping it would hide her vulnerability.

"Are you warm enough?" he asked. The sky was clouded over and the wind off the water was brisk. Waves were pounding the shore, sounding like sonic booms.

"Yes, I'm fine." Erica welcomed the wild weather. It matched the turmoil inside her.

They drifted down to the shore where it was easier to walk on the damp, packed sand. For long moments, neither said anything. They were both shaken by the powerful emotions that had almost erupted.

Finally Mike broke the silence. "What are we going to do about us, Erica?"

"The only sensible thing. Admit that we have nothing in common."

"Beyond the obvious," he said mockingly.

"It isn't enough."

"It's one hell of a good start. I have a feeling we'd be fantastic together. And it isn't true that we're incompatible. We've never had a serious disagreement."

"Because you've always convinced me to do what you want."

"And you're afraid I'll want more?" He turned his head to stare at the pure line of her profile.

She was very conscious of his probing gaze. "Be honest, Mike. You're an extremely virile man. I don't think you would have been patient much longer."

"Even if that was true, why not wait until I stepped over the line?"

"I was trying to avoid the inevitable unpleasantness."

"You'd throw away a friendship on the off chance that I might make a pass at you?" he asked incredulously.

"It would have been very awkward," she murmured. "I thought it was better for us to stop seeing each other before anything . . . regrettable happened."

Mike's body became rigid with anger. His tawny eyes were glowing coals in the darkness, scorching her with his withering stare. "Are you telling me you were afraid I'd rape you if you refused?"

"No!" Erica backed toward the water. He actually looked capable of violence. "I never said that!"

"But you meant it. What did I ever do to make you think I'd try to force myself on you? Any man who would do such a thing is beneath contempt! I didn't realize you lumped me in with all the misfits and perverts in the world."

"I didn't! You're jumping to all the wrong conclusions."

"Am I?" His hard face didn't soften. "Convince me. Because I don't believe you were that spooked by the mere prospect of an argument, no matter how distasteful it might be."

Erica lowered her head and twisted her hands together nervously. If she let the misconception stand, Mike would never bother her again. It had to be that way, but not at such a price. He would remember her with disgust.

"If it's that hard to think of another explanation, there isn't any," he said sardonically. "I wanted an answer and I got one. Come on, I'll take you home."

What could she do to redeem herself without telling him the truth? The only solution was part of the truth, the part that didn't really matter.

As Mike turned toward the house, Erica said, "I wasn't honest with you when you asked if I ever had a bad experience. It wasn't anything as devastating as rape, but it left scars all the same."

He turned back. "Would you like to talk about it?"

"I never have, but maybe you won't judge me so harshly if you know." She stared down at the water that swirled around her ankles before receding, burying her feet in the sand. The tide was coming in. "We met in college. He was a senior and I was a lowly freshman. Jordan was handsome and popular, his family was wealthy, he had it all. I couldn't believe it when he asked me for a date."

Mike started to say something, then thought better of it.

"We began to go together and at first everything was wonderful. Looking back, I realize it was because I always let him have his own way. Jordan didn't like foreign films, so we didn't go. He didn't like most of my friends, so we didn't see them."

"He sounds like a real charmer," Mike commented sardonically.

"I was very young. And I thought I was in love."

"Sex can easily be confused with love when you're young. I presume you hadn't had much experience with men."

"I was a virgin," she said simply.

"Even worse," Mike muttered. "I hope he initiated you gently."

"I don't know. It wasn't what I expected from reading romantic novels. Maybe it was my fault, but I always thought sex was overrated." Until she met Mike, Erica thought privately.

A puzzled look overcame his disgust. "But that was a long time ago, and you picked a loser. After you realized it, you must have met some caring men who loved you the way you deserve."

That was as much of the story as she could safely tell him. He mustn't find out about her marriage—and especially its aftermath.

When she didn't answer, Mike looked at her in disbelief. "Are you saying you haven't been with a man since?"

He might conclude that she was frigid, but it was better than finding out the real reason she'd never dared allow anyone to get close to her. She tried evasive tactics. "Jordan was very controlling, the way you are. I went along with his decisions even when I didn't want to."

"*That's* why you decided to stop seeing me?" Mike exclaimed. "Because you thought I was like your pathetic boyfriend?"

"You must agree that you have a very strong personality." She gave him the ghost of a smile.

"I'd say we were evenly matched. You made me work for every date you agreed to—including this one."

"I'll admit you were right about tonight. It's better to clear up our misunderstandings. I'd really like to part friends."

"We haven't cleared up a damn thing! So you had a lousy relationship. Does that mean you'll never take a chance on anybody again? I don't think you're that timid."

Erica suppressed a sigh as she was forced to surrender the rest of her pride. "I believed Jordan when he said he loved me. And then I found out he was cheating on me regularly. I've seen it happen to other couples, too, after they've been together for a while. Men seem to get bored when the chase is over. You and I had a lovely relationship. I wanted it to end on a happy note." Her excuse was rather thin, but it was the best she could come up with.

Mike shook his head in disgust. "If I had that guy here right now I'd hold his head underwater for about fifteen minutes. What happened to him? Did you finally come to your senses and dump him?"

"He's long gone," Erica answered, without elaborating.

"But not forgotten, I can tell. You're a warm, responsive woman, sweetheart. No man would want anyone else if he could have you. I'm going to prove it to you."

When he reached for her, Erica backed away, unaware that she was now in water up to her knees. As she stumbled over a piece of coral submerged in the sand, a large wave broke over her head, knocking her down.

Mike pulled her upright, then swung her into his arms and struggled to shore against the strong undertow. Seaweed was tangled in Erica's hair and she was soaked to the skin.

"Are you all right, darling?" he asked anxiously as she coughed and sputtered.

"I guess so." She started to shiver. "It's cold."

"Hang on, we'll be inside in a minute and you can take a hot shower."

Mike didn't put her down when they reached the house. He carried her through the den and down a carpeted hallway.

"We're dripping sand and water all over everything," she protested.

"Big deal." He set her on her feet in a large, luxurious bedroom.

It was a very masculine room. The king-size bed was covered with a tailored gray spread, and the ebony wood furniture was quietly elegant. None of the surfaces were cluttered with knickknacks, but books were stacked on a table by the window and on a nightstand. The one on the other side of the bed held a silver-framed photograph of

Mike with his arm around a laughing young woman with light brown hair.

Erica pushed the wet hair off her forehead and glanced down at her sodden clothing. "What a mess I am!"

He smiled, plucking a sprig of seaweed out of her hair. "You look like a mermaid."

As his eyes traveled over her, she was suddenly conscious of how provocative she must look. Her wet T-shirt was plastered so tightly to her breasts that her nipples were clearly defined.

She folded her arms over them quickly. "How am I going to go home looking like this?"

He dragged his eyes back to her face reluctantly. "Don't worry, I'll toss your clothes in the dryer. They'll be ready by the time you get cleaned up." He indicated a yellow-and-gray-tiled bathroom off the bedroom. "You can shower in here and I'll use the guest bath. Just hand your clothes out to me."

Erica went into the bathroom and closed the door. It was spacious like the bedroom, big enough for an oversize tub with a built-in whirlpool, and a separate, glass-enclosed shower.

She stripped off her wet jeans and T-shirt. Standing behind the door, she opened it just wide enough to hand them out to Mike.

He took them from her, but when she started to close the door he said, "Where's your underwear?"

"Oh . . . well, it will dry in here."

"Don't be ridiculous, honey. Give it to me. I've seen a woman's bra and panties before."

"I'm sure you have," she said tartly. "All right, wait a minute till I take them off." She stripped to the skin and handed him the two little scraps of lace and nylon.

He gripped the fragile garments tightly, picturing her slim, naked body. Stifling a groan, he turned away.

After putting her clothes in the dryer, Mike returned to the bedroom to get some dry clothes for himself, which he carried into the guest bath. But after hesitating for a moment he went back to the den and poured himself a drink. Time passed while he stood at the window, staring out at the turbulent ocean.

How was he going to convince Erica that all men weren't pond scum like that boyfriend of hers? Any woman would be put off by a guy like that, but a first encounter would be especially disillusioning. Could he break through the wall she'd built around herself? Finally he sighed and went back to the guest room.

Erica's thoughts were equally somber as she took a hot shower and washed the saltwater out of her hair. Being forced to talk about Jordan had brought back all the bitterness and pain. It was bad enough that he'd made her unhappy while they were together; Jordan had also made it impossible for her to have a normal, loving relationship with any other man. Not for the reason Mike thought, but it amounted to the same thing.

She turned off the shower and wrapped herself in a large fluffy bath towel. Using Mike's hair dryer, she blow-dried her hair, telling herself this ordeal was almost over. He would attempt to get her to change her mind, but at least he wouldn't use seduction. That was the one argument she might not be able to resist.

Mike hadn't brought her clothes back to the bedroom as she'd hoped. They should be dry by now, though. It had taken at least half an hour to get cleaned up. Wrapping the towel more tightly around herself, she went into the hall. The shower was running in the other bathroom so she decided to go looking for her clothes on her own. The logical place for the dryer was in the kitchen, or a service porch next to it.

Erica paused to admire the sleekly modern kitchen. It had all the latest appliances, long counters to work at, and a big window over the sink. What a joy it would be to cook here! She could picture Nicky sitting at the round glass table while she prepared his breakfast.

Reluctantly she continued on to the service porch where she found the laundry equipment. Her pants were still a little damp, but Erica couldn't wait any longer. She wanted to be fully clothed when Mike appeared. At least her underwear and T-shirt were dry.

Flinging the the bath towel aside, she pulled on her panties. As she reached for her bra, a strangled sound made her whirl around quickly. Mike was standing in the doorway, wearing only jockey shorts. The brief strip of white made his deep tan more apparent.

They stared at each other as though hypnotized, neither able to move. Erica's heart raced as she gazed at his powerful body, and Mike couldn't drag his eyes away from her pink-tipped breasts.

He finally moved toward her, as though pulled by an invisible wire. "I thought you were still in the bathroom," he murmured.

"I came to get my clothes." The golden glow in his eyes immobilized her. She was incapable of reaching for her T-shirt.

"I would have brought them to you," he said in a husky voice.

"You were in the shower," she whispered.

"I'm here now."

Mike put his arms around her and drew her gently toward him, giving her a chance to pull away. But how could she? Raw desire drove everything else from her mind. She needed to feel his bare body against hers, wanted him to fill her with the ecstasy only he could bring.

"Beautiful Erica, it's going to be so different this time," he said softly. "I'll show you the way it should be between a man and a woman." He kissed her with great tenderness.

With a sigh of anticipation, she clasped her arms around his neck and clung so tightly that their bodies were sealed together.

Mike's embrace tightened and he parted her lips for a deep kiss that drove her passion even higher. Uttering a tiny cry, she dug her fingers into the bunched muscles of his back.

He swung her into his arms and carried her down the hall, kissing her closed eyelids and each corner of her tremulous mouth. When they reached his bedroom he placed her on the bed and joined her without letting her out of his arms.

"I want it to be so good for you, sweetheart." He covered her face with kisses.

"It already is," she whispered.

"Ah, darling, you're so wonderfully responsive." He lowered his head and took one nipple between his lips. "I want to bring you more joy than you've ever known."

After removing her panties he stroked her thighs sensuously, igniting the flames that were licking at her midsection. She quivered as he slipped his hand between her legs and caressed her intimately, making her ravenous for him.

Erica arched her body into his and slid her hands inside the waistband of his shorts, clutching at his tight buttocks. "I've never wanted anyone like this," she moaned.

"My darling love!" Mike kissed her fiercely, then ripped off his shorts and positioned himself between her legs.

When he thrust deeply, she wrapped her arms around his waist and raised her hips to receive all of him. He filled her with such rapture that she called out his name over and over again.

They moved against each other with total abandon as the storm built to an almost unbearable fierceness. Mike waited until she had reached the summit before seeking his own release.

Erica clutched him tightly as wave after wave of sensation swept through her taut body, thunderous at first, then spiraling down to a warm glow of total satisfaction. She smiled blissfully as Mike kissed her closed eyelids.

"Do you see the difference now?" he asked tenderly.

"I never knew it could be like this."

He smiled into her dazzled eyes. "It gets better, too."

"I don't see how it possibly could."

He caressed her body lovingly. "Give me a few minutes and I'll show you."

Erica curled up in his arms, filled with contentment. Reality was waiting to destroy it, but she didn't allow herself to think beyond this moment.

"I'm glad we finally worked everything out, but I wish you'd told me sooner what the problem was," Mike said. "I went through hell, wondering why you wouldn't see me."

"Don't talk, just hold me," she murmured.

"Gladly." He kissed her with deep affection. "But we have to talk, angel. There are things about myself that I haven't told you."

"Whatever they are, I don't want to hear them."

"You have to let me tell you. I don't want any more misunderstandings to crop up between us. We need to be completely honest with each other."

She stirred uneasily. "When people say that, it's usually a preface to something you don't want to hear."

Mike pulled her back into his arms. "I don't have any shameful secrets in my past, honey."

"You don't have to confess them to me, even if you do."

"You're the most important person in my life. I want us to know everything about each other."

"Oh, Mike." Her eyes shimmered with unshed tears. "Why can't we just have this one perfect night?"

"We're going to have a lot more than this one." He kissed her, gently at first, then with growing passion.

Erica responded almost desperately, trying to banish her problems for this short, enchanted time. But when Mike began to work his magic on her, she didn't have to try.

His mouth and hands fanned the embers of her sated desire, bringing her body to pulsing life once more. He seemed to know exactly what she wanted, and took delight in his ability to please her. She'd never guessed her body was capable of such pleasure.

When it was over, even Mike was speechless. He was content simply to hold her close. Erica broke the spell reluctantly, after glancing at the clock next to the silver-framed photo.

"It's getting late. I have to leave."

"Why?" He tightened his embrace. "Stay with me tonight."

"I can't. I have to work tomorrow."

"We'll get up early in the morning, make love, and then I'll drive you to work." He kissed the tip of her nose. "Doesn't that sound like a winner? I'll even make you breakfast first."

"You have it down to a routine," she said lightly.

"You think that's the way I start every day? I couldn't possibly be as sexually active as you imagine," he answered dryly.

Maybe not, but he hadn't learned all he knew by practicing celibacy. Erica glanced unconsciously at the photograph. Was she someone special?

Mike followed her gaze. "That's my sister," he said quietly. "Not the favorite in my harem."

"It's the only photograph in the room," she said defensively. "I couldn't help wondering."

"You should have asked me."

"I didn't have the right. You're free to go out with anyone you choose."

"And you think I chose you to be the designated bed partner for tonight?" he demanded. "You still don't get it, do you? I'm in love with you, Erica."

She stared at him in shock for a moment, then inexpressible joy made her heart soar. Mike loved her! It was like a gift from heaven—until reality set in. This could only complicate matters.

He smiled at the confused emotions on her face. "Now will you stay with me tonight?"

"I wish I could," she said truthfully. "But I really can't. Please don't make it any harder, darling."

He stared at her speculatively. "I have a feeling that if I kept you here I could find out what other secrets you're keeping from me."

Erica tried to smile. "A woman has to retain a little bit of mystery to be interesting."

"I'm already completely under your spell." He lifted her chin and looked at her searchingly. "But you've never said how you feel about *me*."

Her long lashes lowered to hide the truth. "Tonight should have answered that."

"It could have been merely a strong physical need on your part. You're a very passionate woman."

Erica's cheeks warmed as she remembered her uninhibited response in his arms. "You taught me things I never knew before."

"Was that all it was for you, satisfactory sex?"

"I . . . you must know I'm very fond of you."

"I would hope so, since we're having this conversation in bed," he remarked sardonically. "Okay, Erica, call me the next time you're feeling friendly. I'll be glad to oblige."

"I didn't mean to hurt your feelings," she said in a low voice. "I thought I showed you how I felt. It's very difficult for me to put things into words."

"I only want you to use four of them." He gathered her into his arms and tipped her chin up. "Say, I love you, Mike."

What was the point in refusing when it must be written clearly on her face? "I love you, Mike," she said softly.

His embrace tightened and he kissed her tenderly. They clung to each other, exchanging whispered words of endearment between kisses. But when his caresses became more intimate, Erica stopped him reluctantly.

"I really have to go, Mike."

"I still don't understand why, but I won't argue anymore—this time." He followed her out of bed and pulled on his shorts. "When is your next day off? I'll pick you up after work and we'll spend the night together and all the next day."

"Have you also decided what time we'll get up and what we'll have for lunch?" she teased.

Mike's face sobered immediately. "I'm not trying to control your life like that weasel, Jordan."

Erica went over to put her arms around his waist. "I was only joking. There's not the slightest similarity between you two."

"I can see where I might have seemed autocratic," he said slowly. "I refused to take no for an answer a lot of times."

"I'm glad you did." She smiled. "If you'd gotten discouraged and given up, I wouldn't be here now, feeling wonderful."

"I can make you feel even better," he murmured, caressing her bare bottom.

"Do you give rain checks?" She laughed, moving out of his embrace.

"Not usually, but in your case I'll make an exception."

When they reached the hotel, Mike wanted to see Erica to her door, but she wouldn't let him.

"You still don't trust me, even after tonight?" He frowned.

"How can you think a thing like that? It's just that it's late and I really have to get some sleep. I know what would happen when we got upstairs."

"You're probably right." His grin faded. "Am I ever going to see your apartment?"

"I'll cook dinner for you one night," she promised, wondering how long she could put him off with excuses.

Mike was thoughtful on the drive home. Erica was the girl he'd been looking for all his life. She was warm and genuine, completely unpretentious, and disdainful of phony values. All this in addition to being the most gorgeous, sexiest woman alive! His loins quickened at the memory of the night they'd just spent.

But what did he know about her day-to-day life? How did she spend the time when they weren't together? He always had the feeling she was leading a double life. His conscience pricked uncomfortably as he realized the same could be said about him.

Although he had an early-morning appointment, Mike didn't go to bed when he got home. He paced the den floor restlessly, wondering if Erica would be angry when he told her about himself. She had every right to be.

Finally he strode to the telephone and punched out his sister's number.

"Do you know what time it is?" Nancy asked indignantly, after finding out nothing was wrong.

"It's only midnight. You never go to sleep until twelve-thirty or one."

"You might have wakened Steve," she said, referring to her husband. "Or we could have been making love."

"I hope you'd have had sense enough not to answer the telephone." Mike laughed. "Tell Steve I'm sorry, either way."

"It's all right, he isn't here. He went to Maui for a couple of days to do some consulting on an engineering job. What's up, big brother? Why aren't *you* making love at this hour? Isn't that what swinging bachelors do every night?"

"I don't know where you women get your information," he complained.

"Oh? Has some other woman given you a bad time?"

"No. Nothing like that." Mike's softened tone was detectable.

His sister's interest quickened. "Give me an update on your love life. Are you still playing the field, or did some lucky player finally score a goal?"

"How did you guess?"

"It was bound to happen sooner or later. Tell me about her. Will I like her?"

"You couldn't help it. She's sweet and beautiful and intelligent."

Nancy laughed. "If she's also obedient and house-trained, you could be describing Mother's poodle."

"I should have known better than to call you for advice," Mike said disgustedly.

"I'm sorry. It's just so unusual to hear you rhapsodize over a woman. I thought maybe you were putting me on. There *have* been a lot of females in your life."

"None like Erica. This is the real thing."

"Then why do you need advice?"

"Well, the problem is, I haven't been completely honest with her."

"That's good. The last thing a woman needs to hear about is a man's previous affairs. And don't ask about hers. People in love think they want to know those things, but they can come back to haunt you."

"That isn't the problem that concerns me. You see, we met kind of by accident and I didn't tell her who I am."

"You didn't use your right name?"

"Of course I did," he said impatiently. "But Mike Smith is a common enough name. She didn't realize I was Grover Smith's son."

"It isn't your fault that she didn't make the connection."

"Maybe not, but I didn't try very hard to make it clear. She sort of got the idea that I was a wage slave like everybody else, just scraping by. She thinks this house belongs to a friend and I'm house-sitting for free rent."

"She couldn't have gotten that impression out of thin air. Did you 'sort of' tell her that?" Nancy asked ironically.

Mike sighed. "I'm not proud of it, but you know what it's like when people find out your father is Grover Dudley Smith, the man who owns half of Hawaii."

"I wouldn't go that far."

"Okay, so he only has holdings in cattle, cotton and sugar."

"Plus a few allied businesses. Yes, I know what you mean," Nancy agreed. "I had some bad experiences myself before I met Steve."

"Exactly. You never know if people like you for yourself, or for who you are and what you can do for them."

"Erica was attracted to you when she thought you were poor, so you don't have to worry about that. Just tell her the truth."

"Oh, sure! I didn't tell you who I was, sweetheart, because I figured you'd try to take me for everything you could get. That ought to go over big."

"You don't have to say it like that. Explain that you didn't know anything about her in the beginning. You said you met by accident. Where was it?"

"On the beach one night. I had on cutoffs and a torn T-shirt. If I'd told her the truth she wouldn't have believed me, which made it easier to keep up the fiction that I was just an ordinary working stiff. Then when I started to fall in love with her, I was afraid to tell her. What if I couldn't make her understand, and she walked out on me?"

"If you're that serious, you have to tell her."

"That's my other problem. I've tried, but she won't let me."

"I don't understand. How can she stop you?"

"Every time I try to talk to her, she finds some excuse to change the subject, or else she suddenly has to leave. The same thing happens when I ask personal questions of her. She doesn't like to talk about herself."

"Maybe she's an heiress and she's been putting on the same act you have. Wouldn't that be a hoot?"

"Yeah, hysterical."

"Seriously, Mike, I'm sure Erica is a terrific person, but what do you really know about her? What does she do for a living? Who are her friends? Where does she live?"

"She's head of housekeeping at the Haialua Hotel. They furnish her with an apartment."

"That's quite a perk. How do you know it's the truth? Have you seen it?"

He hesitated. "Well, no, I always pick her up in the lobby. But only because it's more convenient that way."

"Maybe, but I think you might have a problem, pal. Before you go off the deep end, you'd better find out why she's being so secretive."

"I think I know. Erica had a relationship with a creep who tried to take charge of her whole life. He had her so brainwashed that she did everything he said. He even made her give up all of her friends for him."

"You wonder why women put up with guys like that, but they do."

"When she finally got free of him, I think she promised herself she'd never get into another controlling relationship. Without ever realizing it, I'm afraid I scared her off."

"You can be very intimidating to people who don't know you're just a big old teddy bear." Nancy chuckled. "But you have to set her straight about your family."

"I've tried to correct my mistake. When we first met, I took her to unpretentious little restaurants where I figured I wouldn't run into anybody who knew me. Then when I realized what a jerk I was, I took her to nicer places, paving the way for a confession. She never gave me an opportunity. Finally I took her to the Catamaran Club, hoping she'd find out for herself. Some of the crowd were bound to be there. It's their hangout."

"I gather that didn't work, either. Don't tell me all your friends were dining elsewhere."

"No, a lot of them were there. They all stopped by the table and talked about yachting races and raising money for charity, but nobody mentioned Mother or Dad."

"What did you expect them to say, 'How's your tycoon father?' Or maybe, 'Did your dad close another million-dollar deal today?'"

"I don't know what I expected." Mike groaned. "All I did was complicate matters. Now Erica thinks I'm a hanger-on, trying to keep up with the Joneses. What the devil am I going to do?"

"I can see where that would be a turnoff. Did it lead to an argument tonight? Is that why you called?"

"No, this evening was . . . everything was fine." His softened voice revealed more than he realized.

"Then my advice is just to cool it for a while. If you keep pressuring her, she'll only get more defensive. It probably reminds her of the other guy."

"You could be right," Mike said thoughtfully. "He left a lot of scars."

"When she feels relaxed with you, maybe she'll be more open about herself."

"You have it backward," he said wryly. "*I'm* the one who's looking for an opportunity to be truthful."

"It wouldn't hurt for both of you to be honest with each other."

"I know all I need to know about Erica," he stated in a voice that didn't invite discussion.

"I wasn't criticizing her," Nancy said cautiously. "But it does seem strange that you pick her up in a hotel lobby. Why doesn't she want you to see where she lives?"

"I knew you'd react this way! That's why I never brought her around to meet you. Just because Erica doesn't belong to our charmed circle, you automatically assume she's a fortune hunter."

"Don't be such a blockhead!" Nancy's annoyance matched his. "You're my brother and I care about you. I don't want you to get hurt."

"You needn't worry." Mike's voice was vibrant. "Erica is the first woman I've ever felt sure about."

Nancy's face was sober after they hung up. Had her brother finally fallen in love—but with the wrong woman?

Chapter Five

Mike was annoyed at his sister for doubting Erica, but her advice was sound. He'd been pushing Erica too hard. From now on he intended to wait until she had confidence in him. His loins pulsed as he recalled the giant step she'd already taken in that direction.

The days that followed—or rather, the nights—were idyllic. Mike picked Erica up after work several times that week and brought her back to his house. Sometimes they went for a swim while the darkening sky was still faintly tinted with pink from the recent sunset, and the first stars were starting to appear.

Afterward they would shower together and take turns soaping each other with a sponge, playfully at first, then more erotically until their passion flamed out of control. When it was too urgent for any delay, they consummated their love right there, under the warm, gentle flow of water.

At other times, Mike would sit on the built-in marble seat of the tub and lift Erica onto his lap, facing him. She would curl her legs around his waist and utter tiny cries of delight as he cupped her breasts in his hands and kissed each sensitive nipple.

Erica would never have believed she could be so abandoned, or that making love could be this mutual act of giving pleasure. She was often the one who guided Mike inside of her, who was thrilled as much by his satisfaction as her own.

One night when they were wrapped in robes, she smiled blissfully. "I never knew bathing could be such fun."

"You never showered with what's-his-name?" Mike exclaimed without thinking. He regretted it when her face clouded over. "The next thing I'm going to teach you is how to barbecue," he said hastily. "Are you hungry?"

"Famished! I seem to have worked up quite an appetite." She grinned.

It was like a honeymoon. They cooked together, took long romantic walks along the beach in the moonlight, and made endless, fulfilling love.

Everything was perfect until the weekend approached. Mike was full of plans to show Erica all that the islands had to offer.

"Would you like to go to the Mauna Kea Beach Resort and play tennis, or would you prefer to hike through a rain forest on Lanai?"

"They both sound rather strenuous," she remarked tepidly.

"Okay, then I have another suggestion. We could take a boat to the Leeward Islands. There's a whole string of beautiful little atolls that are uninhabited except for birds and an occasional sea turtle. I know of one that's especially romantic. We can swim in the lagoon and make love in a fern grotto." He ran a finger down her spine suggestively. "Can you think of something better to do?"

"No, it's a wonderful plan," she said brightly. "Unfortunately I can't make it this weekend."

Erica had felt only marginally guilty about leaving Nicky that week, since she'd been there to give him dinner and tuck him into bed. Susie had offered to do it, but Erica refused. There was no way she would leave her son on the weekend.

Mike frowned. "Aren't you off on Saturday and Sunday?"

"Yes, but I . . . I've already made plans."

"I see." He struggled mightily to remember Nancy's advice. Play it cool. Don't try to take over her life.

"I'm really sorry, Mike." She braced herself for an argument that didn't develop.

"I understand," he said pleasantly. "We'll do it some other time."

Erica was relieved, but she knew it was only a respite. Mike wouldn't accept such a vague excuse for long. It was only a matter of time until he demanded to know what she did with her weekends. The explosion would come when she couldn't tell him.

Erica took Nicky to a movie that Saturday, and for ice cream afterward. As usual, his happiness chased away her depression. Until he started to talk about his friends at nursery school.

"Why don't I have a daddy like Kevin does?"

"You did have, but he went to heaven before you were born," Erica said. "I already told you that."

"I meant a daddy like Kevin has *now*. The one he had before went away like mine did, but his mother got him a new one. Why don't you do that?"

"We don't really need one," she said, keeping her voice casual. "Don't we have fun together, just the two of us?"

"Yes." The little boy thought it over. "But it would be more fun if I had some brothers and sisters. Everyone at school does. Do you think I'll ever have any?"

"You never can tell." Before he could pursue the subject she said, "Would you like to stop by the toy store after you finish your ice cream?"

Nicky was instantly distracted, as she meant him to be. But his plaintive question raised recurring doubts. Was she depriving him of a normal childhood? What else could she do, though?

Mike tried to be patient with Erica, as he'd promised himself, but things weren't working out according to plan. She continued to refuse weekend dates without any real explanation.

The obvious reason was another man. Mike's jaw clenched at the thought, and yet... in spite of all the indications, he couldn't believe Erica was two-timing him. Their nights together were too incredibly perfect. She gave herself to him completely when they made love. That wasn't the behavior of a woman who had another man in her life.

But in spite of Mike's belief that Erica would eventually confide in him, nothing changed. She never mentioned her private life and she wouldn't let him tell her about his. Mike paced the floor on many a night, trying to figure out a solution. Finally he had an idea.

It bothered him greatly to live a lie, even though it wasn't solely his fault. If he arranged for Erica to find out what he'd been concealing, surely she'd have to be more open about herself. It was a way of killing two birds with one stone.

His parents were lending their estate for one of his mother's frequent charity affairs. Nancy and Steve would be there, too. It was a chance for Erica to meet the whole family and see that he wasn't the social-climbing jerk she disapproved of.

Mike timed the invitation for the beginning of the week, before Erica could make other plans. For extra insurance he waited until after they'd made love. She was lying in his arms with a blissful expression on her face.

"I'll never get enough of you," he said, stroking her cheek.

"We see each other three or four times a week. I keep expecting you to get tired of me." She wanted to hear him deny it.

"Every night would be hardly enough, but I want to see what you look like in the daylight, too."

"You've seen every part of me," she said softly.

Mike was almost distracted when she moved against him, but he used willpower. "I'd be content to spend all our time exactly like this, but I don't want you to get bored. We haven't gone out in ages."

"I'm not complaining."

"I don't intend to wait until you do. We're going to stop being such recluses, starting this weekend. Save Sunday for me," he said casually. "There's someplace I want to take you."

Erica's face assumed its usual hooded expression. "I've already made plans for Sunday."

"This early in the week?"

"Yes, I...I'm afraid so."

"I'd like you to change them. It would mean a lot to me."

She avoided his eyes. "I wish I could, but it's impossible."

"Is there another man, Erica?" he asked somberly.

"No! I told you that before."

"How can I believe you when you're unavailable every weekend? You must be seeing *someone.*"

She could tell he wouldn't be put off this time. If she refused to give him an explanation it might be the end of their relationship. It had been doomed from the beginning, but Erica couldn't bear to see it end yet.

"I do spend my weekends with somebody," she said hesitantly. "But not the way you think. It's someone who depends on me. I've made a commitment and I don't like to go back on it.''

Mike looked puzzled. "You're talking about some kind of volunteer work?"

What a perfect excuse! "It's something I enjoy doing," she murmured.

"Why on earth didn't you tell me sooner? All this time I've been going through hell picturing you with another man!"

"You didn't act like it," she said uncertainly. "You seemed more annoyed than jealous."

"I could have had a great career as an actor. Just the thought of any other man touching you drove me wild."

"You should have known better." She kissed the hollow in his throat. "How could you even think such a thing?"

"I couldn't imagine what else it could be. That became my worst nightmare. I just wish I'd asked you sooner."

"Well, now you know. That's one less thing you have to worry about," she teased.

"I think you enjoy keeping me guessing." He gave her a mock frown.

"A woman is entitled to a *few* secrets," she said lightly.

He took her in his arms, looking at her with a serious expression. "I don't want there to be any secrets between us. That's what causes misunderstandings. I want you to trust me enough to tell me everything."

"There isn't anything else to tell." She stirred in his arms.

Mike had a feeling there was, but he'd learned better than to push too hard. "Okay, now that that's settled, let's get back to Sunday. I'll pick you up at two."

She gave him a startled look. "I told you I couldn't go."

"I think what you're doing is admirable, honey, but you're going a little overboard. Nobody expects you to spend every weekend doing good deeds."

"People count on me to be there."

"Not Saturday *and* Sunday. I'm only asking you to give up one afternoon. I'm sure with a whole week's notice they can get somebody to fill in for you. What is this place, a retirement home, or a senior citizens' center?"

Erica managed to avoid the question. "It wouldn't be fair to ask somebody else to take my place."

They argued back and forth until finally Mike said quietly, "I'm not just being arbitrary. This means a lot to me, Erica. If you care for me at all, you'll come with me on Sunday."

This was the showdown she'd been dreading, and there was no way out. She couldn't leave Nicky even if she would consider it. Susie spent the weekends with her family, visiting with her brothers and sisters and their numerous children. Erica had a standing invitation to bring Nicky to play with the other kids. She'd done it on several occasions and he'd had a wonderful time.

"I'm waiting," Mike said adamantly.

Erica hesitated. Was she being an overly protective mother? Nicky would enjoy a day with Susie's brood. He felt comfortable with her and he liked being with other children. Were his present weekends alone with her really that satisfying?

Mike's eyes were bleak. "If it's that hard for you to decide, I guess I have my answer."

She made up her mind. "I was just trying to think of somebody to take my place. If the one I have in mind is willing, I'd love to go with you on Sunday."

He grabbed her and held her tightly. "You can't believe how happy you've made me! This is going to change our lives, I know it."

Nicky was so delighted to go with Susie that Sunday that Erica knew she'd made the right decision. Every instinct urged her to keep him close and safe, but he had to be allowed to spread his wings.

Erica was curious about where Mike was taking her, but he wouldn't say. When she told him she had to know how to dress, he would only tell her they were going to a party. A luau? A barbecue? He refused to be specific, but after seeing how his friends dressed, Erica decided not to be too casual.

"Do I look all right?" she asked when he came to pick her up.

The answer was evident in his eyes as they traveled over her admiringly. She had bought a new dress for the occasion, a gauzy white frock with lace insets that gave tantalizing glimpses of her slim body. The pink high-heeled sandals she wore provided a touch of color and also matched her pink shell earrings and straw purse.

"You look gorgeous," Mike said as they got in the car. "I can't wait to show you off."

"To whom? You still haven't told me where we're going."

"You'll find out in a few minutes. It isn't far from here." To forestall any more questions he said, "I haven't seen that dress before. It's lovely."

"You haven't see me in much of anything lately." She grinned.

He turned his head to give her a sultry look. "It's your most becoming outfit."

"That doesn't say much for this dress."

"It's almost as beautiful as you are. Everybody's going to love you."

As she was preparing to ask who that might be, Mike turned into a driveway between two impressive gates set in a high stone wall. The palm-lined drive led to a sprawling mansion partially hidden by lush shrubbery. A profusion of bougainvillea matched the red tile roof and contrasted stunningly with the white walls of the house.

The driveway was filled with expensive cars, and music was playing somewhere. Although no one was in sight, the sound of voices indicated a party was in progress.

"What a gorgeous estate. Who lives here?" Erica asked.

Instead of answering, Mike said, "The party is around the back."

He opened the front door without bothering to ring the bell, and led her through the house to a broad terrace fronting the ocean. The view was spectacular. Well-tended green lawns sloped gently to the beach and the ocean beyond where little sailboats bobbed and skimmed like butterflies.

Two red-and-white striped tents were set up on the lawn to dispense food and drinks to the scores of guests milling about. The music was coming from a combo on the terrace, competing with the din of the crowd.

As Mike scanned the little knots of animated people, an older woman detached herself from a group and came toward them. She had a patrician face and a self-assured manner. It was quite evident that she belonged in this social sphere.

"Hello, darling," she called to Mike. "I couldn't believe it when you said you were coming today. I know how you hate these things."

"No more than having my tax return audited." He grinned and kissed her cheek. "Mother, I'd like you to meet Erica Barclay. Erica, my mother, Phyllis."

"How nice of you to come, my dear." Phyllis Smith extended her hand. "I know you could be doing something a lot more interesting."

"If you know these things are dull, why do you keep giving them?" Mike teased.

"Because I raise a lot of money for charity this way."

"I'll bet you could raise even more if you let everybody just mail in their checks and stay home."

Erica barely heard them. The first shock was finding out this elegant society lady was Mike's mother. The second was that she was their hostess. His parents actually lived in this splendor! Nothing made sense.

"Get Erica a drink and circulate," Phyllis said. "I want everybody to see I really do have a son." With a wave of her hand, she left them.

Erica gave Mike a bewildered look. "That was really your mother?"

"Would anybody claim to be, otherwise?" He laughed.

"I don't understand any of this. If your parents are this wealthy, how can you have money problems? You said you were in debt."

His merriment faded. "I didn't exactly say that. I think I said something like, what *if* I was in debt."

"What's the difference?"

"No matter how I put it, I'm going to come out looking like a jerk—which is exactly what I acted like." He sighed. "Let's get a drink and I'll try to explain."

"I don't want a drink. I want to know what kind of game you've been playing with me."

"I never meant to deceive you. When we first met and I told you my name, I realized you didn't connect me with my dad, which I always consider a bonus. I'm very fond of him, but people treat you differently when they find out your father is Grover Dudley Smith."

"What did you think I'd do if I made the connection?"

"Sometimes it affects a person's perspective," he said carefully. "I was afraid it might change our relationship."

"We didn't have one at the time." Erica gazed at him with dawning comprehension. "You thought I'd be so dazzled by your wealth that I'd set my sights on you. Mike Smith, the most eligible bachelor on the Islands."

"It sounds extremely pompous when you put it that way," he said uncomfortably. "But it has been known to happen."

"You must have thought it was very funny when I worried about your finances," she said bitterly. "I suppose it was especially hilarious when I offered to pay my own way."

"That's when I realized what a knucklehead I was. I tried to level with you, but you wouldn't let me."

"How hard did you try? All I recall are the lies and deceptions designed to keep me in the dark. You're not really house-sitting for a friend, are you? You own that house!"

"Yes, but it's the only outright lie I ever told you."

"Oh, sure! You were really straight with me," she said sarcastically. "Now that I think back, you were even reluctant to admit you went to prestigious colleges—probably prep school, too. That would explain why you didn't know anything about the public school system."

"Those were all stupid errors in judgment, but they were made before I got to know you," Mike pleaded. "I've handled this entire affair badly, sweetheart. I'm really sorry, believe me."

"How can I? You haven't told me the truth about one single thing!"

"That's not so," he said quietly. "I meant it when I said I love you."

"I'll bet! Why should I believe that when you're someone I don't even know?"

"I'm the same man I was before—only richer," he added with an appealing smile. "You're not going to hold that against me, are you?"

"I'm glad one of us finds some humor in the situation," she answered stiffly.

"Erica, darling." He took both of her hands and held on when she tried to pull away. "I realize today has been something of a shock to you, but I couldn't think of any other way to make you listen. I can only hope these past weeks have made up for all the stupid things I did in the beginning. Will you forgive me?"

"You should have told me," she said weakly, trying to hang on to her indignation.

It was no use. Memories came rushing back. Mike's tender lovemaking, his understanding and anger on her behalf when she told him only a part of Jordan's shortcomings.

"I promise we'll never have secrets from each other again," he said solemnly.

Erica's long lashes swept down. While she was struggling for a reply they were joined by his sister, who was even more attractive than her photograph. She and Mike had the same unusual hazel eyes—although hers were more green than gold—and the same sun-tipped light brown hair. She also had his poise and assurance.

"Didn't anybody tell you this was a party?" She gave her brother a teasing glance. "You're supposed to mingle and have fun."

"You sound like Mother." Mike laughed. "I want you to meet my sister, Nancy," he told Erica, putting his arm around her. "And this is Erica," he said with pride in his voice.

The two women acknowledged the introduction politely, looking at each other with interest. Nancy could understand why her brother was hooked. Mike had known a lot of women, but Erica was definitely special. Her exquisite face was eye-catching; when coupled with a slender yet sexy body, she could dazzle any man.

Nancy had reservations, though. Mike was clearly crazy about Erica, but did she share his feelings? Hers weren't nearly as obvious as his. The entire family wanted to see Mike happily married, but to someone who really loved him. Nancy intended to find out.

"Mike tells me you live at the Haialua," she remarked casually. "It must be fun to live in a hotel. You can call room service twenty-four hours a day."

"That privilege is reserved for guests," Erica said. "I only work there."

"But you do live right on the premises? I believe Mike said you have an apartment in the hotel?"

"Yes, I do," Erica answered briefly.

Mike frowned at his sister, aware of what she was doing. "Where is Steve?" he asked abruptly. "Isn't he with you?"

"He will be. The nanny promised to come back early this afternoon so we could come here, but she's late. He'll join us as soon as she gets home." Nancy turned to Erica. "We have a four-year-old son, Scott."

"Mike told me." Erica smiled naturally for the first time. "He's a computer whiz."

"I wouldn't say that, although he's fascinated by them. Scott has been begging for one, but Steve says he'll treat it like any other toy and get tired of it in a few days. He says we should wait until Scott is older."

"Every child is different, but most of them have a longer attention span than adults give them credit for. Look how long they can work at making something out of those little plastic construction pieces. I wouldn't have the patience."

"You sound as though you've been there." Nancy stared at her curiously. "Do you have children of your own?"

"No, I—my sister has a little boy Scott's age. I've spent a lot of time taking care of him."

"You must like kids," Nancy commented, deciding to be more charitable.

"I do."

"I do, too," Mike said softly.

Erica didn't look at him. "You're very fortunate to be able to stay home with Scott," she told Nancy. "A lot of mothers have to work."

"I work, too. Mike evidently didn't tell you that."

"No, he didn't."

"I had a few more pressing things on my mind." He gave Erica a teasing look.

She pretended to ignore it. "What kind of work do you do?" she asked Nancy.

"I'm an attorney. I just started practicing again recently after taking time off to be with Scott while he was a baby. He doesn't need me around full-time anymore, and I didn't want to turn into one of those doting mothers who won't let their child develop on his own, so I went back to work."

"I realize Scott has the best of care, but do you ever feel guilty about leaving him?" Erica asked earnestly. "I mean, are you ever afraid he might feel abandoned?"

"Children just need to know you love them. As long as they're secure about that, I believe they benefit from contact with all sorts of people."

"I've read that, but I always wondered if it was true," Erica said.

"I think so. It's a little like the situation between adults. You might love somebody madly, but you don't necessarily want to spend all your time with them."

"Don't listen to her. I think my sister's been married too long." Mike laughed. "I'll have to talk to Steve about putting some romance back in their lives."

As Nancy was preparing a withering reply, their mother joined them. "You're still standing exactly where I left you," she scolded her son. "This poor girl doesn't even have a drink." Phyllis raised her hand to summon a waiter bearing a tray of glasses filled with champagne. "Did Steve get here yet?" she asked her daughter.

"No, but he should be." Nancy glanced at the diamond watch on her wrist. "I wonder if I should phone him."

"He probably stopped off at the club to hit a bucket of balls." Mike grinned.

"It wouldn't surprise me," Nancy said. "Would you believe he bought Scott a set of junior clubs and he's been teaching him to swing them?"

"What's wrong with that? A boy needs to learn things from his father. It's called male bonding."

Erica took a big gulp of champagne. It always hurt to hear about fathers doing things with their sons.

"Speaking of fathers," Nancy said. "Where is ours? I haven't seen Dad around."

"He's at an emergency meeting with the governor. Something to do with a short fall in municipal bonds." Phyllis sighed. "He promised to get away as soon as possible, but I'm not counting on it."

"That's too bad," Mike said. "I wanted Erica to meet him."

"You're welcome to stay for dinner, all of you. It would be nice to have the whole family together."

"Sounds good to me," Nancy said.

"Me, too." Mike looked at Erica. "Is that all right with you?"

"I'm sorry, but I can't," she said.

He frowned. "I really want you to meet Dad."

"And I'd like to, but I just can't tonight." Erica was conscious of his mother's and sister's scrutiny. Their expressions were carefully neutral, but she could tell they thought she had a date with another man. At least she could clear that up. "You didn't mention anything about dinner, and I promised a friend I'd take care of her little boy. She and her husband haven't had a night out together in a long time. I simply can't disappoint them." She was becoming a very creative liar, Erica thought despairingly.

"What am I going to do with you?" Mike asked fondly. "She works all week, and then on the weekends she takes care of children and old people," he told the other two.

"I think that's very admirable," Phyllis said. "I wish there were more young people with her sense of responsibility."

"I don't deserve any special credit," Erica murmured, feeling guilty. "A lot of people do more."

The arrival of Nancy's husband took the spotlight off Erica. Steve was accompanied by a small boy who raced toward them, calling out excitedly.

"I came to your party, Grandma! Mom said I couldn't, but Dad brought me anyway. Aren't you glad?"

"I'm always delighted to see you, darling." She leaned down to give him a hug. "This might not have been the time I'd have chosen, however."

"Sorry, Phyllis," Steve said. "The nanny phoned and said there was some kind of crisis at home and she couldn't leave. I didn't know what else to do with Scott, so I brought him along."

"I'd be more inclined to believe her story if she hadn't been so reluctant to give up part of her day off," Nancy remarked. "Even though I promised her an extra day next week."

"Well, it can't be helped," Phyllis said. "I'm sure Scott won't be any trouble, will you, angel?" She smiled at him.

"What a dreamer you are," Nancy muttered. "Steve will just have to take him home."

"No! I don't want to go home." Scott darted off the terrace and onto the lawn, almost colliding with a waiter who was carrying a full tray of food to replenish the buffet.

Erica was closest. Without stopping to think, she sprinted after the child and took his hand. When he tried to pull away, she knelt down and talked to him soothingly. His rebellious expression was replaced by a smile as he commented on whatever she said to him.

His parents watched in amazement. "I don't believe it!" Steve exclaimed. "I never calmed him down that fast. Who is that wonder woman?"

Mike's eyes were shining. "Her name is Erica Barclay, and she's with me."

"If she uses that same technique on grown men, you're a dead duck." Steve laughed.

"Funny, I've never felt more alive in my life," Mike answered softly as Erica returned to the terrace, holding the little boy by the hand.

"Okay, I'll go home, but can I have some cake and ice cream first?" Scott asked.

"Of course you may, angel," Phyllis replied.

"Can I have chocolate? I won't get any on my shirt."

"You will, but that's what washing machines are for." Nancy held out her hand. "Come on, pal, let's go in the kitchen and see what we can find in the freezer."

Steve looked at Erica curiously. "How did you get Scott to give up without a struggle?"

She smiled mischievously. "I merely pointed out that he would have to leave if you said so, but if he didn't put up a fuss there might be some ice cream in it for him. The cake was his own idea."

"My wife, the attorney, would tell you bribery is against the law." Steve chuckled.

"I prefer to think of it as a trade agreement. You have to make some concessions to avoid hostilities, and ice cream seems a small price to pay."

"You know a great deal about children," Phyllis remarked. "Do you have any of your own?"

There was that question again. Fortunately Mike answered it for Erica. "Not yet, but I'm sure she'll be a fantastic mother."

Mike was gazing fondly at her as a young blond woman with rather sharp features approached their group. Her smile was insincere, but her interest wasn't. The woman's eyes darted from person to person, registering every detail of their clothing, jewelry, even hairdos.

"Such a fabulous party, Mrs. Smith," she gushed. "Everyone is positively raving!"

"It's very kind of you to say so." Phyllis introduced her to Erica as Sally Coleman, the society columnist for a local paper. The two men evidently knew her.

"All the big contributors are here today. I'm just sure you're going to raise tons of money for medical research," Sally said.

"I certainly hope so. It's badly needed."

"I don't know what Honolulu would do without women like you." Sally's compliments were perfunctory. She was more interested in the diamond-and-ruby bracelet on Phyllis's wrist. "What a glorious bracelet! Is it new? A gift for some special occasion?" she asked archly.

"No, I've had it for some time."

"Well, it certainly is lovely." Sally was disappointed, having hoped for an item for her column. "Your dress is, too. Is it a Valentino?"

"I really don't recall. I've had *it* for some time, also."

"If you ladies will excuse me, I'm going to collect Scott and split." Steve kissed his mother-in-law's cheek. "We'll be back for dinner."

"And I'm going to get Erica that long-delayed drink," Mike said, putting his arm around her shoulders.

Sally looked at them with sudden interest. "I should have known you were Mike's date. He always gets the prettiest girls."

His jaw clenched. "Stop giving Erica the wrong impression. There haven't been that many of them."

Sally fairly bristled with excitement. "Did I speak out of turn? That sounds provocative. Do I hear an announcement in the offing?"

"If there ever is one, I'm sure you'll be among the first to know," Phyllis interceded smoothly.

Sally turned to Erica. "How do you spell your first name, Erica with a *c* or a *k?*"

Erica's nerves were taut when Mike finally managed to pry her away. This was a nightmare come true, her name in the paper, her private life invaded. It was inevitable, though, if she continued to see Mike. Everything about the Grover Dudley Smith family was news.

"Mother deserves a medal for putting up with that tasteless witch," Mike said disgustedly as they walked across the lawn toward the bar.

"Why does she?"

"For sweet charity's sake. A lot of the guests only come to these things to get their names in the paper and have their designer gowns described. It's tacky, but their money isn't. You'd be amazed at how much Mother raises for her various charities. She's very serious about them."

"She's a charming woman."

"I hoped you'd like each other."

Erica smiled faintly. "She probably didn't give me a second thought. You've evidently brought a lot of women around."

"But no more," he said deeply.

She changed the subject. "I'm sorry I didn't get to meet your father. Is he really at a meeting, or was that just an excuse to get out of playing host today?"

"I'll admit it's not his thing, but this time he has a valid excuse. Wall Street has been reacting to some new laws passed in Washington, and the state's finances are tied to the bond market."

"Does your father do some kind of consulting for the government?"

"Not officially, but he's widely regarded as an expert on the market. Financial papers in New York and other big cities frequently print excerpts from speeches he makes."

"I didn't realize he was that famous outside of the Islands," Erica said slowly.

"Well-known, anyway. Don't be intimidated when you meet him, though. He's a regular guy." Mike glanced over at the crowded bar. "Wait here, honey, and I'll bring you back a drink."

Erica looked at her watch, wondering how soon she could leave without upsetting Mike. Every minute from now on would be torture, knowing it was their last time together.

There really was no other solution. If the local papers started speculating about an engagement between herself and the only son of Grover Dudley Smith, it could be picked up by gossip columns in mainland papers. Then they'd start digging into her background. And that couldn't be allowed to happen. But how was she going to convince Mike that it was over between them? Without telling him why.

By the time the afternoon finally ended, Erica had a pounding headache. It was an effort to smile when she thanked Mike's mother for her hospitality.

"Do you feel all right, dear?" Phyllis looked at her closely. "You look a little wan."

"I just have a slight headache. It's nothing, really."

"Why didn't you say something, darling?" Mike was instantly concerned. "I'll get you a couple of aspirin."

"Don't bother. I'll take some when I get home."

"Do that," Phyllis said. "It was lovely meeting you, my dear. I hope you'll come and see us again."

"Count on it," Mike said confidently.

When they pulled up in front of the hotel Mike said, "It's too bad you have to baby-sit tonight. That's the last thing anyone needs when they have a headache."

"It's getting better," Erica lied.

"Take something for it, anyway."

"I will."

He cupped his hand around her neck and pulled her face toward his. "I want you to take care of yourself. You're very precious to me."

"You'll never know what you mean to *me*," she whispered, touching his cheek with her fingertips—for the last time.

"Darling Erica." He kissed her, gently at first, then with growing ardor as she returned his kiss ardently. Finally he drew back just enough to gaze into her eyes. "I could help you baby-sit," he murmured.

Erica realized she was only making it harder on herself by prolonging the inevitable. Grasping the door handle she said, "Your family is expecting you for dinner. They'd be disappointed if you didn't come. Let's leave things the way they are."

"I suppose you're right, but I'm sorry you can't come, too. I just took it for granted that we'd spend the evening together, but I guess I should have said something."

"It's just one of those things," she said vaguely.

"We'll have dinner with them one night next week so you can meet Dad. I'll check with Mother to find out what night they're free."

"You'd better check with me first. I won't be...there's a chance that I might have to fill in on the night shift."

"Surely they don't expect you to make the rounds, turning down beds and putting chocolates on pillows. You're a supervisor!"

"I know, but we're shorthanded. Let's just put everything on hold for now."

"Does that mean I won't see you tomorrow night?"

"I'm afraid not."

"You knew you had to work, didn't you? Why didn't you tell me sooner, instead of springing it on me at the last minute like this?"

"Because I knew how you'd react. There's nothing I can do to change things, believe me." She opened the car door.

He caught her wrist. "When will I see you?"

"I'll let you know." Erica took a long, last look at his beloved face, then turned swiftly and went into the hotel.

Mike's first inclination was to go after her. He had an uneasy feeling that something was wrong. Then he told himself he was imagining things. She had a headache; naturally she wasn't herself. His face cleared when he remembered their passionate goodbye kiss.

* * *

Susie brought Nicky home a little later. He couldn't wait to tell Erica about his exciting day.

"They had a rubber pool and we went swimming, Tommy and Margie and me. It wasn't a real swimming pool like here, but it was fun. And then we had hot dogs and root beer with ice cream in it, just like a soda."

"That's not all he ate." Susie laughed. "He isn't going to want much dinner."

"I can't thank you enough for taking him," Erica said.

"Any time at all. He was no trouble. You ought to get out more on weekends."

"I'll think about it," Erica said evasively.

"How was your day? Did you have a good time?"

"It was a lovely party. I'll tell you about it sometime. Right now I'd better get Nicky into the bathtub."

"Okay, we'll talk later. I have to get going, too."

Erica's thoughts were somber as she washed the little boy's hair and listened to his animated chatter about his playmates and their parents. Poor Nicky. She wanted him to have everything, but she couldn't give him what he wanted most—a family.

Her own situation didn't bear thinking about. Mike would call persistently for a while. He would probably even come to the hotel again, but this time she didn't plan to see him. And after a while he would give up.

Nicky's clear brow puckered as he looked at her clouded face. "Are you sad about something, Mom?"

"How could I be sad when I have the best little boy in the whole wide world? I'll bet you know his name."

"It's Nicky!" he chortled.

"That's my boy!" Erica's spirits weren't quite so heavy as she lifted her son out of the bathtub.

Chapter Six

Mike reacted the way Erica expected after she started ducking his calls. He phoned repeatedly for the next few days, then showed up at the hotel and asked for her. When the desk clerk followed instructions and told him she was unavailable, Mike became belligerent. It took the combined efforts of the manager and the security guard to persuade him to leave. They also requested that he not return.

Erica shuddered when she heard about it. Mike must have been really upset to make such a scene. Did he blame her for his humiliating experience? Maybe he'd decide he never wanted to see her again. Erica tried to convince herself that the embarrassing incident was a blessing in disguise.

Mike's ego wasn't as fragile as Erica supposed. After storming out of the hotel and blowing off steam, he calmed down and changed his tactics. It was an entirely different man who appeared in the Haialua lobby late the next afternoon. Mike carried an armload of flowers and wore a conciliatory smile as he approached the front desk.

"I hope these will make up for my behavior yesterday," he said, handing one of the bouquets to the reception clerk who had called the manager the previous day. "I had just gotten a speeding ticket, right after my secretary quit without notice. I guess my frustrations simply boiled over and I took them out on you. It's no excuse, but I hope you'll accept my apology."

"I understand." The woman was completely won over by his magnetism, rugged good looks, and the dozen long-stemmed roses. "I'm really sorry I had to call the manager."

"I don't blame you in the least." His mouth curved wryly. "You had no way of knowing I'm completely harmless—especially where women are concerned."

Gazing at his handsome face, she doubted that. He could charm a woman into almost anything.

"Could I speak to the manager for a moment?" Mike asked. "I'd like to apologize to him, too."

"Of course. His office is right over there."

The manager looked wary at first. He was a slightly built man in his fifties, no match for Mike's six feet plus of sinew and muscle.

Mike soon put him at ease. "I just wanted to say you were perfectly right to toss me out yesterday. I was completely off base."

"It was a regrettable incident," the manager said carefully. "Nothing personal, I assure you."

"You're very charitable. I can't believe I created such a ruckus over nothing." Mike rumpled his hair ruefully. "I guess it was kind of the last straw. I'd just lost an argument with my father and I took my foul mood out on the first target. When you get told off by Grover Dudley Smith, it smarts for days."

The manager looked startled. "You're Grover Smith's son?"

Mike nodded. "He's a great father, but it's hard to live up to him sometimes. Anyway, I just wanted to make amends and tell you not to worry. I won't be coming around anymore."

"You misunderstood me! Any member of the Smith family is welcome here at all times. I was merely suggesting that it might be best if you left *yesterday*. Please feel free to visit us at any time."

His father's name wasn't always a liability, Mike thought ironically. "You're very understanding. I just hope Miss Barclay will be, too." He held out the remaining bouquet of roses. "Will you have these delivered to her?"

The two men shook hands and the manager reiterated his standing invitation.

Mike left the office and went to the newsstand where he bought a paper. Poring over it as though deeply interested, he strolled over to stand by the elevator. Several cars came and went while he waited patiently. As soon as a bellman arrived carrying his roses, Mike entered the elevator after him.

He got off when the other man did and followed him down the hall. When the man stopped to knock at a door, Mike quickened his pace and walked past him down the hall. He was turning a corner when Erica opened her door.

"Flowers for you, Erica," the bellman said. "Your boyfriend must be loaded. These long-stemmed beauties don't come cheap."

She stiffened. "Is he still in the lobby?"

"I doubt it. He didn't give them to me personally. Either he dropped them off and left, or else the florist delivered them."

Erica let out her breath. "Thanks for bringing them up, Walt."

"They're pretty, Mom," Nicky said when she returned to him. "Can I put them in water?"

"If you like." She handed him the bouquet. "I'll get a vase." As Erica went into the kitchen, there was another knock at the door.

"I'll get it," Nicky called. He flung open the door and looked curiously at the tall man on the threshold. "Who are you?"

Mike smiled. "I'm a friend of Erica's. Will you get her for me?"

"A man wants to see you, Mom," Nicky called over his shoulder.

Mike's expression changed. He was staring incredulously at the little boy when Erica appeared.

Her face paled. "How did you find me?" she asked tautly.

Mike brushed the question aside. "This is your son? You're not just baby-sitting for a friend?"

"Susie sits with me sometimes, but I'm not a baby," Nicky informed him.

Mike stared from one to the other. "Why didn't you tell me?"

"Go in the other room and play with your toys, honey," Erica told the child.

"I want to stay here with you," Nicky said.

"This will only take a few minutes and then you can help me cook dinner," Erica coaxed.

"Is he going to stay for dinner?"

"No, he...he can't."

"Yes, I can," Mike said firmly. "I have no intention of leaving, so you might as well make the best of it."

"Are you going to help my mom, too?" Nicky asked.

"I'm certainly going to try."

"I don't need any help," Erica said in a low, intense voice. "Just go away and forget you ever met me."

"Can you forget *me* that easily? If so, you're luckier than I am." He moved closer, gazing deeply into her eyes. "My memories will never go away."

"We had fun together, but it's over now," she answered miserably. "As you can see, I have a prior commitment."

"We had a lot more than fun together," Mike stated. "And what does your son have to do with it—unless you also have a husband you haven't told me about."

"She doesn't have one of those," Nicky said unexpectedly. "My daddy went to heaven before I was born."

"Thank you for the information. Lord knows I can't get any out of your mother," Mike said ironically. "I should be asking *you* these questions."

He wasn't serious—or was he? She had to get Mike out of there! "I realize I owe you an explanation, but this isn't the time or the place. I have to prepare Nicky's dinner. I'll meet you later, any place you say."

"I have a better idea. Why don't I keep you company while you make dinner." It wasn't a question. "We can talk after he's in bed."

Short of putting Mike out bodily—which wasn't a physical possibility—Erica had no other option. She turned and went into the kitchen. The other two followed her, Nicky chattering away busily while Mike listened with a bemused expression.

They were having spaghetti, so Erica put the sauce on the stove to warm and filled a pot with water to boil the spaghetti in. When she went to get salad ingredients out of the refrigerator, her nerves were so jangled that the head of lettuce slipped out of her fingers.

Mike picked it up and placed it on the counter. Putting his hands on her shoulders he said gently, "Relax, angel, everything is going to be all right."

Why did he have to make it so difficult for her? she thought despairingly. Her resolutions were so hard to keep when Mike was this close.

"I'm much handier around the kitchen than you are," he teased. "I'll make the salad while you set the table."

Nicky was watching them with fascination. "Would you like to be my new daddy?" he asked Mike.

"You can't just ask somebody to be your father!" Erica gasped.

"Why not? He doesn't have to be if he doesn't want to."

"I'd consider it a privilege," Mike answered gravely.

"You see?" Nicky's eyes shone with excitement. "This is gonna be neat! Wait till I tell all the kids at school."

"Now see what you've done." Erica glared at Mike accusingly. "This isn't a joke to him. He's serious!"

"I am, too." Realizing how upset she was, Mike said to the little boy, "Maybe we'd better get to know each other first. We'll spend some time together and you can tell me all about yourself. What do you like to do?"

"I like to go swimming and play ball in the park, but Jimmy Kanoa says Mommy throws like a girl."

She was momentarily startled out of her distress. "You never told me that."

"It's okay." Nicky gave her a sunny smile. "He doesn't say it anymore. I smacked him."

"Good for you!" Mike said.

"You shouldn't tell him to fight," Erica said helplessly.

"It sounds like he did okay." Mike grinned. "The salad's ready. Sit down and I'll dish up the spaghetti."

Erica had had so many shocks that she was numb. She picked at her food as Nicky and Mike carried on a spirited conversation. The rapport between them had been instantaneous—she knew both of them well enough to know it wasn't feigned on either side. Which only added to her misery.

When it was Nicky's bedtime, he wanted Mike to help tuck him in. "When do you think we'll know each other well enough?" he asked Mike.

"Not long if we work at it. How would you like to bring your mom over to my house for dinner tomorrow night?"

"Maybe some other time." Erica answered for her son.

Nicky's lower lip jutted out mutinously. "I want to go. Why can't we?"

"This isn't a game of one-upmanship," she told Mike bitterly. "You have no right to put me in this position."

"You're absolutely right, although I'm not playing games." He turned to the little boy. "It's my fault for not asking your mother first, but we'll do it some other time. Maybe we'll go to the park, too, and throw a ball around. I was on the football team in college."

"Oh, great!" Erica muttered grimly.

When they were back in the living room she said, "You really fight dirty! Did you have to tell him you were a football player? It's bad enough that you're a man!"

"I can remember a time when you were happy about that." His laughter faded as he looked at her stormy face. "You have a wonderful little boy, Erica, and you've done a great job raising him, but he needs a man in his life. Whether I'm that man or not is up to you, but I'd like to fill the void until the right one comes along."

She stared down at her clasped hands. "I never realized he was suffering because of me."

"That's a little strong. If he flattened that other kid, he can take care of himself."

"I don't want him to turn into a bully, either."

"Is there anything you *don't* worry about?" Mike teased.

"Not when it comes to Nicky." She sighed.

"Why didn't you tell me about him?" he asked quietly.

"In the beginning I didn't think you'd be interested. You were so polished, and you had such a sophisticated lifestyle. I was sure the subject of children would bore you."

"But after you got to know me better, after we made love, you still didn't say anything. You must have known I'd think another man was the reason you'd never stay all night or see me on the weekends. Didn't you care anything about my feelings?''

"Of course I did, but you only put up a token argument. How was I to guess it really bothered you?''

"If you don't know the answer to that, then I must have been doing something wrong all those nights we spent together. I told you I love you, remember?''

"Men sometimes say that...at the time," she murmured.

"You can't possibly believe that. And I don't think *you* said it simply because the sex was satisfying. There has to be some other reason you didn't tell me about Nicky, and I intend to find out what it is.''

Erica's blood chilled as she realized he would do exactly what he said. She had become adept at deception, but she was no match for Mike when he wanted something. Her mind scrambled wildly, looking for an acceptable excuse.

Finally she said, "You talked to Nicky. You saw how badly he wants a father—so much that he'd accept any man I brought home.''

"Thanks a lot," Mike said wryly.

"I didn't mean to disparage you, it's just a statement of fact. Nicky thinks a father would automatically love him and we'd all live happily ever after. I know that isn't always the case, but he's too young to find out yet.''

"What happened to his father? Is he really dead, or did he walk out on you?''

"No, he died before Nicky was born.''

"Not that it matters, but were you married?''

"Yes.''

"Tell me what happened," Mike said quietly.

"The things I told you about Jordan were true. We did meet in college and we had an affair. That's all it should have been," Erica said reflectively. "I wasn't sophisticated or experienced enough for Jordan. He had a reputation for being very sexually active. I couldn't satisfy him.''

"No woman could have." Mike's face was austere. "It isn't about sex with guys like that, it's about ego and power."

"You may be right. He was very possessive. Whenever anyone else showed an interest in me he became more attentive."

"The rest of the time you were simply his property."

"I guess so, although I didn't realize it at the time."

"Did you get pregnant? Is that why he married you?"

"No, I didn't get pregnant until a couple of months later. By that time I knew the marriage was a mistake, but I wouldn't admit it to myself. Then when I found out I was carrying Nicky, it was too late."

"Women do raise children alone. You're a single mother."

"It wasn't that simple. Jordan and I were on an extended honeymoon in Europe. As you'd expect, he handled all the money. He even took charge of my passport. I couldn't have left him if I'd wanted to."

Mike frowned. "Jordan was what, twenty, twenty-one? How could he afford a trip like that?"

"His father kept big sums of cash in a safe at home. Jordan helped himself to a large chunk. Needless to say, I didn't know about it."

Mike was silent for a long moment, struggling not to voice his disgust. Finally he asked, as mildly as possible, "Was there any reason why he'd steal from his own family?"

"He was due to graduate from college that summer, and his father had the rest of his life planned out for him." Erica smiled mirthlessly. "Jordan learned the technique at home. After graduation he was supposed to start work in the family paper mill, learning the various operations from the bottom up so he could eventually take over the company. The problem was that Jordan found the family business extremely dull, but he knew that wouldn't carry any weight with his father."

"What did he want to do instead?"

"Nothing, actually. His idea of the good life was partying every night and collecting his allowance check at the beginning of the month. That would all end when he graduated, so he took the money and ran."

"Why did he take you with him?"

"For all his pseudo sophistication, Jordan was very young. He'd never been to Europe before, and I think he was hesitant about going alone. Another reason could have been that he wanted a live-in bed partner," Erica said matter-of-factly. "He knew I wouldn't go unless he married me."

"He's damn lucky his parents didn't prosecute," Mike said grimly.

"They were pretty angry. That's why we stayed away so long. I was ready to come back after a few weeks. I didn't like the people he fell in with. They were all like Jordan. Glib, insincere people who did everything to excess. But when I mentioned going home, he told me to loosen up and stop being such a prude. We kept traveling from place to place, supposedly in search of more fun. I didn't know it was so his father wouldn't catch up to us."

"Why did he finally agree to return?"

"I became pregnant. Jordan couldn't have cared less about being a father, but the baby was a ticket back into the good graces of his parents. He was an only son, and this would be their first grandchild. Everything was forgiven when we got home."

"Did things improve between you and Jordan?"

"They got worse, if possible. His parents blamed me for everything. They were sure I'd lured Jordan into marriage and forced him to take the money to finance our glamorous adventure. They couldn't believe their son would do such a thing on his own."

"They sound as warped as he was," Mike remarked disgustedly.

Erica stared down at her tightly clasped hands. "It wasn't a happy time, especially since we lived with them. Jordan was out a lot, doing his own thing. As I got bigger and less appealing, he stayed out later and later. I would smell perfume on his clothes, or see a smear of lipstick on his collar when he finally did come home."

Mike looked at her incredulously. "You let him get away with that?"

"Not meekly. We had some rousing arguments, but nothing changed. Jordan got worried when I threatened to leave. He swore he hadn't been with other women and promised to stay home more. As soon as I calmed down he was back to his old tricks again. I stopped arguing and faced the fact that our marriage was over. I made up my mind to leave as soon as the baby arrived. Jordan died two weeks before Nicky was born." Her voice was flat.

"Was it an accident?"

"He wrapped his sports car around a tree at three o'clock in the morning. His alcohol level was off the charts, and there was a woman with him."

Mike reached out and took both of her hands in his. "I'm so sorry," he said in a husky voice.

She merely nodded. "I couldn't leave right away as I'd planned. Jordan's parents were devastated. Even though they didn't like me, Nicky and I were the last link to their son. It seemed cruel not to stay and help them through their grief."

"You're more forgiving than most people would have been."

Erica winced as she recalled the last, nasty scene with her in-laws. "I tried to be, but finally it got to be too much. I took Nicky and moved as far away as I could."

"They didn't object? They must have really doted on their only grandchild."

"Not the way you think. They weren't what you'd call loving grandparents. Nicky was more of a valued possession to them, a male child who would carry on the name and go into the family business. Jordan was a disappointment to them, but they planned to be a lot stricter with Nicky."

"They didn't blame themselves for anything? People like that aren't fit to raise a child!"

"That's why I don't feel any guilt over leaving," Erica said quietly.

"You have no reason to. Any mother would protect her child from vultures like them."

"I'm glad you agree with me," she murmured.

"Wholeheartedly, but you can't go to the other extreme and be overly protective. You have to let people do the things for him that you can't."

"I can do whatever needs doing," she said stubbornly.

"I'm sure you're willing to, but why deprive Nicky unnecessarily? Let me teach him the things boys do together."

"You mean punch each other and see who can spit the farthest?"

"If those are the current juvenile rites of passage. Are you prepared to teach him to spit?"

Erica couldn't help smiling. "I'd rather not."

"Good call. You probably spit like a girl," Mike said fondly.

"Those are fighting words, pardner. Would you like to step outside and spit?"

"I'd rather do this." He took her in his arms and kissed her with great tenderness. "Darling Erica, let me be part of your life and Nicky's."

If only it were that simple, she thought despairingly. "What if you got tired of him and didn't want to be bothered anymore? Children aren't always adorable little angels. They can be cranky and difficult sometimes. You've never had to alter your plans because of a sick child or a meeting with his teacher."

"I've never had the opportunity. That's what I'm asking for. Don't condemn me without giving me a chance. Haven't I already shown you that all men aren't like Jordan?"

Erica melted as she remembered Mike's tender, caring lovemaking. "Yes," she answered softly.

"Then let me be a father to Nicky—on a trial basis, if that's the way you want it. You can always back away if I don't measure up. Bring him to my house for dinner tomorrow night."

"I already told him he couldn't go."

"Tell him I convinced you."

"You always do." She slanted a glance at him. "I'd have to take Nicky home by eight o'clock. We couldn't..."

"I know." Mike smiled. "Doesn't that show you how sincere I am?"

After Mike had left, Erica stood over her sleeping son, gazing down at him with a troubled expression. Had she allowed herself to be persuaded for her own sake or Nicky's? It was hard to be analytical about something she wanted so desperately. Never at Nicky's expense, though. Was she taking another step on the slippery slope to destruction?

Erica sighed deeply as she turned away and prepared for bed.

Nicky was enchanted with Mike's house. He ran from room to room, calling out to his mother whenever he discovered something new. At first Erica followed him to be sure he didn't cause any damage. Until Mike took her by the arm and led her into the kitchen.

"Leave him alone," he said. "This is a home, not a museum."

"I don't want him to break any of your lovely things," she protested.

"Don't worry about it. When I bought this house I hoped to fill it with children some day."

"Then you shouldn't have furnished it so expensively," she said lightly.

Nicky came charging into the kitchen. "Mom, come and see! He's got a swimming pool in his bathroom."

"That's a bathtub." Mike laughed. "It has a whirlpool that churns up the water like waves. You can try it out after dinner if you like."

"I took a bath before I came here, but I'll take another one."

"That's a first," Erica remarked. "He never willingly took two baths in one day."

"See what a good influence I am?" Mike grinned.

The evening was a great success. Mike was a natural with children. He charmed Nicky as effortlessly as he did everyone else, Erica thought wistfully.

After dinner they all went for a stroll along the beach.

"I've never been on the beach when it's dark," Nicky said, clinging to Mike's hand. "It's nice, but you can't find any seashells."

"Then you'll just have to come back on the weekend when there's no school," Mike told him.

"Can we, Mom?"

"If Mike wants us to, we undoubtedly will," she said ironically.

Mike put his arm around her. "Do you have something you'd rather do?"

"I can't think of anything," she answered softly.

When they returned to the house, Mike filled his bathtub and turned on the Jacuzzi. Nicky climbed in tentatively at first, but he was so delighted with this new form of entertainment that he didn't want to get out.

"You'll wrinkle up like a raisin," Erica warned.

"I don't care. I want to do this every day! Can we get one, Mom?"

"I'm afraid not. This thing is the size of our entire bathroom."

"You can come over and use mine any time," Mike consoled him. "But only if your mother says so."

By the end of the evening Nicky's eyelids were drooping from all the unaccustomed excitement. Mike carried him out to Erica's car.

Her heart twisted as she looked at the trusting way Nicky's little arm was hooked around Mike's neck, and the indulgent smile on Mike's face as he gazed down at the drowsy child. Anyone would suppose they were father and son. But Mike wasn't Nicky's father—and never could be.

Mike wasn't aware of any further problems between himself and Erica, but he was careful not to pressure her into marriage. While containing his impatience, he waged a subtle campaign to demonstrate that rich people can have the same family values as anyone else.

He and Erica resumed their pattern of having dinner at his house several times a week. They made tempestuous love as always and their need for each other never lessened. Erica didn't let herself think about the future. The present was too heavenly.

One night after Mike picked her up and they were driving away from the hotel, he remarked casually, "I thought we'd do something different tonight."

"I can't believe you could get any more creative." She grinned.

He reached over and ruffled her hair. "Are you trying to tell me I'm getting predictable?"

"I wouldn't change anything about you," she answered softly.

He turned his head to give her a sultry glance. "I'm beginning to wish I hadn't made plans for tonight."

"Different ones than usual?" she teased.

"Unfortunately, yes. We're having dinner at my parents' house."

Erica's smile vanished. "Not tonight! I'm not dressed." She had on jeans and a pale blue sweatshirt with the hotel's logo on the front.

"You look fine. Mother said it would be casual."

"I can just imagine what her idea of casual is—Giorgio Armani slacks for him, and a Chanel sweater with a diamond pin for her."

"You have the wrong idea about them. They're normal people like everyone else."

"Who just happen to live in a mansion and have a staff of servants. That's certainly normal, all right."

"Why do you have this bias against the wealthy? Most of them lead responsible, productive lives. They're good parents and they love their children. The only difference is, they can give them more of the material things. Is that so terrible?"

"I guess my experience with Jordan's parents left its mark," Erica said slowly. "They gave him everything, and look how he turned out."

"They didn't give him love. Although, Jordan was a bad seed. Do you honestly think affluence had anything to do with making him what he was?"

"It's hard to believe," she admitted.

"Okay, then. Just try to keep an open mind, that's all I ask."

Mike's parents didn't even seem to notice their attire— Mike was wearing jeans, too—but good manners wouldn't have allowed them to comment, Erica was certain.

When they arrived, Mike led her to a screened-in lanai at the back of the house facing the ocean. The incredible view could be better appreciated without the tents and the crowds of people.

But Erica was more interested in her hosts than the view. She focused her curious attention on the renowned Grover Smith, an imposing man with silvered temples and a strong face. He was making the same assessment of her. Although his greeting was pleasant, she had a feeling those enigmatic eyes didn't miss a thing. What his conclusion was, she hadn't a clue.

"It's so nice to see you again, my dear," Phyllis said.

"I must apologize for the way I look. Mike didn't tell me we were coming here for dinner," Erica explained.

"You look charming. This is just a family night. Nancy and Steve should be along any minute."

Erica stifled a groan. "How could you do this to me?" she muttered to Mike as he handed her a drink. She was even more embarrassed when he kissed her cheek.

"Didn't I tell you she was gorgeous?" he asked his father.

"You did, indeed," Grover agreed with a smile, although his eyes still didn't reveal anything.

Erica wanted to tell him not to worry, that she wasn't after his son, but of course that was impossible.

The Smiths were too well-bred to ask personal questions, but Mike proudly told them all about her job and how competent she was to land a managerial position at such a young age.

"Besides all that, the perks are terrific," he said. "Erica gets an apartment and full use of the hotel facilities."

It suddenly occurred to her that he might mention Nicky, since he evidently wanted his parents to know all about her. That mustn't be allowed to happen! While she was trying to think of some way to send him a signal, Mike's sister and brother-in-law arrived.

"Sorry we're late," Steve said. "But I'm not to blame. It was your daughter's fault this time."

"I had a case drag on and on in court," Nancy said. "That's why I'm wearing my sincere clothes. I didn't want to take time to change." She glanced at Erica. "You look comfortable. I envy you."

"Mike didn't tell me where we were going. I might never speak to him again."

"What can you expect from a man? They don't think clothes matter."

"They shouldn't be as important as they've become," Phyllis said. "I can't understand what pleasure people get out of reading about what someone else wore to a party."

"Sally Coleman would be out of a job if they didn't," Nancy remarked.

"Did you clear a lot of money at your charity affair?" Steve asked his mother-in-law.

"It was successful, but not as lucrative as I'd hoped," Phyllis answered.

"People are tightening their belts," Grover commented. "You have to be more creative these days."

Dinner was announced and they drifted into the dining room, discussing ways to raise money and the reasons why people weren't more generous. There were many opinions, the political climate, taxes, the increase in worthy causes.

Erica found she was enjoying herself. The conversation was stimulating and the surroundings were elegant. Although it was a family dinner, the table was set with beautiful china, and sterling flatware. A uniformed maid served, and there was a centerpiece of orchids on the table.

The atmosphere was informal, however. Everyone talked animatedly, sometimes interrupting each other to make a point. It really *was* like a family dinner, except for the luxury.

Erica was feeling relaxed and unthreatened when Mike dropped his bombshell. They were talking about the necessity for good child care for working mothers.

"I really feel for women who have to leave their children with strangers," Nancy said. "How can they be sure the nursery school they choose is a good one?"

"Ask Erica," Mike said. "She can tell you."

Her heart sank as they all stared at her in surprise.

"That day at Mother's party, I thought you said you didn't have any children." Nancy wore a puzzled frown.

Mike stepped in when Erica struggled for an answer. "That was only because she hadn't gotten around to telling *me* yet."

"I thought you two had known each other for quite a while," Steve commented.

"We have, but Erica got the wrong impression of me from the beginning. Part of it was my fault, and part was pure prejudice on her side." Mike grinned at her. "Erica decided I was a rich man's son who didn't really work for a living. I'm hoping you'll set her straight, Dad."

"Gladly. Michael is an important part of the family business. Other companies have tried to lure him away, and I've used everything including appeals to his family loyalty to keep him." Grover smiled at his son.

Nancy was still staring at Erica. "I don't understand. Even if you thought Mike was a playboy, why wouldn't you tell him you have a child? What does one thing have to do with the other?"

"I didn't think he'd be interested," Erica replied. "And the subject never came up." They were all too polite to say so, but she could tell her answer wasn't satisfactory.

"How old is your child?" Phyllis asked.

"He's four, Scott's age."

"You'd love Nicky," Mike said enthusiastically. "He's bright and beautiful, like his mother."

"I'd love to meet him," Phyllis said courteously.

"Yes, so would I," Nancy agreed.

Phyllis changed the subject adroitly and they started to discuss something else. But the evening was spoiled for Erica. She asked Mike to take her home as soon as good manners would allow.

Erica wouldn't have been reassured by the conversation that took place after they left.

* * *

"Well, what do you think of her?" Nancy asked her father.

"She's a very beautiful girl. All of Mike's lady friends are outstanding."

"But this one is special. He's in love with her."

"How many times does that make?" Grover asked dismissively.

"Think about it. When did Mike ever request an intimate family dinner before? This is the real thing, and I'm worried that he's going to get hurt."

"Mike can take care of himself." Steve grinned. "He's had enough experience with women."

"It doesn't pay to get overconfident," Grover observed dryly. "A man is no match for a clever woman, no matter how much experience he's had."

"Then you do agree that she's playing him like a big fish!" Nancy exclaimed.

"I wouldn't know about that. I just met the woman. I do get the impression that she's on guard about something," Grover said thoughtfully.

"It seems strange that she wouldn't tell Michael about her son," Phyllis commented.

"If you're trying to land a guy, you don't present him with a ready-made family until he's hooked," Steve said.

"You think he wants to marry her?" Phyllis asked.

"I think it's a done deal," Nancy stated. "Erica has handled him very cleverly. For all of his sophistication, Mike is as lovesick as a schoolboy. He won't listen to a word against her."

"I think we should reserve judgment," Grover said. "Michael is a mature man, and if this is his choice we must all accept it."

"She seems like a very sweet girl," Phyllis said tentatively.

"And a real beauty. It'll be the wedding of the decade." Steve chuckled. "I can see the society editors salivating already."

"They aren't even engaged yet," Nancy protested. "Anything can happen."

"You're not losing your brother," her husband teased. "You're gaining a gorgeous new sister-in-law. Is that what's bothering you?"

"I just wish I could be sure she loved him," Nancy muttered.

Chapter Seven

Mike was euphoric on the way home from his parents' house after dinner that night. He was sure his family had been captivated by Erica. She had serious doubts.

"I know them better than you do," Mike said confidently. "Take my word for it, they thought you were great."

"Didn't you see their faces when I tried to explain why I didn't tell you about Nicky? Not that I blame them. It even sounded phony to *me*."

"Don't worry, honey, I'll set them straight."

"No! You can't!"

"I won't tell them the whole story. I'll just say that, due to bad communication between us, you didn't feel I was the right role model for him."

"That ought to go over big with your family!"

"They'll understand." Mike grinned. "They know I'm not perfect."

"I think you'd better leave well enough alone."

"I don't want them to blame you for something that was my fault."

Mike was so generous and thoughtful. He always made her feel guilty. "It doesn't matter," she mumbled.

"It does to me." He raised her hand to his lips and kissed it. "I want my family to love you as much as I do."

How could she let him go on thinking they had a future together? His family was more perceptive than he. She'd seen the concern in their eyes. Erica wished there was some way to reassure them that she would never marry their son.

The telephone call from Nancy came as a surprise. Erica was so sure Mike's sister disapproved of her. She sounded friendly enough on the phone, however.

"It was nice getting to spend some time with you the other night," Nancy said. "We didn't really have a chance to talk at Mother's charity thing."

"It was a lovely party, though," Erica answered cautiously, wondering why she'd called.

"Women like big bashes, but men have to be dragged to them. They'd rather be doing something more physical than just lifting a glass. Mother was amazed when Mike agreed to come."

"I think he'd do anything she asked."

"Yes, we're very close. We believe in all those family values people are always talking about," Nancy said evenly.

"I could tell that, even from the short time I've spent with you."

"You and I have never had a chance to get to know each other. Why don't we have lunch one day?" Nancy suggested, as if it just occurred to her.

"I'm afraid I don't get that much time for lunch."

"I can come to the hotel. We'll have a quick bite in the coffee shop, or that little outdoor café."

"I'd really like to, but I use my lunch hour to straighten the apartment and do some marketing, or wash clothes. All the things I don't have time for after Nicky comes home from nursery school.''

"Yes, I suppose it's difficult when you have to do everything yourself.''

"Not really, you just have to learn to budget your time. But thanks for the invitation, anyway.''

"I'm usually too rushed for social lunches, myself, so I just thought of another idea. Why not bring Nicky over here on Saturday? Our boys could get to know each other at the same time.''

"Oh, I don't know." Erica was beginning to feel trapped. No matter how hard she tried, she couldn't distance herself from the Smith family. "You know how children are at this age. They might not get along.''

"Don't be so negative, they'll probably hit it off famously. Does Nicky like hamburgers?''

"Yes, but without onions.''

"Scott, too. See, they have something in common already. I'll expect you at noon on Saturday. Mike will tell you how to get here. Oh, and bring your bathing suits.''

Erica didn't know how she'd let herself be maneuvered into accepting the invitation. There was no pressing reason to turn it down, only her wariness of Mike's family. They couldn't consider her a suitable choice for their only son—a working mother with a child. What was Nancy's real motive for asking them to lunch? To find out more about her, obviously. After worrying herself into a state, Erica decided to think of some excuse for breaking the date.

Mike phoned that evening, filled with elation. "Nancy told me she asked you and Nicky to lunch. I told you my family thought you were great.''

"Did you ask her to invite us?" The thought suddenly occurred to Erica.

"No way, it was strictly her idea. I'm not even invited.'' He chuckled. "Nancy said you wouldn't be able to talk girl talk with me around.''

"I'm sure she'll tell you what she found out," Erica said evenly.

Mike's voice sobered. "You sound like it's an ordeal."

"I didn't mean it that way. I'm just worried that the boys won't get along."

"Is that all? They'll be great pals. Why wouldn't they be?"

"You never can tell. Adults are polite when they get into a social situation that isn't ideal, but kids can be brutally frank."

"Nancy has a big house. In the unlikely event that they don't see eye to eye, you can put them in different rooms. They'll never find each other."

"Why doesn't that reassure me?" Erica asked dryly.

Nancy and Steve lived in Diamond Head, like her parents. Their sprawling pink house was something like Mike's, only on a grander scale. The property was shielded by a high wall, leaving only tall tropical trees and the tile roof visible from the street.

Lush green lawns surrounded the house and framed an oval swimming pool in back. The water was a clear aqua, like the shallower part of the ocean in the distance.

Mike picked up Erica and Nicky at the hotel and drove them to his sister's on Saturday. He parked in the driveway and accompanied them to the front door.

"Did you persuade Nancy to let you stay?" she asked.

"No. It would be easier to stop grass from growing. When Nancy makes up her mind about something, you might as well give in."

"You two have a lot in common," Erica remarked ironically.

"Any regrets?" He cupped her chin in his palm.

Mike was gazing deeply into Erica's eyes when Nancy opened the door. She noticed with concern that Erica looked more troubled than love struck.

Scott was standing beside his mother, staring avidly at Nicky, who was clutching Erica's hand. The two little boys assessed each other silently.

"It's nice to see you again," Nancy told Erica. "And you must be Nicky." She smiled at him. "Scott has been waiting for you."

Erica's fears seemed to be realized as neither child said a word. Their smooth faces were carefully blank. If Scott resented being forced to entertain a stranger, the day would be a disaster!

"Why don't you show Nicky your toys, Scott?" Mike suggested casually.

"Do you want to see them?" Scott looked at Nicky.

"What do you have?" Nicky asked.

"I just got some new bugs."

"Neat!" Nicky's face lit up. "Can I play with them?"

"Sure. Come on, they're in my room."

Nancy laughed at the startled look on Erica's face as she watched the boys disappear down the hall. "Don't worry, they aren't real bugs. They're actually kind of cute, in a gross sort of way."

"What else would appeal to a four-year-old boy?" Mike chuckled.

"What are they?" Erica asked cautiously.

"They're toys shaped like different insects. The spider is pretty awful, but the giant ladybug isn't too bad," Nancy said. "It has long legs, and when you throw it against the wall it kind of slithers down as if it were walking."

"Oh, yuk." Erica made a face.

"Get used to it," Nancy advised. "Once Nicky sees Scott's, he'll have to have one."

"You're undoubtedly right." Erica sighed.

"That's why Nicky needs a father," Mike said. "Women just don't appreciate these things."

"Weren't you supposed to meet Steve at the country club?" Nancy asked pointedly. "He left here half an hour ago."

"Okay, I can take a hint." He kissed Erica's cheek and sauntered back to his car.

"You can't be too subtle with my brother," Nancy told Erica. "Shall we sit out by the pool while the boys are busy getting acquainted?"

"You have a lovely home," Erica commented, glancing to her right and left as she followed her hostess through the spacious house. "Have you lived here long? Everything looks brand-new."

"It's been about five years now. Steve and I bought this house right after we were married, because we felt it would be a good place to raise children."

Erica looked wistfully around at the spacious lawns and the swimming pool filled with toys—a plastic ball, an inflated raft, a large rubber sea horse. Surrounding the pool were umbrella tables, chairs and chaises covered with thick pads.

"I thought we'd have lunch out here," Nancy said. "The boys are having hamburgers, but we can have a salad if you'd prefer."

"Please don't go to any extra trouble for me. I'm not a fussy eater."

Nancy eyed Erica's trim figure. "You must be on a constant diet to stay so slim."

Erica smiled. "I'm one of the fortunate ones. I've never had to diet."

"You *are* lucky. Some of the women I know practically starve themselves to stay in shape."

"I wouldn't have the willpower."

They sat at one of the umbrella tables and made polite conversation until lunchtime. The boys came reluctantly when they were summoned.

A uniformed maid wheeled out a rolling cart that held hamburger sandwiches, potato chips and glasses of cold milk. There was also a large bowl of cut-up fresh pineapple, mangoes and other tropical fruit.

Between bites of hamburger, Nicky asked, "Can I have one of those ladybug things? They're real cool."

Before Erica could answer, Scott said, "You can play with mine if she won't get it for you."

"My mom buys me anything I want," Nicky boasted. "Unless it costs too much."

Scott slanted a laughing glance at his mother. "I always ask my dad if my mom says no."

"Tell me something I *don't* know," she said dryly. "Your father is a soft touch."

"I don't have a dad," Nicky remarked matter-of-factly.

"Who takes you to the bathroom at the movies?" Scott asked.

"Mom makes me go before I leave home."

"Well, who takes you sailing and plays ball with you?"

"Eat your lunch and stop asking so many questions," Nancy instructed her son. "It isn't polite."

"I just want to find out things." He looked curiously at Nicky. "Don't you feel bad about not having a father?"

"No, 'cause I'm gonna have one soon."

"We talked about that and decided we were getting along fine, just the two of us," Erica told her son carefully. "Don't you remember?"

"Yes, but that was before I met Mike. He says he'll be my father as soon as you say it's okay."

"He shouldn't have told you that," Erica said curtly.

"Why not?" Nicky's lower lip jutted out. "I *like* Mike."

"He'd make a good father," Scott said judiciously. "He knows how to do lots of neat things, like my dad."

The two women were both displeased with the way the conversation was going, although for different reasons.

"Finish your lunch so you can go swimming," Nancy said.

"You always say I can't go in right after I eat," Scott objected.

"You can play Chutes and Ladders while you're waiting."

The boys were easily diverted. They rushed to finish their lunch so they could go and play.

After they'd left, Nancy said, "Children can be unintentionally cruel. I hope Scott didn't upset Nicky with all that talk about fathers."

"No, Nicky and I have discussed it. He knows he isn't the only child in that situation. Some of the children in his school have only one parent."

"It must be difficult being a single mother. I'm afraid I'd compensate by giving Scott everything he asked for."

"Not unless you wanted a badly spoiled child."

"True, but you're always the bad guy who has to say no. I suppose there are days when you'd give anything to have somebody to share the responsibility with," Nancy remarked casually.

"If you're suggesting that I'd remarry just to give Nicky a father, you're wrong," Erica said evenly.

"I wasn't trying to—I mean, I was just speaking in generalities." Nancy was uncharacteristically flustered.

"It's all right," Erica said quietly. "I realize that you and your family are concerned about Mike's…interest…in me and you have every right to be. I don't travel in the same circles, or enjoy the same life-style. I work because I have to, it isn't an option."

Nancy took her last remark personally. "That isn't fair. I might not have to support myself, but I take my job seriously."

"I'm sure you do, and I admire you for it. I was merely pointing out some of the reasons why I'm not suitable for Mike."

"My family and I aren't snobs," Nancy protested. "We never considered any of those things."

"You should have, because they're important."

"Not if two people really love each other. I know how Mike feels about *you*, but frankly, I don't get the same vibes on your part."

Erica smiled mirthlessly. If Nancy only knew! "I'm sure his feelings are only temporary. You must have seen your brother fall in and out of love dozens of times."

"Not really—and he never talked about marriage before."

"From what he tells me, your parents mention it a lot. I guess it's like water wearing away at a stone," Erica said flippantly. "They finally made an impression."

"You don't really believe that."

"Then maybe he's simply reached an age when he feels it's time to settle down. You don't have to worry, though, I'm not going to take advantage of his momentary vulnerability."

"If you really don't want to marry him, why do you go on seeing him?" Nancy asked slowly.

Erica's nails curved into her palms, making little crescent marks as she struggled to keep her feelings hidden. "I enjoy his company, and it's nice to have a male role model in Nicky's life, even if only temporarily."

"So you're just using Mike!"

"You should be relieved to find out that's all it is," Erica replied ironically. "You were afraid I was trying to marry him for his money."

"I won't say it didn't cross my mind, but can you really blame me? Mike is my brother and I want him to be happy. We don't really know anything about you."

"Well, at least now you know I don't have any designs on him," Erica said lightly.

Nancy looked at her curiously. "Is it just Mike, or are you put off by men in general? He told me you had an unhappy relationship, but anybody can make a mistake. You're a young woman, surely you don't intend to go through the rest of your life alone.''

"I'm not alone, I have Nicky. He's my major consideration right now.''

"Children grow up and leave the nest, that's the way it's supposed to be. What will you do then?''

Erica forced a smile. "I've got almost fifteen years before I have to worry about that.''

"It sounds like a lonely life to me.''

"I've told you I don't intend to marry your brother. What more do you want?'' Erica asked sharply. "Unless you don't believe me.''

"You've convinced me, but I don't think you made that decision to please me or my family.'' Nancy stared at her appraisingly. "It doesn't sound like it delights *you* either. I don't think you're as indifferent to Mike as you pretend to be.''

Erica took a deep breath to compose herself. She mustn't let Nancy get to her. "I care about him as a friend. I enjoy the time we spend together. I wouldn't go out with him otherwise.''

"Mike has had girls chasing after him since he was a teenager. He must be a really awesome lover by this time. It's rotten of me to say this, but I'm glad to know there's one woman who's immune to him,'' Nancy remarked artlessly. "It's good for his character to get turned down once in a while.''

Erica's pulse quickened at the erotic memories of Mike's lovemaking. She stood abruptly. "I think I'd like to put on my bathing suit. It's getting quite warm, even in the shade.''

"That's a good idea. The boys will be ready to swim any minute now. You can change in the cabana.''

On the other side of the pool was a spacious cabana with dressing rooms at opposite ends. The area in the middle was like an outdoor living room that could be closed off with a sliding glass door. It was furnished casually for people who wanted to get out of the sun.

Erica's hands were trembling as she undressed and pulled on a simple one-piece suit. Was Nancy convinced that her brother was in no danger from a designing woman? Erica didn't know how much longer she could keep up a pretense of indifference. But if Nancy didn't believe her, she might start digging around and asking questions. Her casual remark was chilling: We don't really know anything about you. Nervous laughter rose in Erica's throat. Nancy might be shocked to find out that even a fortune hunter was preferable to a woman wanted by the police.

Erica braced herself before going back outside, but she needn't have worried. The boys were ready to go swimming, and when they were around, serious conversation was impossible. The children had formed an instant friendship, which made things a lot easier.

The rest of the afternoon was surprisingly relaxing. Erica and Nancy swam and played ball with the two little boys in the shallow end of the pool, then chatted idly while they dried off afterward. The children would have stayed in the water all afternoon, but Nancy coaxed them out periodically with lemonade and cookies.

It was during one of these enforced rest periods that Nicky brought up the subject of Mike once more. "Scott says we'd be cousins if you married Mike."

"I can't have any cousins until Uncle Mike gets married," Scott said.

Both boys had excessively innocent looks on their faces, telling Erica it was a setup. "I'm sure he'll get married some day," she said.

"But I want a cousin *now*," Scott insisted.

"You can't always have everything you want," Nancy told him tartly. "That's life. If you and Nicky are finished with your lemonade you can go back in the pool. Stay in the shallow end, though." When the boys were splashing noisily in the water, she said, "They evidently cooked up that little routine together. I'm sorry. It's been an uncomfortable day for you."

Erica smiled faintly. "It wasn't too unexpected. The only surprise was finding someone here who approves of me— Scott. I guess the credit for that goes to Nicky, though."

"Aren't you being overly sensitive? I'll admit I had reservations about you, but I hope I kept an open mind." Nancy looked at her thoughtfully. "We have a lot in common. We're both working women and we each have a child. I think you and I could be friends if you weren't so defensive."

"I only wanted to make my position clear," Erica answered carefully.

"Okay, you've done that. Now tell me about Nicky's nursery school. I've organized various activities for Scott, but I'm wondering if he wouldn't be better off at a good preschool. What do you think?"

The two women talked about schools and child rearing, and then about the way they had to juggle their time.

"You're fortunate to have living quarters right on the job," Nancy commented.

"I know, but your work is more interesting. What kind of cases do you handle?"

"A little bit of everything, and they're not all that fascinating. A lot of it involves drawing up contracts, and filing minor lawsuits that are often settled out of court."

"I guess people think all attorneys handle cases like Perry Mason's." Erica smiled.

"Don't I wish! Civil suits like divorces and child support squabbles don't have that kind of drama."

"Except for the people involved," Erica remarked bitterly and without thinking.

"Yes, I suppose so," Nancy answered, frowning slightly.

"You must need an entirely separate wardrobe for work," Erica said to divert her. "Do you have to wear suits to court, even in this climate?"

They were discussing clothes when the men returned.

"Is it that late already?" Nancy exclaimed.

"That means you two had a good time together." Mike leaned down to kiss Erica. "I knew you would."

She stood hastily. "I'll get Nicky out of the pool. We'll be ready to leave in a few minutes."

The children scrambled out of the water and ran over to greet the men.

"This is my friend," Scott told his father. "Can he stay for dinner?"

"I don't see why not, if it's all right with his mother." Steve smiled.

Erica shook her head. "That's very nice of you, but we have to go home."

As both boys put up a protest, Nancy said, "They're having such fun together, why not let him stay? In fact, Nicky can spend the night and you can pick him up tomorrow. Steve and I are just going to the club for dinner with some other couples. Why don't you and Mike join us?"

"Sounds good to me," Mike said. "How about it, angel?"

Before Erica could answer, the two little boys jumped up and down, shouting, "Yeah! That'll be neat!"

"Not tonight." She tried to sound firm. "Maybe some other time." A storm of objections broke out as everybody tried to change her mind.

"Let's discuss it over a drink," Steve said. "You two, go get dressed," he told the boys in a tone that didn't invite argument.

"You'll have to tell me how you do that." Nancy laughed as the children obeyed, albeit reluctantly.

"I'm just a masterful kind of guy," he said smugly. "What can I fix you to drink, Erica?"

"Nothing, thanks. I really have to take Nicky home as soon as he's dressed. He's had a big day."

"He has to eat dinner, and so do we." Mike gave her a sultry look. "We'll make it an early evening, I promise."

Erica knew what he had in mind. They would finally be able to spend the entire night together. Her fair skin colored as she wondered if his intentions were as obvious to the others.

"My hair is a mess," she said weakly. "I can't go anywhere looking like this."

Mike's eyes were brilliant as he gazed at her curved body, so tantalizingly revealed by the skintight bathing suit. Steve was more circumspect, but his face registered male admiration.

"You'll have plenty of time to go home and wash your hair," Nancy said. "Especially since you won't have to cook for Nicky. Come on, Steve, I'll help you bring out the bar cart."

Erica looked after them helplessly. "Your family is almost as overpowering as you are."

Mike stroked her cheek tenderly. "I like to think you didn't need to be coerced. Was I wrong?"

"No," she whispered, gazing at him with dazzled eyes. He was everything she'd ever wanted in a man.

Nancy paused on the terrace to glance back at them for a moment before following her husband into the house.

"Well, did you give her the third degree?" Steve teased. "What did you find out—besides the reason Mike is so crazy about her. She does wonders for that bathing suit."

"Erica happens to have a lot more to offer than just a terrific figure," Nancy observed tartly.

"You're right. The face that goes with it is pretty spectacular, too." He chuckled.

"Men!" Nancy muttered.

"You've certainly changed your tune. When I left here this morning you were convinced that Erica was a wicked Delilah, out to give Mike a haircut."

"You're exaggerating. I only wanted to find out if she really loves him."

"And now you think she does?"

"I'm pretty sure of it," Nancy said slowly. "But I can't figure her out. She swears she has no intention of marrying Mike, and I believe she's telling the truth. If she loves him, what's the problem?"

"She tried marriage once. Maybe she figures that was enough."

"Anything is possible." Nancy sounded skeptical. "Okay, what do *you* think is holding her back?"

"What if she isn't divorced?"

Steve looked startled. "That would be a real bummer! But wait a minute. Wouldn't Mike know by now if Erica had a husband? Nicky would mention him, even if she didn't."

"Erica has only lived in Hawaii for a few years. Suppose she moved here to get out of an abusive relationship. If she sued for divorce, her husband would know where to find her."

"Isn't that the stuff of soap operas?"

"You read about it in the newspapers all the time."

"True," Steve admitted. "But she could get a restraining order to keep him away. If that's her problem, you can help her."

"Not unless she asks me to, and I'd bet against it. Erica has her guard up already. The family didn't exactly welcome her with open arms."

"You would have taken a dim view if I had." Steve grinned.

"I'm serious," Nancy said impatiently.

"I'm sorry, honey, but I don't know what we can do except show her we want to be friends. If we stop badgering her, she might relax and begin to trust us."

"I guess that's the best idea. Take the bar cart outside. I'll fill the ice bucket and join you in a minute."

The pressure on Erica from all sides was too much to withstand. She reluctantly agreed to let Nicky stay overnight at the Deightons'.

The apartment felt very empty without him. After Mike dropped her off to get dressed, Erica wandered from the living room to the bedroom, gathering up a stuffed animal, putting a pair of small sneakers in the closet.

It was so quiet. A tiny chill rippled up her spine. This is the way it would be if Nicky was ever taken away from her. Trying to shake off her apprehension, Erica went to turn on the shower.

Mike picked up on her mood immediately. As they were driving away from the hotel he said, "What's the matter, angel? You're not worried about leaving Nicky at my sister's, are you? He'll be well taken care of, I assure you."

"I know, but it's the first time he's ever slept away from home."

Mike covered her hand with his. "That's part of growing up. I realize it's hard, sweetheart, but you want to do what's best for him, don't you?"

"I always have, in spite of what anyone else thinks," she said grimly.

He was puzzled by her intensity. "One night is not such a big deal, is it?"

"No." She managed a smile. "You must think I'm overreacting in a big way."

"I think Nicky is lucky to have such a terrific mother," he answered fondly.

Mike was so dear to her, so loving and supportive. She couldn't bear to see that change. "If anything should happen," she began hesitantly. "I mean, if people criticized me for doing what I felt I had to do, you'd keep an open mind, wouldn't you?''

His attention was distracted for the moment. There was a small crowd of people milling around the front of the Catamaran Club. Cars waiting to pull up to the entrance were unable to get to the curb.

"What's going on, Hank?" Mike asked the parking attendant when the man came out to the street to take the car.

"They're making a movie in town, and some of the stars are supposed to have dinner here tonight. Photographers from all the papers are waiting to get a shot of them."

As several flashbulbs blazed, Mike glanced at the couple entering the club. "Those aren't movie stars, that's Charlotte and Herb Johanson."

The attendant shrugged. "I guess they're taking a few shots for the society page while they're waiting."

Erica kept her head down, appearing to rummage in her purse for something as she and Mike threaded their way through the news media. She pretended not to hear a request from a photographer to "look this way." Her face was averted when a flashbulb went off, but the unexpected attention was nerve-racking.

Erica was trembling when they joined Nancy and Steve at their table.

"Nicky is having the time of his life," Nancy announced as soon as they appeared. "You don't have to worry. The boys ate their dinner and now they're watching a Disney movie on the VCR."

"I wasn't really worried, just reluctant to let go." Erica smiled ruefully. "But Mike set me straight."

"You were starting to tell me something in the car before that mob scene erupted. What was it, honey?" he asked.

"I can't remember, so it must not have been important," she said lightly, having had second thoughts about justifying herself. It was a luxury she couldn't afford.

Erica was on guard at first, but it was such a delightful evening that she gradually relaxed. Nancy and Steve were as delightful to be with as Mike. They joked around a lot and treated her like one of the family.

Their friends were nice, too. There were a few speculative glances cast at Mike and her, but nobody was impolite enough to ask awkward questions.

Erica really enjoyed a conversation she had with a woman named Kate who had a new baby.

"Please tell me they finally sleep through the night," Kate begged Nancy.

"You'll survive." Nancy laughed. "Erica and I did. She has a little boy Scott's age."

"How old was he before he ate solid food?" Kate asked.

The three women talked about babies and their experiences as they grew into toddlers. Erica had never had the luxury of friends like herself with small children, something other women took for granted. The evening ended all too soon for her.

As they were waiting for their cars outside, Nancy said, "You needn't come by too early tomorrow. The boys will be fine until you get there."

"I don't want Nicky to wear out his welcome," Erica protested.

"That's nonsense. Sleep late for a change. I'll bet you don't have the chance very often."

"Try never." Erica laughed. "Little boys haven't heard about days off."

"Well, tomorrow is yours. Come over around noon and we'll have brunch." Nancy got into their car and Steve drove off before Erica could answer.

"That was really nice of your sister, but I don't even remember what it's like to sleep late," she said wryly. "I'll probably wake up at the same old time."

"Then I'll just have to think of some way to amuse you."
Mike's voice was like plush velvet. "You *are* going to spend
the night with me, aren't you?"

"I was hoping for an invitation," she said demurely.

"You have one—any time, any place," he answered
deeply.

A full moon had turned the golden sand to silver outside
Mike's den window. The deserted beach had an eerie beauty,
like some exotic landscape on a distant planet.

Erica gazed out with dazzled eyes. "I've never seen it this
lovely out."

"Would you like to walk along the beach?" Mike asked.

"I'd love to, but I'm not dressed for it." She ruefully indicated her high heels and panty hose.

"No problem. I'll give you one of my sweatshirts to
change into. That's all you need. It'll come down to your
knees."

"I could try one and see."

They went into his bedroom where Mike took a navy
sweatshirt from a drawer. "This should do it." He held it up
to her appraisingly. "Just roll up the sleeves. While you're
changing I'm going to get my messages from the answering
machine. One of our managers was supposed to call and
leave a report."

Erica undressed completely, since it felt weird to leave her
bra on when she didn't have any panties. The shirt covered
her more than adequately, from her neck to just above her
knees, but it felt slightly erotic to be completely nude underneath.

Mike was writing some figures on a pad when she returned to the den. He glanced up and smiled. "You look a
lot sexier in that shirt than I do."

"You'd look sexy, too, if you didn't have anything else
on."

"That can be arranged." He started toward her.

"I suppose this means we aren't going for a walk," she teased.

"I want to do whatever makes you happy." He curled his hands around her neck and kissed her lingeringly.

Erica melted the way she always did. But before she could clasp her arms around him, Mike nibbled her ear playfully.

"Give me a couple of minutes to change and I'll be right with you," he said.

Erica wandered outside, happier than she'd ever hoped to be. There was no tomorrow, only this enchanted night with Mike. It would be a memory to cherish for the rest of her life.

He joined her a few minutes later, wearing the same cut-offs he'd worn the night they met. She commented on the fact.

"Was that why you didn't want to have anything to do with me?" He laughed.

She smiled reminiscently. "It seems funny now that I thought you were a beach bum."

"I think we set a record for misunderstandings." He took her hand and squeezed it as they strolled down the beach. "But no more. Everything is smooth sailing since we started being completely honest with each other."

Erica turned her head to gaze out at the water. "It's hard to believe we're in a big city. We could be on a desert island somewhere."

"I can't think of anyone I'd rather be stranded with," Mike said fondly, drawing her into a loose embrace.

"Or a better place to be marooned," she agreed. "Of course we wouldn't have your beautiful house to live in. We'd have to build a shelter out of palm fronds and live on fish and coconuts. No custom-tailored suits or high-powered cars, either."

"A small price to pay for Paradise on earth." His hands slipped under the hem of her shirt to caress her bare bottom. "Who needs clothes anyway? We'd spend all of our time making love like Adam and Eve."

"They wore fig leaves," Erica said faintly as Mike's erotic caresses made her heart beat rapidly.

"If Eve had a body as beautiful as yours, I don't know why she bothered."

He strung a line of arousing kisses down her neck while his hands slid up her sides to cup her breasts. Erica linked her arms around his neck and tilted her head back, feeling a surge of desire rising in her like a warm tide.

Mike's embrace tightened and his eyes smoldered as he gazed down at her parted lips. "You're so beautiful!"

His mouth covered hers urgently while he molded their bodies so closely that every hard muscle in his rugged frame made its impression against her. Their passion mounted as they inflamed each other with tantalizing, intimate explorations that aroused without satisfying.

Finally Mike stripped off her sweatshirt, groaning. "I can't wait any longer."

"I don't want you to," she whispered, unsnapping his shorts.

Moonlight gilded their nude bodies as they gazed at each other with throbbing expectation. Then Mike feathered her body with his fingertips from the tips of her breasts to her thighs, which he stroked sensuously.

Erica caught her breath and reached out, wanting to experience him in the same way. Her hands glided lovingly over his muscular chest and slim hips, but when she stroked his burgeoning manhood, Mike uttered a hoarse cry and crushed her against him, capturing her mouth for a passionate kiss that left her clinging to him. Erica's legs felt boneless when he finally dragged his mouth away.

"I've waited all my life for you," he said huskily. "Tell me you're mine."

"There will never be anybody else for me," she answered with a catch in her voice.

His face lit with elation. After hastily spreading their sweatshirts on the sand, he lowered her onto them and covered her body with his.

Erica welcomed him into the core of her being, raising her hips to seal their union even closer. The rise and fall of their bodies was in rhythm with the restless water that advanced and receded against the shore. Excitement built in a gathering storm that burst like the cresting wave that foamed a few feet away.

They were totally relaxed afterward. Bathed in a glow of satisfaction, they clung to each other wordlessly.

Finally Mike rolled over onto his side, taking Erica with him. "Do you know how wonderful you are?" he asked, kissing her tenderly.

"I wouldn't mind being told." She smiled.

"I'm going to tell you every day for the rest of our lives."

Her smile faltered. "That's a long time."

"Aren't we lucky? Just think how many good years we have ahead of us."

Erica sat up. "It must be late. We should go back to the house."

"If you like, although this is a special night." Mike stood and extended his hand to her, his nude body gleaming in the moonlight like a perfectly formed statue of an ancient Greek athlete. "We can do anything we want."

"I already have," she answered softly.

Chapter Eight

Mike and Erica were still asleep the next morning when the telephone rang about ten o'clock. They'd spent a wondrous night of tender, passionate lovemaking that had lasted until almost dawn.

"You sound funny," Nancy said after Mike had fumbled for and found the phone.

"I never did speak clearly in my sleep," he drawled.

"My, aren't we grumpy this morning."

"Could you come to the point? I have things to do." Mike smiled down at Erica, lying curled up in his arms with her head on his shoulder.

"They can't be too urgent if you're still in bed at this hour," Nancy said.

"I'd be happy to debate the point with you at some other time. Goodbye, Nancy."

"Wait, don't hang up! I need Erica's phone number. Steve is going down to the marina to inspect some work he had done on the *Lucky Lady,* and the boys want to go with him. I need to check with Erica to be sure it's all right with her."

"I'll have her call you back."

"Why can't you just give me the number and I'll phone her myself?"

"She . . . uh . . . don't bother, I'll do it."

Erica's warm drowsiness had vanished when she realized the call was from Nancy. "Is Nicky all right?" she whispered urgently.

"Do you have someone with—oh, I see!" Nancy chuckled. "Okay, but have her get back to me on the double, the boys are champing at the bit."

Erica was adamantly opposed when Mike relayed the conversation to her.

"It's your call, naturally, but Nicky will be perfectly safe with Steve," Mike said. "He takes Scott on the boat with him all the time."

"Two active little boys are a lot different than one. Call Nancy and tell her I'd rather Nicky didn't go." She swung her legs out of bed. "I'll get dressed and go over and pick him up."

"Nancy will insist on talking to you. I know my sister. Do you want me to dial the number for you?"

Erica hesitated, sensing his disapproval even though he hadn't voiced it. "You think I'm wrong, don't you?"

"I understand your concern," he said simply.

"But you think I'm being overly protective."

"You're a wonderful mother," he answered indirectly. "Nicky is a delightful, well-adjusted little boy, but there are limits to what you can do for him all alone. He needs to be part of a family that cares about him."

"Nancy and Steve aren't his family," Erica said stubbornly.

Mike avoided pointing out the obvious—that they could be. "Maybe not, but Nicky is comfortable with them. He won't understand why he can't go with Scott and Steve."

Erica sprang out of bed and paced the floor distractedly. Everything Mike said was true. She'd tried to be all things to Nicky, but it wasn't possible. He wanted a family.

Mike looked at her compassionately. "It's not that big a deal, honey. I'll call Nancy and tell her Nicky can't go. He'll get over it. We'll take him to the zoo, or the aquarium or somewhere, and he'll forget all about the boat."

"No, tell her Nicky can go," Erica said slowly.

She'd never denied her son anything. How could she deny him the illusion of a family, if nothing else? Maybe it could work out. A lot of people had close relationships for years and years without getting married. In time, maybe Mike could be persuaded to accept the situation, she thought with a rush of hope. That might be the solution to everything. She wouldn't have to give him up!

"If you're really sure," he persisted. "I don't want you to be unhappy."

She gave him an enchanting smile. "How could I be when I'm with you?"

Mike got out of bed and came over to take her in his arms. Their nude bodies merged, then heated at the intimate contact. When Erica moved against him and kneaded his buttocks, Mike's reaction was unmistakable.

"Let me get Nancy off our backs and I'll try to make you even happier," he murmured.

Nicky was eager to tell his mother about all the exciting things he'd done. "Uncle Steve has the neatest boat! He says he'll take me and Scott fishing sometime if it's okay with you."

"We can talk about it later," Steve said diplomatically. "You two better get washed up for lunch." When the children had dashed off, he said to Erica, "He's a nice little kid."

"The boys were perfect angels," Nancy agreed.

"Sure, because they were with me all morning," Steve teased.

They were relaxing around the pool, joking back and forth, when the older Smiths arrived unexpectedly.

"This is a nice surprise," Nancy exclaimed. "Will you stay for brunch?"

"We don't want to intrude on any of your plans," Phyllis answered. "Your father and I just wanted to spend a little time with our grandchild."

"You're always welcome," Steve said affectionately.

"We're flattered," Nancy remarked. "I can't believe you and Dad have a free day."

"Part of one, anyway," Grover remarked dryly. "Your mother is dragging me to a cocktail party this afternoon."

"He always complains about going, and then he enjoys himself more than anyone," Phyllis said.

"Just once I made the mistake of saying I had a good time," Grover grumbled. He gave Erica a smile. "It's nice to see you again, my dear."

While they were all chatting, Scott appeared and took a flying leap into the older man's arms. "Grandpa! When did you get here?"

"Just a few minutes ago." Grover hugged the child closely. "Have you been a good boy this week?"

"I'm always good," Scott declared.

"Give me a break!" Nancy tousled her son's hair playfully.

"He's Grandmother's little angel," Phyllis said, holding out her arms. "Come and give me a kiss."

Erica's heart twisted as she glanced at her son. Nicky was hanging back with a wistful look on his face as he watched Scott with his grandparents.

Mike moved forward and took Nicky's hand. "Mother, Dad, I'd like you to meet Nicky, Erica's son."

Phyllis looked at him with interest. "It's nice to meet you, Nicky. I've heard a lot about you."

When the child clung shyly to his hand, Mike said, "This is my mother. She likes little boys."

"Grandpa does, too," Scott said. "He brings me presents. Did you bring me something today, Grandpa?"

"He doesn't have to give you something every time he comes," Nancy said swiftly, nodding toward Nicky almost imperceptibly.

"What if I give each of you a nice, crisp dollar bill?" Grover said.

"Cool!" Scott exclaimed.

"What do you say?" Erica prompted as Nicky examined his with pleased surprise.

"Thank you," he said dutifully before turning to Scott. "You're real lucky to have a grandfather."

"Don't you have one of those, either?" Scott asked.

"I guess I do, but I've never seen him."

"Gee, you don't have anybody at all."

Nicky squared his small jaw. "I've got my mom."

Mike cleared his throat, and Nancy blinked rapidly. "Run in the kitchen, both of you, and tell Mrs. Halsey we're ready for brunch," she said.

"He's a fine young man," Grover told Erica. "You should be very proud of him."

"I am," she answered with a lump in her throat.

"Nicky is such a handsome little boy," Phyllis said. "He looks just like you, except for that pretty blond hair."

"He got that from his father." Erica touched her own hair self-consciously, even though she'd checked just yesterday to be sure her blond roots weren't showing.

"That's the *only* thing Nicky ever got from that creep," Mike muttered.

The boys returned, followed by the maid who had served lunch the previous day. The subject was dropped as they all moved to the cabana where a table was set with place mats and colorful napkins.

Scott climbed onto the chair next to his grandfather.

Grover patted the chair on his other side. "Come sit by me, Nicky. I want to hear all about you."

The child was a bit intimidated by the imposing older man, but after looking at his mother and receiving a reassuring nod, he did as he was told.

"What do you want to be when you grow up?" Grover asked.

"I'm gonna be a fireman and make a million dollars so I can buy my mom a house," Nicky said.

"I'm gonna be an engineer like my dad," Scott said. "What did *your* dad do before he went to heaven?"

"I don't know." Nicky looked at his mother in perplexity. The subject had never come up.

"Why not?" Scott asked.

"Nicky's father died before he was born," Mike said swiftly. "He never got to know him."

As Scott was poised to ask more questions, Grover said, "Perhaps both of you boys will come to work for me when you finish college."

"Is this your way of telling me my days at the firm are numbered?" Mike chuckled.

"By then you'll be the head of it, and I'll be enjoying a long-anticipated retirement."

"You'll never retire, Dad," Nancy said fondly. "What would you do with yourself?"

"Maybe I'll whip your mother's charities into shape." He gave his wife a mischievous look. "They don't return nearly the profit they should, considering that most of the work is done by volunteers. I'd like to run *my* business without a payroll."

"That's an oversimplification and you know it!" Phyllis said indignantly. "Our costs are kept to a minimum, but we do have unavoidable expenses. Take our annual fashion show and luncheon. The hotel is donating the ballroom, but we still have to pay the waiters and kitchen personnel."

"You're a brave man, Grover." Steve grinned. "If I ever criticized *my* wife's management skills, I'd be sleeping in the den for a year."

"Stop teasing Mother," Nancy chided her father. "You know you're proud of the work she does."

"She knows it, too." Grover gave his wife a melting smile.

Phyllis's answering smile told he was forgiven. Turning to her daughter, she said, "Actually I'm glad your father brought it up because I've been meaning to talk to you about the fashion show. We decided to do a repeat performance the next night. Last year's affair was so successful that we thought, why not have a dinner and invite the husbands who couldn't make a luncheon show?"

"I take it that's a rhetorical question." Steve grinned.

"Don't pretend you're reluctant," Nancy said. "It will give you and all the other husbands a chance to stare openly at pretty girls."

"I hope it isn't asking too much of the models," Phyllis said.

"Don't worry, they'll love another chance to ham it up. Most of the models are junior members of the organization," Nancy explained to Erica. "It's great fun. We get to wear high-fashion gowns and pretend we're celebrities once a year."

"Perhaps you'd like to be one of the models," Phyllis said to Erica. "With your lovely figure, you'd be an asset."

"That's very flattering, but I can't," Erica declined. "I have to work."

"Can't you take a day off?" Nancy asked.

"It would be more than that, I'm afraid," her mother said. "There will be fittings and rehearsals."

"That's right, what a bummer!" Nancy exclaimed. "I know you'd enjoy it. Bridget and Kate are modeling." She named two of the women whose company Erica had enjoyed the night before.

"It would have been nice. Maybe next time," Erica said.

"Too bad, but at least you can come to the dinner," Nancy said.

"We'd be delighted to have you brighten up our table," Grover told Erica. "Steve and I—and Michael when we can get him to give up his lunch hour—sit in lonely male isolation. Phyllis promises every year to sit with us, but they're always shorthanded backstage and she has to help out."

"There's an idea!" Nancy said to Erica. "You could be one of the wardrobe mistresses. You won't get any applause for it, but at least you'd be part of the group. We really have a great time. How about it?"

"I don't see why not. That's more my kind of thing anyway," Erica said. "I haven't had any experience modeling."

"You couldn't be any worse than Theresa Ryder." Nancy grinned at her mother. "Remember when she flipped her train around at the end of the runway and dislodged Schyler Livingston's hairpiece?"

"I do, indeed. It fell into his soup and he was so embarrassed that he got up and left. Schyler used to be a big contributor to our organization," Phyllis added ruefully.

After brunch the women discussed details of the fashion show while the men took the two boys to the park to play ball. Grover went along to umpire.

Erica noticed with a twinge that Nicky was clinging trustingly to the older man's hand, and Grover was treating him like a second grandson. They were all so kind and compassionate. Erica crossed her fingers and prayed nothing would ever happen to change their opinion of her.

The days that followed were unbelievably happy—except that Mike kept pressuring Erica to marry him.

"What are you waiting for? Nicky likes me, and I'm crazy about both of you." He gave her a stirring kiss to prove it. "What's the problem?"

She stirred restlessly in his arms. "Everything is perfect just the way it is. Why do we have to get married?"

"Because I want to live with you and have children. You must know me well enough by now to trust me. Marriage isn't going to turn me into a monster like Jordan."

It was the only thing they argued about, and sometimes Erica became discouraged. Was it only wishful thinking to hope Mike would become accustomed to their relationship and accept it indefinitely? But he always backed off from forcing the issue.

The approaching fashion show and dinner took her mind off her worries. She and Nancy were on the phone together constantly in the evenings, discussing the details. Apart from Susie, it had been a long time since Erica had had a close woman friend and she was enjoying it thoroughly.

"We got our first look at the clothes today and they're to die over!" Nancy said. "I get to wear this absolutely gorgeous slinky gown with a slit all the way up the thigh. I'm considering buying it, although there's a turquoise suit that's a lot more practical."

"Go for it. You don't need to be practical."

"I like your thinking. There's also a black chiffon number that would look divine on you."

"Forget it." Erica laughed. "I *do* need to be practical."

"Not if you married Mike. You two are made for each other. Anybody can see that. Why won't you marry him?"

It was the first time Nancy had ever come right out and asked. Erica was startled, but she decided this was a good time to test the water, so to speak.

"A lot of couples choose not to get married these days," she said tentatively. "It's a lot less complicated. After all, if two people really love each other they don't need a piece of paper to prove it. They can live happily ever after without one."

"How about children? Movie stars have them quite casually, but Mike is an old-fashioned kind of guy, in spite of appearances. He wants his children to bear his name. My advice is, marry him, but I promise that's my last word on the subject."

Erica sincerely hoped so, although she wasn't counting on it.

"Plan on bringing Nicky over after nursery school on Friday," Nancy said. "We have to be at the hotel early to start getting ready for the show."

The fashion show was as much fun as Nancy promised. It was held in the grand ballroom where a runway had been constructed to extend from the bandstand into the audience.

The large room looked very festive. Round tables for eight were covered with pink tablecloths centered by bowls of red and pink anthuriums. At each place setting was a party favor, a small box tied with satin ribbon, pink for the ladies, red for the men. Waiters were busily attending to last-minute details, although the ballroom looked ready for the festivities to begin. Unlike the atmosphere backstage where chaos reigned.

A large dressing room was filled with animated young women jostling each other to get to the mirror. Some had fat pink curlers in their hair, others were being combed out by a hairdresser. The noise level was high.

Nancy introduced Erica, then led her to a rack crowded with dresses for every occasion. "I have to show you the one I was telling you about." She held up a glamorous, black chiffon gown.

"It's spectacular," Erica agreed.

"They all are. I'm going to buy most of the outfits I'm modeling." Nancy turned her head as someone called to her. "Take a look through them. You won't be able to resist splurging."

Some of the things were wildly impractical, like brief sequinned shorts with mesh tank tops, meant for evening wear—by whom, Erica had no idea. But she fell in love with most of the outfits. A pale blue satin suit was outstanding. It had a short, bias-cut skirt and a black lace camisole.

The wardrobe woman came over to her. "That was a good choice for you. It will be very effective with your black hair and blue eyes."

"I'm not one of the models. I was just looking at it." Erica hesitated. "Would you know how much this costs?" The woman named a price that made Erica gasp. "Are all of these things that expensive?"

"More or less," the woman answered laconically.

Nancy beckoned to her from across the room, and from then on Erica was kept busy. She removed rollers, zipped up dresses and tied scarves. As show time neared, a buzz of conversation came from the guests outside.

Erica took a peek through the curtain to see if she could locate Mike. It was an imposing crowd. Every table was filled with people in evening attire. Mike was seated with his relatives at a choice table next to the runway, but the three men weren't alone. There were several other people there. Erica's attention focused on the glamorous young woman sitting next to Mike. She was talking to him animatedly, and he was listening with a smile on his face.

A fierce stab of jealousy gripped Erica—accompanied by a dreary premonition. There would always be women waiting to console Mike if he lost patience with her, or even if they had a misunderstanding.

It was like a sore spot she couldn't help probing. While she was helping Nancy into a knit dress a few minutes later, Erica said, "Your mother will be pleased. It's a full house out there. Mike is sitting with a very attractive redhead," she added casually.

"I know," Nancy said. "I peeked out to be sure he and Steve showed up. They were really going to hear from me if they just sneaked in when the show was over."

"Do you know who the redhead is?" Erica persisted.

"That's Jennifer Lawrence. Mike dated her for a few months a while ago." Nancy held up a hand mirror to view the back of her hair. "She was crazy about him," she remarked absently.

"I don't think it's past tense," Erica said in a pinched voice.

Nancy's attention snapped back. "She had her shot at him and she missed. Mike is only being polite. You know what a gentleman he is."

Erica didn't have time to dwell on her problems when the orchestra began to play and the show started. Nancy and the other models sauntered down the runway at a leisurely walk, but when they returned backstage the pace picked up frantically.

Changes had to be made with lightning speed, and sometimes accessories were misplaced. The models weren't professionals, so they tended to panic. Erica calmed them down by finding the missing belt or brooch, or whatever was needed. And if the article couldn't be found, she substituted something adequate.

"I don't know how we ever managed without you," Phyllis said gratefully.

Erica had located a lost scarf and tied it artfully around a model's waist when the young woman fumbled with it awkwardly.

"You're the only calm one here," Phyllis declared.

"That's because I don't have to go out there." Erica laughed. "If I did, I'd be the biggest basket case here."

"I don't believe that for a moment. You don't give yourself enough credit."

As a grand finale, all the models lined up on stage while the audience applauded. Phyllis came out and gave a gracious speech, thanking everyone for their participation—the models, the hotel for donating the room, all the people who had volunteered their time.

It was a standard speech, and the audience clapped dutifully while flashbulbs popped. The press was covering the affair, since it was attended by a large segment of Honolulu's society and business figures.

Phyllis ended her speech by saying, "I'd like to give special thanks to someone who's new to our group. Without her, our little show wouldn't have functioned nearly as smoothly. I hope you'll all join me in thanking Erica Barclay. Come out, Erica."

She was frozen to the spot, unable to move as Phyllis gestured to her. Finally someone gave her a little push.

Erica did the only thing possible. She put her hand up to shield her face, as though the lights were blinding her. When Phyllis held the microphone out to her, she lowered her head to say a quick thank-you, then moved in back of the line of models.

"Damn!" Stu Haoki lowered his camera. "I can never get a clear shot of that woman. She always has her hand up to her face or else her head is turned away. It's almost like she doesn't want her picture taken."

"That would be a change!" Sally Coleman said derisively. "Most of these society dames eat up publicity with a spoon."

"Well, everybody likes to see their picture in the paper," Stu commented mildly. "It's human nature."

"It would be nice if just once they did something to deserve it. All these women do is sleep until noon and plan the next party over lunch in some fancy place."

"What are you complaining about? You get to go to their parties for free."

"And be treated like a servant," Sally answered bitterly. "They only invite me because they want to get their names in my column."

Stu shrugged. "Isn't that what you get paid for? You'd be out of work if they *didn't* give parties."

"Big deal," she sneered. "You think I want to do this for the rest of my life? When I started at the *Chronicle* they promised me a shot at some real stories. But here I am two years later, still sucking up to rich women who think they're better than I am."

"Aren't you exaggerating?" Stu raised his camera to get a shot of Phyllis, table hopping among her acquaintances. "Mrs. Smith seems like a real nice lady."

"She's not so bad, but her family thinks they're Hawaiian royalty just because they own so much of the Islands. Oh, sure, they're polite, but they always act like it's a terrible faux pas to ask what designer made their gowns, or how many carats their new diamond rings are. I'm just doing my job, for God's sake!"

"It's all in a day's work," Stu said dismissively. "Don't take it personally."

"That's fine for you to say. They don't make you feel like an outsider they have to put up with." Sally's eyes strayed to Mike across the room. He was surrounded by a group of friends, looking handsome and vital. "Do you think the heir to the Smith dynasty even knows I'm a woman?"

"Maybe you're just not his type." Stu started to pack up his gear. "I happen to like brunettes. Maybe he does, too."

"He likes socialites, like himself. But if there's any justice in this world, someday Mr. Michael Smith is going to meet someone he can't have…I only hope I'm around to see it."

"Don't hold your breath," Stu advised. "Well, my work's done here. I'm leaving."

Erica was shaken by her moment in the spotlight. But the pictures were all taken from a distance; nobody could recognize her. Besides, it was only a local charity event. Who would be interested, outside of Honolulu?

"Wasn't that a blast?" Nancy asked when they were back in the dressing room. "Next year you really should model.

If you give your boss enough notice I'm sure you could get some time off."

"It's possible," Erica answered neutrally. Who knew what could happen in a year. Would she and Mike still be together?

"Okay, I'm ready." Nancy took a last look in the mirror. "Let's go accept our well-earned adulation."

The redhead was still monopolizing Mike. Her annoyance was evident when he stood and kissed Erica's cheek. He introduced the two women who eyed each other coolly.

"Mike and I have been having such fun catching up on old times," Jennifer remarked. "I hope you don't mind."

"Why should I mind?" Erica asked evenly.

"Some women feel threatened if their date shows an interest in another woman. Especially one he's had a... relationship... with."

Mike frowned and started to speak, then checked himself. As a gentleman, he could neither admit nor deny it.

Erica had no such prohibitions. She gave a tinkling laugh. "I can't imagine what the threat would be. There's nothing deader than a romance that's over with. Trying to revive it would be rather pathetic."

As Jennifer's face reddened unbecomingly, Nancy tried to turn a snort of laughter into a cough. A few moments later the redhead made up an excuse and left.

Mike breathed a sigh of relief, turning to Erica. "We didn't have a grand passionate affair as Jennifer implied."

"She was just a casual acquaintance?" Erica asked cynically.

"Well, no, I took her out a few times."

"Nancy indicated it was more than a few."

"My sister talks too much," he said in irritation.

"She didn't tell me anything I couldn't have guessed. You might as well have had a target painted on your forehead."

Mike gave her a melting smile. "She would have missed."

Erica craved further reassurance. "Even at such close range? She was practically sitting in your lap."

"That was your fault."

"*My* fault!"

"Exactly." He grinned. "If you'd let me tell the world we're engaged, I wouldn't have to fight off predatory females."

She hadn't seen that one coming. "You're big enough to fight your own battles," she said weakly.

"No man is proof against a determined woman." He laughed. "I'm considered a great catch. If you don't snap me up, somebody else will."

That was exactly what Erica was afraid of. There would be more Jennifers down the road. Would one of them take Mike away from her if she continued to refuse his proposals?

Phyllis returned to the table and the conversation became general, focusing on how successful the evening had been.

"You mean I don't have to make up the deficit?" Grover chuckled.

"My wife did it for you," Steve remarked dryly. "She bought all the outfits she modeled."

"I liked that light green thing that Kate wore," Mike said to Erica. "It would look good on you."

"You mean the pale green silk tunic with the slim pants?" It was one of her favorites, too.

"That's the one. Why don't you get it?"

"A few hundred reasons," she answered ruefully. "All those zeros on the price tag."

"Let me give it to you in appreciation for all your help this evening," Phyllis said. "It was quite invaluable."

"I wouldn't think of it!" Erica gasped. "I was more than happy to help out. Besides, I enjoyed it immensely."

"It would really give me a great deal of pleasure," Phyllis said graciously.

"Let her do it." Grover patted Erica's hand. "Otherwise she'll buy you something you might not like as well."

Some people came over to their table, ending the discussion, much to Erica's relief. It wasn't the amount of money involved, although the price was mind-boggling. She was more troubled by this evidence that Mike's family expected them to marry eventually. Phyllis would scarcely offer a gift like that to just any volunteer. Erica genuinely liked all of the Smiths, and it bothered her to deceive them so cruelly.

When the party broke up, Nancy said, "Let's get together tomorrow for brunch at the club so we can rehash everything."

"Like why so and so wore the same dress she wore last week?" Steve teased.

"Something like that." Nancy grinned. "How about it?" she asked the others.

"I have a better idea. Why don't you come to my house?" Mike said casually. "Erica and I will whip up something."

After discreet but meaningful glances at each other, they all accepted.

Erica was less than pleased with Mike's suggestion. On the way home she told him so.

"Why did you ask your parents for brunch? They're bound to guess I spent the night at your house."

"So what? They might seem a little formal, but they aren't stuffy. I'm sure they thoroughly approve."

"Only because they think we're going to get married."

Mike turned his head to look at her steadily. "Aren't we?"

"I hope so...in time."

"That's the first encouraging sign you've given me. How much time?"

"About fourteen years." Nicky would be out of high school by then—and out of harm's way.

"Why fourteen years?" Mike asked curiously.

"It sounded like a nice round number," she said lightly.

"Round or square, if you think I intend to wait that long you're sadly mistaken. What are you doing on your lunch hour Monday?" When she gave him a startled look he laughed. "I wasn't suggesting a quickie wedding, I merely thought we'd pick out your engagement ring. I almost bought you one, but then I decided it would be better to let you make your own choice."

"You don't have to buy me a ring," she said swiftly.

"Why won't you ever let anyone do anything for you?" he asked with a baffled look on his face.

"You've done more than you know," she answered softly. "You've brightened my whole life."

"I hope so, because you've given new meaning to mine," he said in a husky voice.

Erica was filled with poignant happiness as she entered the house with Mike. It felt like coming home. If only, she thought, if only. But all wistfulness vanished when they reached the bedroom and Mike took her into his arms.

His kiss was slow and savoring at first. "This is what I've been wanting to do all evening."

"Even when Jennifer was blowing in your ear?" Erica teased, supremely confident of his love.

"Especially then. It reminded me of how you react when I do this." He explored the inner curves of her ear with the tip of his tongue.

"Is this my reaction?" She pulled his shirt out of his trousers and raked her nails lightly up his spine.

"Sometimes you get more familiar than that."

"Let's see if I can remember." She untied his tie and began to remove the onyx studs in his dress shirt. It was more painstaking work than simply unfastening buttons. When Mike started to help, she wouldn't let him. "It's my turn to undress *you* this time."

"Be my guest." He grinned. "Any time you feel like it."

After she had removed his shirt, Erica ran her palms over his broad chest, enjoying the feeling of his warm, smooth skin. Mike caught his breath sharply as she leaned forward and kissed his flat nipples. But when he tried to draw her close, she resisted, slowly unfastening his belt.

"I'm not through yet." She smiled seductively.

Mike forced himself to remain still as she unzipped his tuxedo pants and watched them slide to his ankles. His control was challenged when his briefs followed the trousers. But when she caressed his rigid thighs, erotically skirting his hard arousal, all attempts at control vanished.

With a hoarse cry he pulled her into his arms and captured her mouth for a scorching kiss. The tables were turned as Erica felt her own passion flare. Mike's tongue was laying siege to her mouth and his taut virility found the juncture of her thighs.

"How can I want you more every time?" he muttered.

"Don't ever stop," she begged, digging her fingers into his buttocks.

"Not ever. You're mine and I'll never let you go!" He unzipped her dress and dipped his head to kiss the valley between her breasts while he unclasped her bra. "I never get used to the perfection of your body," he said huskily.

Erica wound her fingers in his hair as his mouth moved over her breasts. She moaned softly when his tongue curled around one nipple and his lips suckled gently.

"You're so beautiful," he said, almost reverently. "I want to touch every inch of you."

He knelt and rolled her panty hose down, lifting one foot and then the other to remove them completely. When she was completely nude, he stroked her body sensuously.

Erica's legs were trembling so much that she could hardly stand. She cried out when he circled her hips and drew her body close for an intimate kiss that sent a shock wave through her.

"I do know how to please you, don't I, darling?" He looked up at her with blazing eyes.

"I never knew there was this much pleasure in the world!" She pulled him to his feet and wrapped her arms around him so tightly that their bodies were fused.

"Do you have any idea of how much I love you?" he asked. "I'm going to spend the rest of my life making you happy."

Erica didn't want to be reminded of the future. "Just love me," she whispered.

"Always, my dearest one. Nothing will ever change that."

She clasped his head in her hands and covered his mouth with hers. And for a little while the future ceased to exist.

Mike carried her to the bed and covered her body with his. They were fused into one person, sharing the same driving excitement, the same throbbing escalation, and finally, the same rocketing fulfillment.

They were totally relaxed afterward, too content to speak. Mike stroked her hair languidly, and she rested her head in the curve of his neck.

"I'm almost sorry now that I invited everybody for brunch tomorrow," he said finally. "I'd like to stay in bed with you all day."

"We couldn't have done that anyway. Have you forgotten that I have a son?"

"He's one of the reasons I want to marry you," Mike teased. "I'll have a head start on a family."

"With your expertise you won't have any trouble starting one of your own." She smiled.

"There's an idea! If I got you pregnant you'd have to marry me."

"It's not one of your better ideas."

Mike's face sobered. "I've been wanting to talk to you about Nicky. After we're married I'd like to adopt him, if that's all right with you."

It was so perfect that Erica had a lump in her throat. Poor Nicky. Mike would have made such an ideal father.

When she didn't answer immediately he looked at her with a slight frown. "Are you worried that his grandparents might object?"

"They've never been interested in what's best for him."

"Then you'll let me adopt him?"

"I think it would be the best thing that ever happened to Nicky," Erica answered truthfully.

"Good. Now that that's settled, we can start making the arrangements, beginning with your ring. What time do you go to lunch?"

"Well, I . . . it varies."

"I'm flexible," he said calmly. "I can pick you up any time you say."

"All right," she answered reluctantly. "But call me first."

Erica felt as if she were on a juggernaut speeding out of control. The pressures on her were increasing from all sides. Everything in her life was so ideal now, but she couldn't avoid a feeling of impending disaster.

Then Mike kissed her and murmured, "I love you, sweetheart."

And the fear disappeared.

Chapter Nine

Erica was fast asleep when Mike got up the next morning. He smiled tenderly at her flowerlike face on the pillow, and got out of bed carefully in order not to awaken her.

Much later, after preparations were under way in the kitchen, he returned to kiss her awake. "It's time to get up, sleepyhead, unless you want to be in bed when the family gets here."

Her eyes opened slowly and she smiled at him. Then his words registered. She sat up in bed, glanced at the clock and gasped. "Why didn't you wake me sooner?"

"You were sleeping so peacefully. I didn't want to disturb you."

"I'll take a quick shower and then I'll help you with brunch."

"There's no hurry. Everything's under control." He put his arms around her waist and slid his lips over her shoulder.

"Everything except you." She laughed.

"Do you want me to be?" he murmured, caressing her bare body.

"No," she answered softly, clasping her arms around his neck. "I don't ever want you to change."

"Count on it!" He kissed her tenderly, then with mounting desire. Reluctantly he drew back. "Damn! I wish we didn't have company coming."

"But we do," she said with equal reluctance. Their need for each other never diminished.

Erica showered and dressed swiftly. Fortunately she kept a few casual things like shorts and bathing suits at Mike's house, since she and Nicky were there so often.

After making the bed she hung up their clothes from the night before, smiling at the memory of why they'd been discarded so carelessly. When the bedroom and bath were neat, she went into the kitchen to help Mike.

He was whistling as he moved from sink to stove, wearing an apron tied around his narrow waist. It didn't detract from his virility. Erica stood in the doorway for a moment, admiring the grace of his perfectly coordinated body.

"What can I do to help?" she asked.

His smiling eyes traveled over her brief white shorts and long legs. "Just sit on that stool over there and look beautiful while I scramble the eggs."

"You can't cook eggs ahead of time. They get hard and rubbery."

"Not when you use a little trick I picked up from the chef at the country club. I always wondered how he kept large quantities of eggs hot and moist at their buffet brunches, so I asked him. The secret involves sour cream and a couple of other things."

"Aren't you going to give me the recipe?"

"No." He kissed the tip of her nose. "I want to be indispensable to you."

"You already are," she said tenderly.

* * *

Mike's family arrived a short time later, without the boys.

"They wanted to stay home because Mrs. Halsey said they could make ice cream," Nancy explained. "You can buy it in any grocery store, but they were so excited they barely said goodbye to us." When she saw the expression on Erica's face, Nancy said uncertainly, "I guess I should have asked you first, but I didn't think you'd mind."

"No, it's all right," Erica said, covering her disappointment. She'd barely seen Nicky all weekend.

Everyone sat around the den drinking Bloody Marys and chatting comfortably together for a while before going into the dining room for brunch.

Mike had done a good job. The eggs were perfectly cooked and kept warm in a covered casserole on a long heating tray. Other casseroles offered crisp bacon and thick slices of grilled tomatoes. The buffet also held pitchers of juice, an assortment of bread and muffins, and halved papayas filled with strawberries.

"Everything is delicious," Phyllis told Erica.

"I can't take any of the credit," she answered. "Mike did it all."

"Bad strategy." Steve shook his head in mock disapproval. "This will be expected of you after you get married."

"I think it's admirable for a man to help his wife," Phyllis chided gently.

Nancy looked at her father with mischievous eyes. "What did you ever do, Dad?"

His own eyes twinkled. "I helped your mother bring two beautiful children into the world."

"I can help out there, too." Mike chuckled.

Erica's cheeks turned pink as they all laughed.

After brunch they took their coffee into the den and Mike tuned the television set to the finals of a golf match. While the men drew closer to the set, the women grouped together at the opposite end of the big room.

The conversation turned inevitably to the affair the night before, and Erica repeated how much she'd enjoyed it.

"I hope you'll join in some of our other activities," Phyllis said. "A lot of the events are held on the weekend."

"It's very nice of you to ask me, but I almost never leave Nicky with sitters during the day."

"He can always stay with us," Nancy said. "The boys get along famously together."

"I'm happy about that, but I feel I'm not spending enough time with him," Erica said carefully.

That part was true, but it was only part of the story. She was paving the way for refusing future invitations to big events where photographers were as thick as flies.

"I'm sorry. You're upset because I didn't insist that the boys come with us today," Nancy said soberly.

"Not at all! I'm delighted that Nicky's made a good friend. I hope we can get them together often. Maybe you'll bring Scott over to the hotel to play on the beach once in a while."

"Try to make some time for Grover and me, as well," Phyllis said. "They're both adorable children."

Erica was greatly relieved at having settled her most pressing worry without alienating any of the Smith family. She genuinely liked them, and it was so good for Nicky to have a surrogate family. If Erica realized she hadn't really solved her problem, she refused to think about it.

The days flowed by in a golden stream. On the weekends Mike took them to places they'd never been, like the Big Island of Hawaii. He flew them there one Sunday in the company plane.

"I didn't know you could fly!" Erica exclaimed when she found out. "Is there anything you can't do?"

"Nothing, as long as I have you," he answered tenderly.

The small six-seater plane was excellent for sight-seeing. Nicky squealed with delight as Mike flew low over miles of dense rain forest, broken only by an occasional deep gorge with brilliant flowering bushes at the base. One impressive cliff had twin falls cascading down its sheer side.

"Look, look!" Nicky pointed excitedly.

"Those are the Hi'ilawe Falls," Mike explained. "They feed a big river down below. A long time ago people used to catch fish there with their bare hands."

"I want to try," Nicky declared.

Mike smiled. "Maybe next time."

After a day of sun and swimming on the crescent beach in front of the luxurious Mauna Kea Beach Resort, they flew home over equally stirring scenery.

Another weekend Mike took them on his boat to the Leeward Islands, the string of mostly tiny atolls to the northwest of Honolulu. They were uninhabited and could only be reached by relatively small boats.

"It's like being on a deserted isle," Erica marveled after they left the yacht in a postcard perfect lagoon and hiked through overgrown vegetation. The dense green was punctuated by brilliant flashes of exotic, climbing orchids, and the only sounds were birdcalls.

They ate a picnic lunch on a secluded beach inhabited by gooney birds, blue-faced boobies and dozens of other varieties of colorful birds.

"Has anyone ever lived on these islands?" Erica asked.

"Not in modern times, because of the lack of drinking water," Mike explained. "But archaeologists have found temple remains, beautifully carved stone statues, and a lot of other artifacts from an early culture. You can see them in the Bishop Museum. We'll take Nicky there one day."

Erica couldn't have asked more of life. Every day was so idyllic that she wanted to knock on wood. Could anything this perfect continue?

The only thing even resembling an argument that she and Mike ever had was over an engagement ring. She always managed to thwart his attempt to take her shopping, but he refused to give up. Finally one night he handed her a small, blue velvet box.

"What's this?" she asked, although she already guessed. Inside the box was a magnificent, pear-shaped diamond ring.

"I hope you like it. I got tired of waiting for you to pick one out yourself."

"It's gorgeous!" she gasped. "But you shouldn't have."

"Wrong. This is what I should have done a long time ago." Slipping the ring onto her finger, he said with satisfaction, "Now everybody will know it's official."

Erica looked at her finger despairingly. It was the most beautiful ring she'd ever seen. "I wish you hadn't done this, Mike."

"You don't like it? That's why I wanted you to go with me. We can exchange it for an emerald, or anything else you'd prefer."

"It isn't that. I love it, but it's . . . it's too expensive. The people I work with are all in modest circumstances. How would it look?"

"Like you're going to marry a very wealthy man." Mike grinned. "This is only the beginning, sweetheart. I want to give you all the lovely things you deserve."

When he kissed her tenderly, Erica didn't have the heart to argue with him. She'd pick a better time.

In the days that followed, the ring posed a problem. It was too costly to just leave in a drawer, but she couldn't wear it. The reason she'd given Mike was valid, although there was another even more pressing one. It would be disastrous if the story got out that she was engaged to marry the son of the prestigious Smith family.

Erica finally settled for wearing the ring on a thin chain around her neck, underneath whatever she had on. It solved the problem, but the first chink had appeared in the idyll. The big diamond was a constant reminder that she was living on the edge.

Erica told herself not to borrow trouble. Little glitches were bound to occur, but she could handle them.

The dinner honoring Mike's father was one of those unforeseen events. She couldn't very well refuse an invitation to attend with the family. Grover was being given the Man of the Year award from a prestigious organization. It was quite an honor and would be a large, newsworthy occasion.

Erica was always leery of photographers at the big bashes, but this wasn't a purely social affair where they snapped pictures indiscriminately. The majority of the guests would be businesspeople, politicians, and members of the intellectual community. It was unlikely anyone would be interested in her.

She and Nancy discussed the event together. They'd become good friends and talked on the telephone frequently. The two couples also went out together regularly.

"I'm so glad you're going to the banquet," Nancy said. "I know you don't like those big affairs."

"Not especially, but this is different. I wouldn't miss seeing your father receive such an impressive award."

"He'll be pleased that you came. What are you going to wear?"

"I don't really have anything suitable. I'll have to buy a dress."

"Good, I'll tag along. I never pass up an opportunity to go shopping."

"I don't plan to look in the couture department," Erica warned. "It would be foolish to spend a lot of money when I have so little occasion to wear a long gown."

"You'd have plenty of chances if you weren't so stuffy about big dinner dances."

"What can I do? I'm not a party animal," Erica answered lightly.

"Okay." Nancy sighed. "Bring Nicky over on Saturday and we'll hit the stores."

Erica had every intention of buying something simple and sensible. She wouldn't even have gone into the exclusive dress shop Nancy patronized, but they passed it on the way to a department store.

"Do you mind if we stop in here for just a minute?" Nancy asked. "I want to see if the dress they're altering for me is ready."

Erica accompanied her inside, but it took more than a minute. The saleswoman wanted Nancy to try on the gown to be sure the alterations were satisfactory.

While Nancy was in the dressing room, Erica's attention was caught by a flame red chiffon gown. The strapless top was draped Grecian-style over a long fluid skirt.

"That would be perfect for the banquet," Nancy remarked, coming out of the dressing room.

"And afterward I could wear it when I take Nicky to the pizzeria for dinner," Erica answered ironically.

"For once in your life, do something rash!"

"I already did." Erica grinned. "I let you go shopping with me."

"I'm serious," Nancy said impatiently. "There's no reason for you to be so frugal. Mike is a very wealthy man."

"He doesn't pay for my clothes, I do."

"He will soon—when you're married, I mean."

"That's somewhere in the future. Until then I pay my own way."

"That sounds rather indefinite. You *are* going to marry him, aren't you?" Nancy looked at her sharply.

"It's a distinct possibility, but I don't see any point in rushing into anything. A lot of great friendships have been spoiled by marriage." Erica smiled to indicate it was a joke.

Nancy's austere expression didn't change. "Mike expects to spend the rest of his life with you. I can't believe you're just stringing him along."

"You must know me better than that!" Erica protested.

"I thought I did." Nancy continued to stare at her implacably.

"You needn't worry about Mike. He's the most wonderful man I've ever known. I would never want to hurt him," Erica said quietly. When Nancy didn't look entirely convinced, she forced a smile. "We're supposed to be shopping for a dress for me. I knew it was a mistake to let you come along. I won't be satisfied with anything after seeing this red dress."

"I'm sure you'll find something you like," Nancy answered coolly.

"I suppose it wouldn't hurt to try it on." Erica was looking for some way to get back on their former, friendly footing. "Do you think red is a good color for me? I usually feel more comfortable in pastels."

Nancy's reserve gradually vanished as she accompanied Erica into the dressing room and they started to discuss clothes.

The red dress fit perfectly and was wildly becoming. Erica gazed at herself with pleasure, feeling like an entirely different woman, someone glamorous and carefree.

"It's stunning on you," Nancy pronounced. "I'd wear silver sandals with it. You could get red ones dyed to match, but I think that would be too much."

"Yes, I do, too." Erica looked at herself wistfully.

"You *are* going to take it, aren't you?"

"Why not?" Erica said impulsively. "If Nicky spills tomato sauce on me at the pizzeria, it won't show."

Mike was very complimentary when he came to pick Erica up the night of the party. He kissed her bare shoulder and paid her extravagant compliments.

But when she reached for her evening bag, he frowned. "You're not wearing your ring."

She'd put it in a drawer for that one night, since there was no place to hide it under a strapless neckline. "Oh, well, I . . . I was afraid to wear it to such a large gathering," she said lamely. "People get held up in parking garages, or even on the street."

"You're being ridiculous," he said impatiently. "Go put it on."

Erica didn't want to precipitate an argument—especially one she wouldn't win. Her excuse had sounded thin, even to her own ears. It didn't really matter, anyway. There would be so many jewels at the event, who would notice one more ring?

The grand ballroom, of a different hotel this time, was crowded with tables jammed closely together. Mike and Erica were placed at a table with his sister and brother-in-law and some older couples Erica didn't know. Friends of the Smiths, no doubt. Phyllis and Grover were seated at a long head table, along with a state senator and other notables.

When Erica and Mike arrived, Nancy looked her over approvingly. "That dress is perfect on you. Now aren't you glad I talked you into it?"

"Yes, but I have a feeling I won't be when I get the bill." Erica laughed.

Nancy's gaze sharpened on Erica's ring. "That's not the only thing new you have on. Let me see."

Erica reluctantly held out her hand for Nancy's inspection.

"It's lovely. My brother has good taste. But why on earth didn't you tell me that day we went shopping?"

"Mike just gave it to me recently."

"I feel slightly foolish after the lecture I gave you, but you're partly to blame. You sounded pretty vague about where you and Mike were headed."

"Oh, well . . . I thought he should be the one to tell you."

Nancy turned to him. "I just found out you're engaged. Congratulations, it's about time. When is the wedding?"

"You'll have to ask Erica," Mike said.

"We haven't had time to discuss it, and I think the program is about to start," Erica said hastily.

"In your dreams!" Nancy said. "Everybody hasn't shown up at the head table yet. This thing will go on for hours."

"Your mother must be very proud that so many people turned out. I've never seen such a big crowd."

"Dad deserves it," Nancy said affectionately. "There are a lot of successful men who don't care about anything except making money, but Dad isn't like that. He'll always take time to help somebody out of a jam."

Mike nodded. "Like that fellow who embezzled money to pay for his wife's operation."

Sally Coleman stood against the wall a short distance away. She had seen Nancy pick up Erica's hand and examine the large, glittering diamond.

Stu Haoki strolled over to Sally. "I didn't expect to see you here tonight," he said. "This isn't your standard charity bash."

"A lot of the old dowagers are here, and they'll expect to see their names in the paper tomorrow. If they don't, guess who will hear about it?" Sally asked sourly. "If I get cut off their guest lists, I'm out of a job."

"Why didn't you just copy the names off the reservation list?"

"Because I have to describe what they're wearing and tell them how smashing they look."

Stu's wandering glance focused on Erica. "That wouldn't be a hardship with the lady in red, the one with Mike Smith. She's a real looker. I've seen her with him before."

"That's Erica Barclay. I think they just got engaged."

"He's a lucky guy."

"If you ask me, it's the other way around. The Smiths are loaded."

"Maybe it's a love match. You're just guessing that she's mainly interested in his bank account. She might have money of her own."

"Not like his. The Smith family is so rich I'll bet they don't even know what they own."

"After a certain point it doesn't matter," Stu observed. "What business is her family in?"

"I have no idea. I only met her once before, at a charity function at the Smith estate. All I could find out was that she isn't a native—and even getting *that* out of her was like pulling teeth. She sure didn't make my job any easier."

"Maybe she's just shy."

"None of them are, take my word for it." Sally stared at Erica's table. "Look at her, yakking it up with Mike's sister."

"I meant, shy around the press."

"She'd better learn to live with publicity if she intends to marry Grover Smith's son," Sally said tersely. "When the old man gets a cold in Hawaii, the commodity market sneezes in New York."

"What makes you think they're getting married? I've snapped Mike's picture with a dozen different women."

"She was showing his sister the big rock on her finger. Does that tell you something?"

"You ought to be happy about it. You'll have all kinds of new parties to write about."

"I can hardly wait," Sally remarked sardonically.

Stu looked at her with a raised eyebrow. "You sound like an ex-girlfriend. Did you have something going with the guy?"

"Are you kidding? My blood isn't blue enough."

"Well, you can't win 'em all." He switched his attention back to Erica. "If you're right about this engagement thing,

I'm glad I got a shot of her earlier. She isn't easy to catch off guard. It's almost like she knows when you're going to take her picture.''

Sally frowned thoughtfully. "You don't have any shots of her?''

"Not clear ones. I should have been able to get a good one when Mrs. Smith called her onto the stage after that fashion show event, but the lights were so bright she had her hand up to shade her eyes.''

"I remember, now that you mention it. But the lights didn't bother any of the other women," Sally mused.

"Not enough to spoil their picture." Stu grinned.

Sally's eyes began to sparkle with excitement. "Why do you think Erica Barclay doesn't want her picture taken?''

"I don't know if that's true. I just said it was hard to get a clear shot of her.''

"Because she doesn't want you to! I wonder why.''

He shrugged. "There could be all kinds of reasons.''

"Name one.''

"Well, she might come from some old-line family that frowns on publicity. Who was it who said a lady should only have her name in the paper twice—when she's born and when she dies.''

"I don't know who said it, but they didn't live in today's society.''

"You honestly think Erica has something to hide?''

"I don't know, but I'm going to find out," Sally said with ill-concealed malice.

"Well, good luck to you. I've got to go to work. It looks like the show is about to start.''

Sally could hardly wait to begin questioning Erica. This time she intended to push—albeit discreetly—for answers. These people had to be handled with kid gloves, but if there was a story here, who knew what opportunities it might open up for her? Unfortunately the program started before she could put her plan into action.

There were a lot of people who wanted to pay tribute to Grover. His family glowed with pride as speaker after speaker praised him to the skies.

When everyone had finished and Grover came forward to accept his award, the entire audience rose to their feet in respect and admiration. His acceptance speech was short, but dynamic. Its conclusion was especially moving.

"My life has been blessed by many things, but most of all by my wonderful family. They've always surpassed the high standards I've set for them. Their accomplishments have pleased me, but their outstanding character and trustworthiness have made me even prouder."

"The old man really delivered, didn't he?" Mike's voice was husky.

"You'd better not let him hear you call him an old man," Steve joked, to cover his own emotion.

At the end of Grover's speech he'd looked directly at their table, including Erica along with the others. While they were basking in his praise, her guilt mounted. She wasn't worthy of Grover's trust, but she hoped he'd never find out. Erica didn't want to be the one to bring him pain.

"Let's go up and congratulate Dad," Mike said.

"There's such a mob around him," Nancy objected. "We'll never get through."

"I'll run interference." Steve grinned. "I didn't play right tackle for nothing."

Sally watched in frustration as they disappeared into the crowd around Grover.

"Nice going, Dad," Mike said when they finally got a word with him.

The older man smiled. "I don't mean to sound ungrateful, but a testimonial dinner is like getting a preview of your own funeral. People have to say nice things about you."

"I'm sure they meant every word," Erica protested.

He patted her cheek. "Perhaps, but at least I know my family is sincere. Thanks for coming, my dear."

More people came to congratulate Grover, and Erica and Mike made way for them.

"Are you ready to cut out?" Mike asked her. "We've done our duty."

"It wasn't a chore," she scolded. "Your father is a wonderful man."

"Agreed, but we've already told him so." He put his arm around her waist and murmured in her ear, "The rest of the night belongs to us. Unless of course you really want to stay."

"No, I'm ready to leave. Let's say good-night to Nancy and Steve."

"I already told them we were going home."

"Pretty sure of yourself, aren't you?" She tilted her head to smile up at him.

"Are you kidding? You always keep me guessing. I just hoped it was an offer you couldn't refuse."

"You were right," she murmured.

Sally was across the room, trying to make her way through the crowd. She saw the seductive looks Erica and Mike exchanged, then watched in frustration as they left the ballroom before she could get to them.

"Damn!" she muttered. "That woman is harder to pin down than a sumo wrestler. Well, there's more than one way to trap a fox."

People were starting to leave as Nancy and Steve drifted back to their table. "It looks like the party is breaking up," he said. "I hope we can leave soon."

"It was your idea to drive my parents here," Nancy told him. "Now we're stuck till the bitter end."

"I should have told Mike to do it."

"Fat chance! He and Erica couldn't wait to get out of here." She grinned. "Isn't love grand?"

"I was beginning to think Mike was immune."

"You make it sound as though love is a disease."

"Some of the symptoms are the same." He laughed. "Rapid pulse, difficulty sleeping, anxiety attacks."

"Aren't you glad we're past all that?" she asked dryly.

"Are you trying to say the magic has gone out of our marriage?" he teased.

"I hope not."

"If we ever get out of here I'll show you it hasn't," he murmured.

Sally's appearance at that moment wasn't exactly welcome, but Nancy was too well-bred to be rude. She greeted the woman politely.

"Your father's speech was absolutely magnificent," Sally gushed. "I was positively spellbound."

"It's nice of you to say so," Nancy answered tepidly.

Steve got up from his chair, saying something vague about having to speak to somebody. Nancy sent him one of those meaningful glances that husbands and wives understand without words—don't leave me alone with this woman! But Steve chose to ignore it.

If Sally realized her reception was less than warm, she didn't let it bother her. "I especially liked the part where your father mentioned his wonderful family," she continued as Steve beat a hasty retreat. "It had special meaning for me, since I've had the privilege of getting to know all of you. I've seen firsthand how devoted you are."

"Yes, we're a very close family."

"Actually I don't really know the newest member of the Smith clan. Or should I say prospective member?" Sally asked archly.

How had the woman found out so fast? Nancy wondered in annoyance. Their parents hadn't even been told yet! "I don't know what you're talking about," she said coolly.

"Oh, I'm so sorry!" Sally exclaimed in mock distress. "Erica was here with Mike, and they were sitting at your table. I just naturally assumed the family approved."

"We *do* approve!" Too late, Nancy realized that she'd given Sally the information she was fishing for. "I mean, Erica is a lovely person. We'd be very pleased if she and Mike got married, but I don't know what their plans are."

"I understand." Sally lowered her voice conspiratorially.

Nancy had only been trying to protect Erica's privacy. But if this dreadful woman really thought they considered Erica unsuitable, who knew what she might print in her column?

"I don't think you do understand," Nancy said carefully. "Erica and I are good friends. Our children play together. Doesn't that tell you something?"

Sally fairly quivered with the excitement she tried to hide. "Erica has children?"

"One child, a boy."

"Your brother has dated so many local girls. It's ironic that a divorcée from the mainland should be the one to carry off the prize," Sally said artlessly.

"Erica is a widow." Nancy knew she was being pumped, but so skillfully that she couldn't avoid answering without leaving a wrong impression. The woman was good, she had to give her that.

"How sad." Sally looked properly solemn. "She's so young, too."

"I don't know how old Erica is, so I can't tell you," Nancy said sardonically, anticipating the next question.

"I wouldn't dream of asking! I was only wondering how old her little one is."

"Nicky isn't a toddler. He's the same age as my son." Nancy gave a sigh of relief as her mother approached. "Are you ready to leave?" she asked her.

"In a few minutes." Phyllis nodded to Sally before slipping gratefully into a chair. "Your father is still accepting good wishes."

"It was such a lovely event," Sally said.

"I thought it went off well, although I must admit I'm glad it's over." Phyllis looked around the rapidly emptying room. "Where are Mike and Erica?"

"They left a little while ago," Nancy said.

Sally saw her opening and seized it. "We were just talking about Erica. I didn't realize she was a widow. Did you know her husband?"

"No, I was told he died before Nicky was born. It wouldn't surprise me if she came here to get away from all the memories."

"Such a tragedy," Sally remarked unctuously. "Was it an accident?"

"I don't know. Erica never talks about him, and of course one doesn't ask."

"Certainly not! It must have been very hard for her to leave all of her family. Do they live very far away?"

Nancy had been sending her mother little signals, trying to tell her to be more discreet. But Phyllis wasn't aware of them.

"I believe Erica comes from someplace on the East Coast," she said. "I don't think her relatives even visit her. She's quite alone here, poor dear, except of course for her darling son."

"And you and your family."

"Yes, we're very fond of both of them."

"It's kind of you to get her involved in your charitable events. I suppose she wouldn't know what to do with herself otherwise."

"Quite the contrary. Erica holds down a full-time job, takes care of Nicky, and still finds time to do volunteer work. She's quite an amazing girl."

The tip of Sally's nose twitched, like a rat terrier who's gotten a fresh scent. "That really is amazing. What kind of work does she do?"

"We have to go, Mother," Nancy said abruptly.

Phyllis looked at her daughter with a slight frown. "Your father isn't here yet."

Sally leaned forward, aware that her window of opportunity was about to close. "You were telling me what Erica does for a living."

"She has some kind of position at the Haialua Hotel. Do you know what her title is?" Phyllis asked her daughter.

"No, I don't." Nancy took her mother's arm and hauled her unceremoniously to her feet. "We really have to leave. Dad is probably waiting for us to rescue him, and Steve wants to go home." She dragged her mother off before she could object.

Sally watched them go with a smug expression. They could run, but they couldn't hide. She'd gotten what she wanted.

"Where are your manners, Nancy?" Phyllis exclaimed, when they were out of hearing. "It was terribly rude of you to drag me off in the middle of a conversation."

"You needn't worry about hurting that vulture's feelings," Nancy answered curtly. "She doesn't have any."

"I realize you don't like Sally, but that's no excuse for bad manners."

"Wake up and smell the roses, Mother! She wasn't making polite conversation, she was trying to uncover some dirt about Erica."

"Why on earth would she do that?"

"Because Mike and Erica got engaged tonight."

Phyllis's face lit up. "How wonderful! Your father will be so pleased."

"We all are, but I got the impression that Erica didn't want to announce it just yet."

"Why not?"

"I don't know and I didn't ask. You know how she is when you ask personal questions. Erica has opened up a lot since we've become friendly, but she's still the most private person I've ever met."

"What makes you think they're engaged?"

"Mike gave her an eye-popping ring. I hope it will give Steve some ideas for my birthday next month." Nancy grinned.

"I don't understand. If Erica is wearing Mike's ring, how can it be a secret?"

"Maybe I'm wrong. It was just a feeling I had that she preferred not to go public with the news. Whatever her reasons are, I think she and Mike should be the ones to announce it, not some snoopy gossip monger whose only interest is a scoop for her column. That's why I tried to head you off."

"I couldn't have told Sally anything," Phyllis protested. "I didn't know it myself."

"She was pumping you for details about Erica's background." Nancy's forehead creased in a worried frown. "I wonder why."

"That's fairly standard procedure. When a young couple gets married, the newspapers carry a little paragraph about them, what schools they went to, what clubs they're members of, who their parents and grandparents are. You have a clipping like that in your wedding album."

"Maybe that's what Erica is trying to avoid."

"Why would she? It makes a nice little souvenir to show your children."

"If you don't have anything in your background you'd rather people didn't find out about."

"Don't be ridiculous! Erica is a charming, wholesome woman. What could she possibly have to hide?"

"You never know," Nancy said soberly.

* * *

Nancy's feeling of uneasiness would have escalated to alarm if she'd heard the call Sally made from a phone booth in the hotel.

Stu Haoki's voice was grumpy when he answered. "Yeah, who is it?"

"It's Sally Coleman. I want to talk to you about that picture you took of Erica Barclay."

"Who?"

"The woman in the red dress," she said impatiently. "Mike Smith's date."

"Oh, yeah, I remember. What about her?"

"You said you got a picture of her. I want a copy."

"I said I *thought* I got a good shot. I won't know how clear it is until I develop the film tomorrow. The conditions weren't ideal, with all those people popping up unexpectedly in front of the camera."

"I'll take it even if it's fuzzy. Can you develop it tonight?"

"Are you crazy? It's almost midnight. I put in a long day and I'm beat. I was just getting into bed when you called."

"It's really urgent, Stu. I'll make it worth your while."

"Forget it, Sally. I don't know what *you* intend to do, but I'm going to bed."

"Wait! Don't hang up. If you won't develop the film tonight, when *will* you do it?"

"When I get around to it," he said irritably.

Her chin set grimly. "I don't happen to be sleepy. I can call you every hour to find out."

"All right already," he grumbled. "I'll drop it by your office tomorrow morning around ten. *Now* can I get some sleep?"

Chapter Ten

Sally was in the newspaper office early the next morning, although she'd only had a few hours' sleep. Excitement had kept her awake. Anything connected with the Smith family was news, but a gut feeling told her she was onto more than an engagement.

Bill Garvey, the *Chronicle*'s crime reporter, didn't come in until late in the morning. Sally knew the nature of his job made his hours erratic, but she could barely contain her impatience.

"I have to talk to you, Bill," she called, before he'd even reached his desk. "I think I might have a big story, but it's more up your alley than mine. I need to know how to go about cracking it."

"Is one of your socialites serving watered-down drinks?" He chuckled.

"I'm serious! Suppose you suspect a person is covering up something in her past. How do you find out what it is?"

His mouth thinned with distaste. "That's gossip column stuff. Go ask somebody on one of the tabloids."

"I'm not talking about a cheating husband or wife. This person is almost paranoid about her privacy. She avoids being photographed and nobody really knows much about her. She's only lived here a few years, so whatever she's hiding probably happened someplace else. How do I find out what it is?"

"I don't investigate crimes, I report on them, but I suppose you'd start with her hometown, or wherever she came from. You'd have to go there and nose around, talk to people who knew her."

"That's the problem. Even if I had the time and money to do that, I don't know where she came from. The people close to her are suspiciously vague. All I could get out of them was that it's someplace on the mainland, the East Coast."

"I suppose you could talk to the police, although I doubt if they'd check her out without more to go on than just your hunch. You better be real careful, kid. If this woman turns out to be a solid citizen she might sue the pants off you."

"Only if I'm wrong, and I don't think I am."

"You've been on the social beat too long. This might come as a shock to you, but not everybody gets off on seeing their picture in the paper."

"Maybe not, but they don't run like a rabbit whenever they see a camera."

"If that's all you have to go on, I'd advise you to forget it. Perfectly normal people have quirks. It doesn't make them criminals."

"I don't want advice, I want information. How do the police track down suspects?"

"Through a lot of grunt work. They run fingerprints through their own files first, then they contact law enforcement agencies all over the country. The computer can tell them if the suspect has any aliases or prior arrests, and also checks for outstanding warrants. There are all kinds of high-tech methods for running someone down. But you don't have those resources."

"I'll find a way," Sally said grimly. "There's something funny going on and I intend to expose it. The beautiful people should have to play by the rules like the rest of us."

Bill stared curiously at her flushed face. "It sounds like you have a personal agenda here."

Sally took a deep breath to calm herself. "You're damn right I do! This story will be my ticket to a decent job on this rag."

"You're sure that's your only reason?"

She smiled maliciously. "I want the job I was promised. And if it means digging up a little scandal on one of those snooty blue bloods, so much the better."

"Okay, but it's going to cost you." He scribbled something on a piece of paper. "Here's the name of a private detective I know. He's an ex-cop, like a lot of P.I.s, so maybe he can get a little unofficial help from the police department."

"Thanks, Bill, I owe you one."

"Don't thank me until you get his bill. You might be sorry you opened up this can of worms."

"No way!" She snickered. "It's a dirty job, but I'm just the gal who can do it."

Erica was mercifully unaware of Sally's suspicions, but she had other problems. Persuading Mike to delay the announcement of their engagement was taking all of her ingenuity. He fluctuated between gentle argument and downright impatience.

Except for that, life couldn't have been more ideal. Nicky adored Mike and the feeling was reciprocated. When Erica went somewhere with Nancy, Mike took care of Nicky as if he were the child's father.

Erica was so happy that she told herself it couldn't last. But she didn't really believe that. When her world came crashing down on a Wednesday afternoon, it was totally unexpected.

Disaster struck without warning at the end of her working day. She had finished checking supplies in the laundry room and gone down to the lobby to meet Nicky. The van always dropped him off promptly.

Erica had no reason to notice the two large men lounging in a corner of the lobby, except for the fact that they were wearing dark suits and ties. Even so, she would have dismissed them as tourists who were waiting for their rooms to be ready.

Her attention was focused on the entrance where Nicky was scrambling out of the school van. A moment later he came racing through the door, bursting with news about a birthday party he was invited to. She was bending down to give him a hug when the two men approached.

The blond one, Pete Parker, drew a shield in a leather case out of an inside pocket. "Caroline Hardwick, you're under arrest for kidnapping, illegal flight to escape prosecution and defying a court order."

Erica's arms closed around Nicky, pulling him tightly against her. She'd lived this moment in her nightmares—but this time she wouldn't wake up.

"How did you find me?" she whispered.

"We got a tip," Stan Kanowsky, the dark-haired member of the team, answered briefly. "You'll have to come with us now. We have a warrant authorizing us to take you and the boy back to New York." He reached out for her arm.

Erica shrank back. "I need time. I have to pack first—for Nicky, anyhow. He'll need clothes and things," she said distractedly.

"We'll arrange for everything to be packed up and shipped."

"At least let me get Blinky, his stuffed rabbit. He can't go to sleep without Blinky."

"Don't make me handcuff you, Mrs. Hardwick," the big man said ominously.

Nicky clutched at her skirt. "Mommy, what's wrong? Who are these men?" He only called her Mommy in moments of extreme stress.

Erica tried to appear reassuring, although she was trembling so badly that even her voice shook. "They're going to take us on an airplane ride. Won't that be fun?"

"No! I don't want to go. I don't like them!"

"You'll get to see a movie on the plane, and have dinner on a tray right in front of your seat," she coaxed.

Her fear had transmitted itself to him, but this new idea was intriguing. He hesitated for a moment. "Do I have to take a bath first?"

"No, we'll leave for the airport right now."

"We need to fill out all the paperwork first," Parker said. "We won't be leaving for the mainland until tomorrow."

It was only a small reprieve, but she welcomed it, too dazed to realize that she was going to be locked up. "Then I'll have time to pack Nicky's things after you bring us back here tonight." When the men exchanged a glance without answering, Erica's blood chilled. "I'm not coming back, am I? You're taking me to jail. But what about Nicky? You can't put a four-year-old boy in a jail cell!"

They looked uncomfortable. "Don't worry, Child Services will look after him."

"No!" Erica clasped Nicky convulsively. "You can't just turn him over to strangers. I won't let you!"

"Be reasonable, Mrs. Hardwick," Parker said. "You wouldn't want to see him put behind bars. You said so yourself."

Nicky began to cry. "Make them go away. I don't want to go anyplace with them."

Erica was overwhelmed with grief and helplessness. The law said she was guilty, and even though it was a terrible miscarriage of justice, there was no way she could stop them from carrying out their orders. All she could do was try to make it easier for Nicky.

Drawing a deep breath, she said, "There's nothing to be upset about, darling. These aren't bad men, they're policemen. They're going to give us a ride to the police station, and you'll get to talk to real officers in uniform. I'll bet you've never done that before."

Nicky looked at her doubtfully, but his tears stopped. "Why don't these men have uniforms?"

"We're federal marshals," Stan Kanowsky said. "But we have badges just like policemen. Would you like to see mine?" He took it out and offered it to the child.

Nicky examined it with interest. "When you get older, will they give you a uniform, too?"

"You never can tell." Stan smiled. "Would you like to sit in the front seat with me?"

A potentially volatile situation was averted as he smoothly maneuvered Nicky out to the car. His partner followed with Erica.

She fought back a feeling of hopelessness as she got into the back seat with Parker. This was no time to give up. There had to be some way to keep the authorities from placing Nicky with strangers—which would be a disaster! He'd feel both abandoned and betrayed. No amount of explanations on her part could prepare him. She had to do *something*.

"Do I get to make a phone call?" she asked Parker in a low voice.

"I'll see to it," he promised.

Nicky was momentarily alarmed when a policeman prepared to take Erica away to be fingerprinted and photographed. But the marshals helped her reassure him.

"Your mom has to make a telephone call," Stan said casually. "Why don't you stay here with us? There's a candy machine in the other room. Maybe you'll see something you like."

"Let Mrs. Hardwick make a phone call before you book her," Pete told the policeman in a lowered voice as he took Nicky's hand.

The little boy looked uncertainly at his mother. "Is it all right, Mommy?"

"Yes, honey." she forced a smile. "It's okay."

Erica looked at her watch, praying that Nancy would still be at her office. She tapped out the number with a shaking finger. After a heart-stopping couple of moments, Nancy's secretary answered and put her call through.

"Hi, Erica, you just caught me," Nancy said. "I was getting ready to call it a day."

"Thank heaven you're still there!"

"What's up? You sound tense. Is my brother being difficult about something?"

"I'm in terrible trouble," Erica said tautly. "I need a lawyer. Will you help me?"

Nancy's casual tone vanished. "Of course I will. What's wrong?"

"I'll tell you when you get here. I'm at the Central Police Station. Can you come right away?"

After a shocked pause Nancy said, "This isn't some kind of joke, is it?"

"If only it were! Please hurry, Nancy, they're going to place Nicky with Children's Services."

"Where is he now? I'll go pick him up."

"He's with me. That's what I'm trying to tell you!"

"He's at the police station? Dear Lord! Does Mike know?"

"No! And you're not to tell him. Promise me!"

"Okay, don't panic. Just hang on, I'll be right there."

Erica didn't feel quite so alone after talking to Nancy. It helped her through the indignity of having her fingerprints taken, and being photographed in a harsh light against a white wall with measurements on it that showed her height.

The worst part was when they put her in a cell. She felt like a trapped animal. But despite a feeling of suffocation, concern for Nicky was uppermost in her mind. He would be starting to ask for her. If only they'd let him spend the night with Mike's sister instead of strangers. Maybe Nancy could post some kind of bond so they'd let her take him out of this place.

Erica paced the small area distractedly, consumed by fear for her child. It seemed like an eternity until Nancy got there. Actually an officer came to unlock her cell only a short time later.

The man led Erica to a room with a scarred oak table, a couple of chairs and a watercooler. Nancy was waiting inside.

As soon as he left them alone she said, "What on earth is going on? The desk clerk told me you're wanted on a charge of kidnapping and flight to avoid prosecution. Is that true?"

"I'll tell you the whole story, but first, can you get them to let you take Nicky home with you?"

"I can't answer that without knowing all the facts."

Erica stared down at her tightly clasped hands. "I haven't been completely honest with you. To begin with, my name isn't Erica Barclay, it's Caroline Hardwick, and Nicky's legal name is Jordan Hardwick, Junior. I changed both our names when I came here, shortly after he was born. Nobody knows this, not even Mike. I hoped nobody would ever find out."

"That's a terrible way to live! If your husband was abusive, why didn't you divorce him instead of running away? You're not the passive victim type."

"I didn't run away from *Jordan*. He died before Nicky was born, as I told you. That part was the truth." Erica sighed. "I'll have to start at the beginning."

She told Nancy the same, limited portion of the story that she'd finally told Mike, and Nancy reacted with the same disgust. Erica paused before coming to the hard part—the events responsible for her arrest.

"You stuck it out longer than I would have," Nancy said sympathetically. "Why didn't you just take Nicky and go home?"

"There was nowhere to go. My parents were killed when I was in high school, and I was an only child. I've been on my own for most of my life."

Nancy gave her a puzzled look. "I seem to remember either you or Mike mentioning that you had family in California."

"When I came to Honolulu I thought it would look suspicious if I just dropped out of nowhere, with no family ties, no background. So I made one up."

"It must be hard to be so alone," Nancy said in a muted voice.

"I always missed having a family, but it made things easier when I decided to take Nicky and start a new life. It would have been cruel to keep him from seeing my parents if they'd been alive. I couldn't have stayed away from them, either."

Nancy slanted a glance at her. "Lord knows I'm not criticizing you, but isn't it also rather unkind to keep your husband's parents from seeing Nicky? I realize they're very unpleasant people, but a brief visit now and then doesn't sound too unreasonable."

Erica sprang up from her chair and paced back and forth. "The Hardwicks don't know the meaning of the word reasonable. It's their way or not at all. That's why I had to get Nicky away from them."

"Look, Erica, I'm on your side all the way, but I can't agree that you did the right thing—or rather, the compassionate thing."

"Let me tell you about Joseph and Miriam Hardwick. You know how people coo over babies and talk baby talk to them? They never even wanted to hold Nicky."

"That's not so terrible. Older people are sometimes afraid to handle an infant."

"Oh, really? When Nicky cried and I went to him, they told me I was spoiling him," Erica continued stoically. "A boy's character was formed in the cradle, and I was making a sissy out of him. I'd learned by that time, that there was no use arguing with them, so I ignored their criticism. That was overconfidence on my part. They hired a nanny, with instructions to keep me away from my son if I didn't follow their rules.''

"You're joking!"

"Do you see me laughing?" Erica asked ironically. "It was the last straw. I hadn't said anything when they made plans to send Nicky away to boarding school in the winter and camp in the summer. I foolishly thought I'd have something to say about it when the time came. Why argue about it now? But when they tried to practically remove me from his life, I realized it had to stop. I told them I was taking Nicky and moving out.''

"That must have provoked a major row!"

"It did. They started out by calling me ungrateful, among other things, and ended up by accusing me again of marrying Jordan for his money. They swore I'd never get a penny from them, so I'd better think twice about biting the hand that fed me. The only way I could support a baby was by selling my body—and the next man wouldn't be fool enough to marry me.''

"Really classy people," Nancy said grimly. "I hope you didn't take their abuse meekly.''

Erica smiled briefly. "That isn't my nature. I got a few of *my* grievances off my chest. The argument raged for hours, but I knew this was one I had to win. Finally I told them to get used to it, there was nothing they could do to stop me. I was Nicky's mother and I could take him and leave if I wanted to.''

"Good for you," Nancy said with satisfaction. "What did they say to that?"

"It pretty much shocked them. They'd never thought about *my* rights before.''

"So they just caved in? That seems out of character."

"You're more perceptive than I was," Erica said bitterly. "I was so relieved to have the unpleasantness over with that I didn't realize they'd only changed tactics. When they asked me to let them have just a few more days with Nicky, it seemed mean-spirited not to agree.''

''Something tells me you were too trusting for your own good.''

''I was young and inexperienced. I didn't know people could be that devious.''

''Let me guess. After pretending to agree, they made your life a living hell?''

''No, the atmosphere was tense, but I thought they'd resigned themselves to the inevitable. Which didn't mean they liked it. I could tell they detested me. You can imagine what those last few days were like. I spent them counting the hours to freedom.''

''Didn't you have any friends you could go to for moral support?''

''Not in New York City. I came from a small town upstate. When we returned from Europe and moved in with Jordan's parents, I didn't know anyone in the city. Jordan's friends were pretty much like him and I didn't have the opportunity to meet anyone else. Then after he died, I spent all my time alone with the Hardwicks. When an old friend of Jordan's called unexpectedly and asked me out to dinner, I jumped at the chance to get out of the house for a few hours.''

''That's understandable, but didn't your in-laws throw a fit?'' Nancy asked. ''People like that would expect you to remain a grieving widow for the rest of your life.''

''Surprisingly, they didn't seem to mind, which should have given me a clue. But Jordan and Derek Cogswell had been friends since they were boys together. I thought maybe the Hardwicks regarded him as nonthreatening, or maybe they felt the way I did—that they wouldn't have to see me for a few hours. Anyway, I accepted the date. Derek wouldn't have been my first choice, but he'd always been pleasant enough. And he'd never come on to me the way some of Jordan's so-called friends did before my figure disappeared.''

"They sound like real charmers," Nancy said disgustedly.

"I could tell you stories you'd find hard to believe."

"I suppose Derek tried to make up for lost time."

"No, he was a perfect gentleman. We had dinner at a nice restaurant and talked about all kinds of things. I was so starved for company that I didn't want the evening to end. When he asked me to his apartment for a nightcap I was tempted, just to avoid having to go home. I thought it might give him the wrong idea, though, so I said no. He didn't try to pressure me, but he said he had some snapshots of Jordan when he was a teenager. Derek said he knew Jordan hadn't been the greatest husband in the world, but maybe I'd like to have the photos to give to Nicky. That seemed like a valid reason, so I said okay."

"How long did it take until he swarmed all over you?" Nancy asked cynically.

"No, his behavior was exemplary. When we got to his apartment he sat me down with a photo album while he made us each a drink. We looked at the pictures together and he told me where they were taken. Then after a while he offered me another drink, but I said no. He seemed annoyed at first and tried to coax me into it."

"I thought he sounded too good to be true," Nancy murmured.

"That's what I began to think. I remembered all the times Jordan told me I was a prude and a poor sport. But Derek backed off. He laughed and said he'd forgotten that I wasn't a real drinker, but he had a new chocolate liqueur that was practically nonalcoholic. I told him I really didn't want anything else to drink, but he insisted that I try it. He went into the kitchen and came out with two glasses of the stuff. It seemed easier to take a sip than to argue about it, so that's what I did. It really was delicious. I drank the whole glass."

When she didn't continue, Nancy asked, "What happened then?"

"The next thing I remember is waking up in my bed at the Hardwicks' the next morning," Erica said somberly. "I had a monstrous headache and a terrible taste in my mouth."

"He drugged you! But why?" Nancy's expression changed. "Did he rape you?"

"No, fortunately that wasn't part of the plan." Erica's mouth curved sardonically. "The Hardwicks came to my room before I was even out of bed. They had pictures to illustrate what happened at Derek's apartment. They were horrible!" Her steely composure started to disintegrate. "He'd undressed me and taken the most disgusting photos of the two of us, I suppose with one of those cameras where you can set a timer and get in the picture."

"Derek gave the photographs to the Hardwicks?" Nancy asked incredulously. *"Why?"*

"It didn't occur to me to ask. I tried to tell them what really happened, but they pretended not to believe me. When I said I intended to go to the police, they said Derek would say I'd had consenting sex with him, and they'd back up his story. I finally realized they'd paid him to stage the whole thing."

"How do you accept payment for doing a thing like that?" Nancy demanded.

Erica shrugged. "Derek was just like Jordan, constantly short of cash and not too particular what he did to get it. Whatever the Hardwicks paid him was worth every penny, because they now had the upper hand. They told me they would go to court and have me declared an unfit mother if I didn't clear out and give them full custody of Nicky. Of course I refused. I didn't think even *they* would stoop so low."

"How much lower could they get after what they did to you?" Nancy remarked contemptuously.

"I didn't stand a chance in court. The pictures alone would have been proof enough that I was a depraved person, but their lawyer piled on the evidence. He told the court about our elopement to Europe on stolen money. Without actually saying so, he inferred that the whole thing was my idea. And the judge believed him. It's difficult to conceive of a son stealing from his parents unless someone practically forced him into it."

"They awarded custody of Nicky to the Hardwicks?"

Erica nodded. "I was granted supervised visiting rights once a month."

"Didn't you have an attorney? Was he out to lunch while all of this was going on?"

"Clarence Darrow couldn't have won my case," Erica said wearily. "By the time the Hardwicks got through presenting their twisted evidence, I was lucky the judge didn't order me to be tarred and feathered. I realized at that moment that I couldn't depend on anyone but myself. I took Nicky and got as far away from New York as I possibly could. He was only a few months old, so it was easy to change our names. I dyed my hair black to fit in with the majority of the population, and to alter my appearance. I'd never supported myself, but I got a job and kept a low profile. Everything was going so smoothly. I was beginning to think no one would ever find me."

"How did they?"

"I don't know. The marshal told me they got a tip."

Nancy frowned. "I wonder who told them. Well, I suppose it doesn't matter now."

"Nicky is the only one who matters. I can't let the Hardwicks get their hands on him. Can you get a court order or something to keep him here?"

"On what grounds? They were awarded legal custody."

"I don't care!" Erica declared passionately, jumping to her feet. "You heard what they're capable of. Would you want people like that to raise Scott?"

"They won't get Nicky," Nancy said, with a confidence she didn't feel. "Let me talk it over with Mike and see what we can come up with."

"No, you mustn't tell him! I couldn't bear to face him after the way I let him believe we had a future together. He won't want anything to do with me anyway after he finds out I'm a wanted criminal.''

''You're being ridiculous! You know Mike. Do you honestly think he'll just let you disappear without finding out what happened to you? I'll get in touch with Dad, too. He has a lot of clout.''

''Do you have to tell your whole family?'' Erica asked despairingly.

''Listen to me. You'll need a lot of help, not to mention money, if we're going to get you out of this mess. Keep your chin up and let me make some phone calls.''

Nancy was so dynamic that Erica allowed herself to hope—until she was returned to her cell. Then black gloom enveloped her. What could anyone do? She just prayed that in time, Mike wouldn't hate her too much.

Hate wasn't the emotion Mike displayed when Erica was brought back to the same room a short time later. Without waiting for the policeman to leave, he took Erica in his arms and held her so tightly that she could hardly breathe.

She clung to him desperately, knowing it might be for the last time. When he loosened his grip slightly she whispered, ''I'm so sorry.''

''For what? Going through hell? Nancy told me the whole story. I just wish *you* had told me.''

''I was afraid,'' she murmured.

''When will you learn to trust me?''

''I do, but it's too late now,'' she said sadly.

''Don't you believe it! Nothing and nobody will ever take you away from me,'' Mike said confidently. ''After we clear this up, we're getting married, and I don't want to hear any arguments out of you.''

''That's what I've always wanted, but it wasn't possible. I'm just glad you understand now why I had to keep putting you off. At least we had a little time together before somebody turned me in.''

"We're going to have a whole life together, sweetheart." He kissed her tenderly. "Starting soon. It's very lonely in that big bed without you."

Erica tried to believe she'd lie in Mike's arms again. It would be too cruel to have found the love of her life and have only memories to sustain her.

"Don't look so sad, darling. Everything's going to be all right. If I ever find out who ratted on you, I'm going to take him apart, limb by limb," Mike said grimly.

Nancy entered the room in time to hear his threat. "Our rat is female, and I'll gladly help you dismember her."

"You know who the informant is?"

"I think so. Sally Coleman was snooping around earlier, and I doubt if she's doing an article on haute cuisine in the Honolulu jail system."

Mike looked at his sister blankly. "Why would she jeopardize her livelihood? She's a society reporter."

"Have you ever seen the expression on her face when she thinks nobody is looking? She's not a happy camper. It must be hard to suck up to people who only tolerate you. I think our Sally is tired of the social world and wants to move up to the crime beat."

"Not on the *Chronicle,* she won't," Mike said curtly. "I happen to be on the board of directors."

"I don't think any responsible editor would fire her because of a personal vendetta," Nancy said doubtfully. "Even if you are a director."

"Who said anything about getting her fired?" Mike's smile would have done credit to a wolf. "I plan to give her a glowing recommendation. Sally Coleman will stay on the society circuit for the rest of her career. Unless she leaves town—which might not be a bad idea."

"A masterful move. Remind me not to get on your S-list." Nancy laughed. She turned as the door opened. "Oh, good, here's Dad."

Grover Smith brought an air of authority into the room. Erica tried not to shrink under his gaze, although it wasn't judgmental.

"Suppose you tell me what this is all about," he said. After they had given him an abbreviated version of Erica's story, Grover looked at his daughter. "How serious is the situation?"

"Very serious." She slanted an uncomfortable glance at Erica. "They have a fugitive warrant for her arrest. They're going to take her and Nicky back to New York on a morning plane."

"I'll go with them without a struggle if you can convince them to leave Nicky here. It's worth going to prison if I know he's safe from the Hardwicks."

"It's not going to come to that," Mike said firmly.

Grover held up his hand and looked again at Nancy. "Can you file a writ of habeas corpus and get her out on bail?"

She shook her head. "A writ of habeas corpus can't be used as protection against illegal imprisonment in this case. Erica violated a court order and fled the state. There's no question of her guilt."

"Just a damn minute!" Mike said angrily. "You're talking about Erica as if she's a common criminal."

"I appreciate your feelings, but this isn't your field of expertise," Grover said. "Let your sister and me explore the possibilities." As Mike subsided reluctantly, Grover asked Nancy, "What are the chances of having the custody verdict set aside on grounds of collusion? I understand that's what happened."

"That's what I plan to do, but it's going to be difficult to prove. In the meantime she's in violation of the law. There's no way I can stop them from taking her back."

"But what about Nicky?" Erica's hands were clasped so tightly her knuckles were white. "Is there any way you can keep *him* here?"

"I don't see how," Nancy said regretfully. "I'd gladly keep him at my house, any of us would take him, but we aren't family. There's no justification."

"I'm not so sure." Grover looked thoughtful. "Erica and Mike are engaged. Which practically makes me Nicky's grandfather."

"That's really reaching for it," Nancy said dubiously. "I don't think it will fly. You might conceivably challenge the custody case on that basis, but Nicky will have to return to the Hardwicks until the court considers the merits of your claim. You'd have to appear in person as the plaintiff," she warned.

"I'd be more than willing to do that. Unfortunately I have pressing business here in Honolulu for the next few days. When that's wrapped up I will appear in New York with my future grandson," he said smoothly.

"Even *you* couldn't pull that off, Dad," Nancy said.

"Watch me." His eyes twinkled. "What good is influence if you can't use it for a good cause now and then? Get my attorney on the phone for me. No offense to you, my dear, but he's a little more adept at arm twisting."

When Nancy went to use the phone, Erica gazed at Grover with tears in her eyes. "I don't know why you're willing to help me after the lies I've told all of you, but I want you to know I'll be eternally grateful."

"Wait until you see if I've overstated my importance." He smiled.

"It doesn't matter. You were willing to try, that's what counts." She looked at him searchingly. "Tell me one thing. Why are you doing this?"

"I think those who can help other people have an obligation to do so." His rather formidable expression softened. "But in your case I have an added incentive. You're a brave young woman and I'm looking forward to having you in our family."

Tears rolled down Erica's cheeks as Mike gripped his father's hand convulsively before taking her in his arms.

Nancy stuck her head in the door. "I have Roger Standish on the phone, Dad, and I clued him in on the details. He's all yours." When Grover left the room she said, "Now we cross our fingers and pray."

"Piece of cake," Mike said confidently, to reassure Erica. "Dad can call in a lot of favors."

"If he is successful, will you keep Nicky for me?" Erica asked Nancy.

"You know I will. Scott will be ecstatic."

"It might be for a long time," Erica said hesitantly.

"You're not to think like that," Mike ordered.

"I have to be realistic. What will they do with me?" she asked Nancy soberly. "Will it do any good to hire a lawyer?"

"You already have one. I'm going back with you." She glanced at her brother. "I assume Mike is, too."

"You've got that right!" he stated.

Erica smiled through her tears. "If I wasn't so miserable I'd be counting my blessings. You're good friends."

Mike tipped her chin up and looked at her tenderly. "I want to be everything to you, your friend, your lover, the father of your children."

Nancy got up from her chair. "I can take a hint. I'll go see how Dad is doing."

Mike took her in his arms and they kissed and whispered words of love. It was a poignant moment because they both knew the future was uncertain.

Nancy and Grover were gone for a long time. When they finally returned he said, "I'm sorry it took so long. I had to make a couple of long distance calls."

"It also took a little time to smooth some ruffled feathers." Nancy grinned. "Judges are as cranky as anyone else when you wake them up."

Grover returned her smile. "They shouldn't be so testy. Older people aren't supposed to need much sleep."

Erica glanced at her watch. "It's only seven o'clock."

"Not in New York," Nancy said.

"Did you get the indictment against Erica dropped?" Mike asked tensely.

"I couldn't do that," Grover answered. "It's a serious charge. I did, however, ensure that she'll be granted bail pending the hearing."

"Well, thank God for that!"

"How about Nicky?" Erica asked anxiously. "Will he have to go back to New York?"

"Not in the foreseeable future," Grover said. "My attorneys are filing a number of petitions that could keep him here indefinitely." His eyes twinkled. "Shakespeare was right when he spoke of the windy side of the law. It can take an amazing amount of time to resolve a dispute."

Mike's face was exultant. "I knew you could do it, Dad!"

"I hope I can continue to justify your confidence," the older man said dryly. "Erica's case is by no means an easy one to win. You mustn't get too euphoric. As of now, they have her dead to rights."

Erica brushed that aside impatiently. "Did you see Nicky? What have they done with him?"

Nancy frowned in concern. "We've been so occupied with your problems that I didn't think to ask."

"Find out where they've taken him and get him back!" Erica said urgently. "He must be terribly frightened by now."

Mike put his hands on her shoulders. "Don't worry, honey, I'll take care of everything."

After he left the room, Erica continued to fret. "His whole routine is upset. Look at the time. He should have had dinner long ago."

"I imagine somebody fed him," Nancy soothed.

"I wish I could be sure."

"Nicky isn't a helpless baby," Grover said gently. "You've made him a remarkably self-reliant young man."

"I hope so." Erica sighed. "He might need to be."

Mike returned holding Nicky by the hand. With a glad cry, Erica leaped to her feet and gathered him in her arms.

"Are you all right?" she asked anxiously.

"Sure." He wriggled free. "Pete and Stan bought me a candy bar, and then this other policeman gave me a coloring book and some crayons. He had a big gun, but he wouldn't let me touch it."

"I should hope not!"

"He was nice, though. We all had dinner together, only they had coffee and I didn't. How old do I have to be until I can drink coffee?"

"See? I told you somebody would feed him," Nancy said. "What did you have for dinner, Nicky?"

"Pizza and a can of soda pop and some chocolate chip cookies that Barry's wife made. He's my friend, the policeman."

As the women groaned, Mike grinned and said, "What's so bad about that? The four food groups have to be represented in there somewhere."

While the others enjoyed this small break in the tension, Erica drew Nicky toward her. "I have a surprise for you. You're going to stay at Scott's house for a while."

His face lit up. "Oh, wow, super!"

"I want you to be a good boy and mind Nancy."

Nicky's excitement dimmed. "Aren't you coming, too?"

"Not right now. I have to take a little trip."

"I want to go with you."

"You wouldn't have much fun. I have to take care of some business matters. You'll have a much better time with Scott."

"No, I won't. I want to go with *you*," he insisted. The small boy's face clouded and he seemed on the verge of tears.

Mike hunkered down next to him. "You'd be missing a bet, pal. Steve will teach you to play golf, and when I come back I'll take you out on my boat."

"You're going, too?" Nicky wailed. The tears started to flow in earnest now.

When Erica seemed about to join him, Grover picked up the child and put him on his lap. "You love your mother, don't you, son?" When Nicky nodded wordlessly, he said, "It makes her very unhappy to see you cry. Is that what you want?"

Nicky gulped and dragged the back of his hand over his eyes. "No, but I don't want her to leave me."

"She wouldn't unless she had to. You're the most important person in the whole world to her. You can give her a kiss and make her happy, or you can cry and make her miserable. It's up to you."

Nicky looked at him doubtfully. "Will she come back?"

"A great big gorilla couldn't keep her away," Grover said, avoiding a direct answer. "Have you ever seen a gorilla?"

"I saw one at the zoo once, but it was a long time ago."

"I'm planning to take Scott to the zoo," Grover said casually. "If you decide to stay with Nancy, you can go with us."

After a moment of indecision Nicky said, "Okay, I'll stay." When he walked over and kissed his mother, there wasn't a dry eye in the room.

Nancy swallowed hard and held out her hand. "Let's go home and tell Scott our big surprise. He doesn't know you're coming."

After they left, Mike said with great feeling, "You're the greatest, Dad. What more can I say?"

Grover smiled. "Don't give me a testimonial, give me another grandchild."

Mike laughed exultantly and hugged Erica close. "That's an order I can't refuse."

Chapter Eleven

Mike was furious when he found out they wouldn't grant Erica bail. He refused to be reasonable when his father explained that she was considered a flight risk.

"That's a bunch of garbage! Can't you use some leverage, Dad?"

"I'd have to call in a lot of favors we might need for more important issues," his father explained patiently.

Mike waved his arms and shouted, "You don't call leaving Erica to rot in jail important?"

"I don't think she'll rot overnight," Grover remarked dryly.

"I'll be fine," Erica assured Mike hurriedly. "If you want to be helpful, bring me a toothbrush and a few other things from the drugstore. I'll give you a list."

"I'll do better than that. I'll go to your apartment and pack a bag for you."

"Don't bother. Nancy said she'd do it when she stops by

to get Nicky's things. You can bring it to the airport in the morning.''

Erica spent the night alone in a jail cell. It was a sobering experience. With Mike and his family around her providing support, she'd begun to think everything might work out. But the middle of a sleepless night brought grave doubts.

She was tense and drawn when an officer unlocked her cell door the next morning. It was an added shock when Pete handcuffed her.

''I'm really sorry about this,'' he said. ''I realize your family is influential—only somebody with major clout could have kept Nicky off that plane—but we have to go by the book.''

''It would mean our badges if we didn't,'' Stan agreed. ''The rules say we have to cuff you. For what it's worth, Mrs. Hardwick, I wish we could make it easier for you.''

''You can call me Erica. I never liked the name Hardwick.'' She tried to smile. These men had been very kind to Nicky.

Mike's short fuse ignited all over again when they met at the airport and he saw the handcuffs. ''This is too much! Why are you treating her like a common criminal?'' he demanded.

''It's standard procedure, Mr. Smith,'' Stan answered.

''I don't give a damn what you call it. Take them off!''

''Don't give us trouble, sir.''

The three men faced each other grimly, all tall, lean and muscular. But Mike was outnumbered.

''Don't make a scene,'' Erica pleaded, glancing around. A few onlookers were staring at them curiously. ''They're just doing their job.''

''Do they need handcuffs to do it?'' Mike's hands balled into fists as he swung back to the marshals. ''What's the problem, are you afraid she'll overpower you without them?''

''No, sir, but she might be able to outrun us,'' Pete said stoically. ''This is an airport. Somebody with a private plane could easily help her to escape. We'll take off the cuffs when we get on the plane.''

''How do you know I won't slip her a parachute?'' Mike asked sarcastically.

Nancy grabbed his arm. ''Stop acting like a dork. Come on, they're loading the plane.''

Mike had wanted to buy first-class seats for all of them, but the marshals declined. So Mike and Nancy changed to tourist class. Fortunately the plane wasn't crowded and they were able to move to seats directly in back of Erica and her escorts.

A tense moment ensued when the marshals wouldn't let Erica sit with the Smiths.

''Proper procedure again?'' Mike drawled.

''Exactly. Of course she's free to talk to the other passengers if she chooses,'' Pete added.

''That's good, because we have to map out our strategy.'' Nancy leaned over Erica's seat. ''I plan to try to have the custody case thrown out on grounds that the Hardwicks conspired with that toad Derek to deny you rightful custody as Nicky's mother. That would make the kidnapping charge invalid. Well, iffy anyway. At least it gives us room for debate. We'll worry about the unlawful flight part later.''

''I'll arrange for bail,'' Mike said. ''They'll grant it, won't they?''

''It's up to the judge, but I don't anticipate any trouble. Dad's phone calls last night will pay off. What we have to worry about is proving Derek was paid by the Hardwicks to frame Erica.''

''If he lies on the stand he's committing perjury,'' Mike said.

Nancy shrugged. "He wouldn't be the first one. It's his word against hers."

Mike's jaw squared. "Maybe I can persuade him to tell the truth. I'd like ten minutes alone with him anyway."

"That's all I need, a battered witness. Do me a favor and don't help me."

"What if we offered him money?" Mike suggested.

Nancy shook her head. "It's too risky. The guy's a loose cannon. It would be just like him to go to the Hardwicks and start a bidding war."

"I don't care what it costs."

"The point is, it might backfire on us. The Hardwicks could go to the district attorney and accuse us of doing what *they* did, suborning perjury. What we really need is something to tie them all together. Even if we can prove Derek drugged Erica and took nude photos of her, that doesn't incriminate the Hardwicks. They can admit they bought the pictures, but only to destroy them to protect their late son's memory."

"Nobody who knew them or their delinquent son would believe a phony story like that," Mike said scornfully.

"A judge might. He doesn't know them."

"It's hopeless, isn't it?" Erica groaned.

"Not at all. I'm just playing the devil's advocate. A good attorney always anticipates the opposition's strategy. Now we have to figure out our own. Tell me everything you know about this Derek jerk. Has he ever been in trouble with the law?"

"Not that I know of," Erica said. "He's a pretty heavy drinker. I wouldn't be surprised if he had some drunk driving arrests, but I doubt if he ever got more than a fine and community service."

"You said he's always short of money. Doesn't he work?"

"He sells real estate, which isn't too lucrative these days. And during dinner that night he told me he'd been divorced twice and both of his wives took him to the cleaners."

"A guy like that deserves more than cleaning," Mike said grimly. "He needs fumigating."

Nancy gave him a quelling look. "Okay, we can prove motive. Now for the method. Even in this age of the disposable camera, many people have camera equipment that lets them take delayed action pictures. Did Derek mention any special interest in photography? That might be incriminating. Before we go after his connection to the Hardwicks, we have to nail him for his part in the scheme."

"He showed me a photo album," Erica said. "That's why I went to his apartment. But they were just ordinary snapshots."

Mike looked thoughtful. "Even if he was an expert photographer it wouldn't prove anything. It's a popular hobby. But not many people keep knockout drops handy."

"That's right!" Nancy exclaimed.

"Derek thought he might need them because he knew I wasn't a big drinker," Erica said excitedly. "Jordan and his crowd were always making fun of me. After one or two drinks I switched to ginger ale while they all got smashed."

"That solves the puzzle of why Derek didn't just keep pouring drinks into Erica until she passed out," Mike said.

"We know what happened, but how do we prove it?" Nancy asked. "Derek isn't about to admit it."

"What do you bet he bragged about it to his friends?" Mike said bitterly.

"That doesn't help us even if we could locate one," Nancy said. "It would be inadmissable as hearsay."

They all fell silent, their enthusiasm dampened. They'd practically forgotten the two marshals who had been listening with covert interest.

"Have you seen those new recording devices, Pete?" Stan asked unexpectedly. "They're so small a woman can hide one in a flower on her lapel."

"Yeah, I heard about a woman who got this guy to admit he'd committed a criminal act, because he thought she could never prove it," Pete said.

The other three stared at them with dawning excitement. "It's certainly worth a try!" Nancy said. "If Erica goes to see Derek alone, he might tell her the whole story."

"Why would he?" Erica asked, her expression sobering.

"Who knows? Maybe to clear his conscience."

Erica laughed scornfully. "If he had one, would he have done such a thing?"

"She's right," Mike said. "Creeps like that don't give anything away. We have to provide an incentive. Something besides money, but what?"

"We'll find one," Nancy said confidently. "You guys are a lifesaver," she told the marshals.

"Hey, we were just shooting the breeze," Pete said.

"Yeah, don't quote us," Stan warned.

"Not to worry, we won't," Nancy promised. "Okay, let's brainstorm," she told the others.

By the time the plane touched down in New York, all the details had been worked out.

Nancy went with Erica and the marshals, while Mike was persuaded, over his vigorous objections, to go and book three hotel rooms. He didn't want to leave Erica for any reason.

She was glad he wasn't with her when they arrived at the police station. The Hardwicks had been informed of her return, and they were waiting to take charge of Nicky. A nasty scene ensued after they discovered he wasn't with her.

"Where is my grandson?" Joe Hardwick demanded. "You'd better not try any delaying tactics. I left an important meeting to come down here."

"I hope they put you in prison for a good long time!" Miriam's thin mouth was compressed. "We've spent a fortune trying to track you down."

"Nicky is fine, thank you," Erica said mockingly.

"Who?" Miriam looked at her blankly.

Joe's face got very red. "Did you dare to change my grandson's name?"

"It was the name I wanted to give him when he was born," Erica replied steadily. She realized they couldn't intimidate her any longer, no matter what they did to her.

"Was Nicky the name of one of the men you carried on with behind my son's back?" Joe sneered.

When Erica turned away rather than continue the ugly dialogue, he grabbed her arm and yanked her back. "Don't you dare walk away from me, you little tramp."

Nancy had had enough. "Take your hands off her," she said sharply.

"Stay out of this," he ordered. "It's none of your business. Who the hell are you, anyway?"

"I'm her attorney, and I'm telling you to let her go."

"A lawyer won't do her any good. She's going to prison like the common thief she is."

"When did you decide to add theft to your charges?" Nancy drawled.

"She stole our property!" Miriam shrilled. "What would *you* call it?"

Nancy stared at them in amazement mixed with revulsion. "If I ever thought Erica was exaggerating, I apologize. She didn't begin to describe how warped and offensive you are. Come on, Erica, let's go someplace where the air is cleaner."

Mike was waiting anxiously for them at the hotel. He relaxed when he saw Erica. "I was afraid there might be a problem about the bail."

"No, Dad came through again. Everything went smoothly," Nancy said. She and Erica had agreed not to tell him about the encounter with the Hardwicks.

"I got three rooms like you told me to, but I don't know why," Mike said. "You're crazy if you think I intend to let Erica out of my sight."

"Just be sure to rumple your bed so it looks like it's been slept in," Nancy said. "We don't want to give the Hardwicks any more reason to attack her reputation."

Mike scowled. "You act as if there's something wrong with our relationship."

"*I* don't think so, but they're the kind of people who believe sex is something little boys snicker over, and decent women shouldn't enjoy." She held out a hand for her key. "Let's get cleaned up and go out to dinner. We can review our plan again to be sure there aren't any slipups."

It was still early in Honolulu, but Erica was emotionally drained by the time they returned to the hotel.

"Get into bed, sweetheart." Mike smoothed her hair tenderly. "I want to check on a couple of things with Nancy. I'll be back in a little while."

Erica decided to take a bath first, hoping it would relax her. Seeing the Hardwicks again had brought back a lot of unhappy memories. Why hadn't she left Jordan while she was still pregnant? Then none of this would have happened.

But then she wouldn't have met Mike. Erica closed her eyes and thought about the first time they'd made love. She'd never known she was capable of such pleasure. Mike had been so understanding, so caring. He taught her that sex could be beautiful when two people were in love. It was such a joy to stroke his splendid body and watch it swell with passion.

Mike's deep voice made her open her eyes. "It's good to see you smile again. You must have been thinking nice thoughts."

"I was." She held out her arms to him.

He lifted her out of the tub and wrapped her in a towel while he dropped kisses all over her face, her neck, her shoulders. When she removed the towel and pressed closely against him, his body sprang to instant life.

"How is it possible to love someone this much?" he groaned.

"I've never loved anyone else," she whispered. "I never will."

After hugging her convulsively, Mike lifted her in his arms and carried her to the bed, kissing her with equal parts of passion and tenderness.

There was a special quality to their lovemaking that night, an unspoken understanding that the unthinkable could happen and they might be separated. Mike seemed to be storing up memories. He caressed her lingeringly, tracing the shape of her breasts, stroking the softness of her inner thighs.

Erica did the same to him. If it was to be the last time, she needed to feel the shape and firmness of his lean body. Her hands wandered restlessly over the triangle of his torso, then moved lower. When she cradled him in her palms, Mike uttered a hoarse cry and slid her body beneath his.

Erica raised her hips eagerly to receive him, shuddering with ecstasy as he filled her completely. They were lost in their own magic world, sharing the fiery, escalating rapture of love.

When it was over they relaxed contentedly in each other's arms. Finally Erica stirred reluctantly.

"I'd like to ask a favor of you, Mike."

"You don't have to ask, it's yours."

She tried to smile. "You shouldn't commit yourself until you hear what it is."

"It doesn't matter. I'm committed to you for a lifetime."

"I hope so," she said soberly. "But if it doesn't work out, will you make sure the Hardwicks don't get Nicky? I've heard of court cases dragging on for years. Maybe you could hold them off until I get out of prison." She sat up in bed, her body tense once more. "I don't know how long it might take, and I'll be in a worse position than ever to win custody, but at least he won't be so helpless by then."

Mike drew her back into his arms. "You're not going anywhere except back to Hawaii as my bride."

"But if the case goes against me . . ."

He realized she needed assurance in words. "Then I'll take care of Nicky, we all will. And I'll wait for you, my love, no matter how long it takes."

Erica's taut body relaxed as Mike kissed her with great feeling.

Nancy got up before them and went out to do some shopping. Erica and Mike were having breakfast in the room when she knocked on the door.

"Wait until you see the recording gizmo I bought," Nancy said. "It's no bigger than a dime. The man also sold me a costume jewelry pin to fit over the thing. It's designed to hide the device while allowing the sound to get through."

They all examined the tiny recording mechanism and marveled at how clever it was. Erica was less complimentary about the pin. It was a large, garish piece made of fake gold and studded with imitation precious stones, emeralds, rubies and sapphires. Not at all up to Nancy's usually impeccable taste.

When she commented on the fact, Nancy laughed. "It will go with your outfit."

"Hardly. You only packed tailored clothes for me, things I can wear to court."

"At the time, I didn't think anything else would be called for. While I was out today I bought you an outfit that's less . . . severe, shall we say?"

Erica was puzzled by the mischievous look on her face. The reason for it became clear when she opened the packages. They held a skinny, black turtleneck sweater and a very short, black leather skirt.

"You've got to be kidding!" she exclaimed. "I've never worn anything like this."

"The old Erica wouldn't have, but you've changed, remember? Derek has to believe you've become hardened and cynical."

"Yes, I suppose you're right."

"The pin is just the kind of tacky accessory someone would wear with an outfit like that. It won't seem out of place. When he catches a glimpse of you in this sweater, Derek won't be looking at a pin, anyway, which is the general idea."

Mike frowned. "I scarcely think all this is necessary."

"Don't go getting macho on us now," Nancy said. "Erica can take care of herself. The next thing is to get in touch with Derek. Let's look in the phone book."

Mike glanced at his watch. "It's almost ten o'clock. He'd be at work by now."

"Not necessarily," Erica said. "Derek was never very gung ho about working. That's probably why he chose real estate, because the hours are flexible. If we can find him in the book, I'll try him at home."

"Here it is!" Nancy said triumphantly. "Derek J. Cogswell—*J* for *jerk*, no doubt. There can't be two guys with that name. He lives on West Seventh Street, that's in the Village, I think."

Erica dialed the telephone and waited, her fingers clamped rigidly around the receiver. Nicky's entire future depended on this call. She had to overcome her revulsion and put on the act of her life. But the phone rang on and on, and nobody answered.

She was about to hang up when Derek said in a sleep-thickened voice, "Yeah, who is it?"

"You'll never guess," Erica replied archly. She looked at the others, wrinkling her nose in disgust.

"It's too early in the morning to play games," he growled.

"Oh, Derek, you'll never change." She laughed merrily. "It's ten o'clock and you're still in bed—alone, I hope. I didn't catch you at a bad time, did I?"

"Who the hell is this?"

"It's Caroline, Caroline Hardwick."

After a pause he said, "I never expected to hear from *you* again. The last I heard, the police were looking for you.

Why did you come back?'' His voice was alert now and wary.

"I have some business to take care of.''

"Isn't that rather dangerous? Or did you settle things with the Hardwicks?''

"No, but I intend to. That's what I want to talk to you about. Can we meet somewhere for a drink?''

"Well, I . . . I'm afraid I'm pretty busy right now.''

"You're still in bed,'' she pointed out.

"Yes, but I . . . uh . . . I have an appointment. I overslept and now I'm late.''

"I understand, but I do need to see you,'' she said firmly.

He hesitated. "I know how you must feel about me, but what's done is done.''

"Don't worry, I'm not harboring a grudge, Derek. I'll admit I was pretty bitter in the beginning, but I've had a long time to think about it. I don't blame you anymore.''

"That's hard to believe,'' he answered, with obvious skepticism.

"I know. I really hated you at first, until I started to think clearly and realized the Hardwicks victimized you, too.''

"They *what?*'' He was clearly caught off base. "How do you figure that?''

"It's a long story, and you're in a hurry. Meet me for a drink and I'll tell you all about it.''

"To be perfectly honest, Caroline, I'd rather not. I have to admit I'm not proud of what happened, but it won't help anybody to rehash the whole thing.''

Her eyes narrowed in anger, but she didn't allow it to show in her voice. "That's not what I want to talk about. You're right about burying the past. What I'm interested in now is the future.''

"What does that have to do with me?'' His voice hardened. "If you think I owe you something, you're trying to shake down the wrong guy. I'm just getting by, myself.''

"Is that supposed to surprise me?'' she asked lightly. "You've been short of money ever since I met you.''

"Can I help it if I have champagne tastes and a beer wallet?" He chuckled, relaxing his guard momentarily.

"What if I could show you how to make so much money you could bathe in champagne?"

"Why would you do a thing like that for me?" His wariness was back.

"Look, I asked you a question. If you're not interested we'll forget the whole thing." Erica held her breath.

After a moment's silence he said, "I didn't say I wasn't interested. It just seems kind of funny that you'd want to do me a favor."

"It isn't pure altruism. I expect to benefit, too. There's enough money in it for both of us."

"What's the deal? I'm not interested in anything illegal." He laughed self-consciously. "I'm too nervous to rob banks."

"You won't have to break a single law," she assured him.

"Okay, what's the story? I'm listening."

"Meet me later and I'll tell you." When he didn't answer immediately, Erica said dryly, "You can pick the place, somewhere public where you'll feel safe."

"That wasn't why I hesitated," he said defensively. "I was just trying to... to figure out when I'll be through with my appointments. Let's see. How about seven o'clock at the Red Lion? It's a bar on Ninth Street."

"Seven o'clock is fine. I'll be there."

Nancy was exuberant when Erica hung up. "You were great! He bit and you played him like a giant swordfish."

"Don't celebrate too soon. He doesn't trust me. The only reason Derek agreed to meet me was the siren song of cash."

"So the plan is working," Nancy said.

"We've only won the first round," Erica warned. "He might freak when I tell him where I intend to get the money."

"Not if you offer to share it with him," Mike said contemptuously. "I still think it would be faster to beat the truth out of him."

"We've been through all that," Nancy said impatiently. "Take Erica out for a nice long lunch somewhere. She needs to relax. Afterward you might drop in at the Whitney Museum. I read in the paper this morning that they're having a retrospective of American Impressionists."

"That sounds interesting." Erica tried to sound enthusiastic. Her nerves were indeed tied in knots. "Where shall we have lunch?"

"You and Mike can decide that," Nancy said. "I'm going to have my hair done and then work on my brief for the hearing tomorrow."

That day was the longest one of Erica's life, although Mike did his best to make it easier. He took her to lunch at one of the most exclusive restaurants in the city, then to the museum and for a stroll along Madison Avenue afterward, where they browsed through the elegant shops. He wanted to buy her everything she even glanced at, but Erica wasn't really focusing on the expensive clothes and jewelry. Her mind was on the crucial meeting that lay ahead.

Finally Mike stopped trying to make light conversation. He just held her hand tightly, giving her silent moral support.

The minutes and hours seemed to inch by, but finally it was time to go. Mike and Nancy rode in the cab with her. When they got to the bar he insisted on going inside and getting a table nearby, in case something went wrong. And this time Nancy agreed with him. Erica assured them she could handle Derek, but it made her feel better to know they were there.

Mike objected vigorously when she and Nancy discussed ways to induce Derek to take her to his apartment. They were both afraid the noise in the bar might interfere with the quality of the tape. They finally calmed Mike down by pointing out that Derek's apartment was only a couple of blocks from the bar. If Erica persuaded him to take her there, they could follow her and wait outside in case they were needed.

The argument with Mike distracted Erica momentarily, but her nerves tightened when she walked into the bar alone. She expected to get stares because of her sexy attire, and she did. But they were looks of admiration; hers wasn't the only far-out getup in the place.

A glance around the crowded room brought a lot of offers of a drink, but not from Derek. He wasn't there. Erica found an empty table and sat down, setting her chin grimly. She knew where he lived, and if necessary, she'd camp in front of his door until he agreed to see her.

After keeping her waiting for fifteen minutes, Derek finally appeared. At first he didn't recognize her. After glancing around the room without locating her, he looked relieved. When Erica raised her arm and called to him, he did a double take.

"I never would have known you." He slid into the chair across from her. "You didn't tell me you dyed your hair."

"I guess I forgot. It's been this way for a long time."

"Well, here we are." His reluctance at being there was evident, although he did show male interest when his gaze traveled over her breasts, prominently outlined by the tight sweater. "Long time no see."

It was the kind of trite remark she might have expected from him. "You haven't changed, Derek." She concealed her irony under a pleasant smile. "You still look great."

"You do, too." His eyes took another circuit. "But you've changed. You look different . . . more with it."

Erica laughed gaily. "I really was a drag in the old days, wasn't I?"

"I didn't mean it that way," he protested.

"It's all right, I admit it. I was a real wet blanket, always nagging at Jordan to stop drinking so much, and wanting to go home just when the party was getting good. I don't know how all of you put up with me."

"Well, you were pretty young then." He slanted a glance at her. "Where have you been all this time?"

"I went to Hawaii. You'd like it, it's a real swinging place."

"You had a child," Derek said hesitantly. "It must be pretty big by now."

He didn't even remember if Nicky was a boy or a girl, Erica thought bitterly. How could you trash somebody's life and just forget all about them? She fought to keep her smile from slipping. "Yes, he's growing like a weed," she said brightly.

"Is he here in New York with you?"

"No way! I'm not that stupid. The Hardwicks would just love to get their hands on him."

He slanted a glance at her. "They were looking for you, too. I heard there was a warrant out for your arrest. Isn't it dangerous for you to be here?"

"No problem. I'm not a naive little college girl anymore. I have a hotshot attorney working on my side. It won't be a slam dunk for the Hardwicks this time."

"Well, uh, that's good." Derek was clearly uncomfortable as he struggled for an apology of sorts. "I was really sorry you got into so much trouble. I didn't think you'd do anything crazy like bolting with the kid."

Erica fought back her rising rage. "It seemed like a good idea at the time," she answered.

Derek's eyes narrowed suspiciously. "You're damned casual about the whole thing. If it was me, I'd be pretty steamed."

"What's the point?" She shrugged. "Stuff happens."

"Maybe, but you've been on the run all this time and you don't blame anybody for it?" he persisted. "You're more forgiving than *I'd* be."

"I didn't say I don't blame anybody. I have every intention of getting even with the Hardwicks. They're evil people. They find everybody's weakness and then use it against them. With me it was my youth and inexperience. They intimidated me until I couldn't fight back. With you it was your lack of money. The Hardwicks knew you were being squeezed from all sides. They exploited your need for their own disgraceful ends." Erica was afraid he wouldn't swallow such a pitiful excuse, but her fears were groundless.

Derek was only too happy to justify himself. "That's right!" he said eagerly. "I never would have gone along with them if I wasn't desperate."

"You should want to get even, too."

His caution returned. "Yeah, well, like you say, what's the point?"

"Satisfaction, for one thing—plus about a hundred thousand dollars or more."

Derek reacted initially with excitement. It was replaced by prudence. "If you're talking about blackmail, count me out. I told you, I'm not interested in anything illegal. You know the Hardwicks. It would be my word against theirs. They'd play hardball, and I'd be the one who ended up in trouble."

"I'm not talking about blackmail." Erica leaned forward and lowered her voice. "My scheme is going to pay off in one great big beautiful lump sum."

"Yeah? How?"

She glanced around furtively at the tables near them. "I don't want to advertise my plan. This place is awfully public. Why don't we go someplace quieter and I'll run it by you?"

"Nobody's paying any attention to us. You can tell me here."

"You obviously don't trust me, which is kind of ironic. After everything that happened, I'm willing to take a chance on *you*." Erica decided to gamble. "Maybe it's a sign that I should forget the whole thing. If you're not interested, somebody else will be."

As she gathered up her purse, Derek said, "No, wait! My apartment is only a couple of blocks from here. We can go there."

Erica relaxed, but only momentarily. As they walked out of the bar, Mike followed close behind. She could feel his glowering stare burning into Derek like a laser beam. If only Nancy could keep him in check!

Erica breathed a sigh of relief when they were inside Derek's apartment. She refused a drink, then made a hasty explanation when he raised an eyebrow. Her new persona would have accepted.

"I'll have a drink afterward to celebrate. Right now I want a clear mind so I don't forget anything."

"Okay, you have my full attention." He smiled. "I find any discussion of money fascinating. What do I have to do to earn this bonanza?"

"Two fairly simple things—find out when the Hardwicks' housekeeper goes on her day off, and ask Joe and Miriam out to dinner on that night."

Derek looked at her in surprise. "That sounds like you intend to rob the house."

"Joe has a lot of cash stashed in his safe in the den, perhaps as much as a quarter of a million dollars. Jordan told me his father keeps two sets of books at the mill. He's been skimming money and hiding it from the I.R.S. for years. I figure after everything the Hardwicks put me through, I deserve that money. Besides, it's the only way I can really hurt them. Money is their god."

"If you want revenge, why don't you just turn him in? Doesn't the Internal Revenue Service pay a reward?"

"Not two hundred thousand dollars."

Derek was torn between greed and fear. He licked his dry lips. "You don't know that he keeps that much in the safe."

"It could be even more. Where else is he going to put it?"

Derek took a deep breath and jammed his hands into his pockets. "This is crazy! I'm not going to be part of a robbery."

"I don't want you to. You don't have the nerves for it," she said, unable to hide completely the contempt she felt. "*I'll* clean out the safe."

"Then what do you need me for?"

"To get the Hardwicks out of the way, obviously. I could hang around and watch them go out, but that's too chancy. I need somebody who will make sure they don't come back unexpectedly."

Derek nodded. "That makes sense. When are you planning to pull this off?"

"First I have to know if you're with me or not. I wasn't born in a pumpkin patch. You'll get the details when I'm sure you won't run straight to the Hardwicks with them."

"After the way they used me? You said so, yourself."

Erica pretended to be in a quandary. "To tell you the truth, Derek, I don't really trust you. I have to decide whether you have the guts to go for the gold, or whether you'll turn chicken and take the piddling reward the Hardwicks might give you for ratting on me."

"That wouldn't be good business—and I'm never stupid when it comes to money. Unless you really expect me to do more than you're letting on," he added prudently.

"No, I told you what your job is. Let me know when the housekeeper will be off and we'll firm up the details. Your part is a piece of cake. I'll be long gone by the time you bring the Hardwicks home, and you'll be in the clear since you were with them all night."

"How are you going to get into the safe? An explosion would alert the neighbors. They'd be sure to call the police."

"Not to worry, I have the combination. I got it from Jordan. Joe would have no reason to change it, since they don't know I have the combination," she said, anticipating his next question.

"How do you plan to get into the house?"

"I still have my front door key. The Hardwicks would never expect me to come back to that house willingly," Erica said with bitter mockery. "So, again, they'd see no need to change the lock."

Derek examined the plan for flaws. He found only one. "Once you get the money, what's to stop you from getting on a plane with the whole score? Why would you split it with me?"

"Not by choice, believe me! Frankly you don't deserve half for the minuscule amount of effort you'll be contributing. But I know that's what you'd hold out for, and I don't have time to look around for somebody else. Just in case my lawyer can't get the indictment against me dismissed, I want to be able to leave town at a moment's notice. And I'll need ready cash to swing it. I have no intention of going to prison."

"That doesn't answer my question. How do I know I'll get my cut?"

They had anticipated his distrust. Erica reluctantly took her engagement ring out of her purse. The huge diamond glittered, even in the subdued indoor lighting.

"This is about equal to your share. I'll leave it with you for good faith."

Derek's eyes widened. "Is that thing real?"

"Very real, but I don't expect you to take my word for it," she said dryly. "You can have it appraised before you go through with your part of the bargain."

"This wouldn't be some kind of setup, would it?" he asked slowly. "I mean, if the ring is hot and I took it to be appraised, I could be arrested. Having a rock like this in my possession would get me a charge of grand larceny."

"That does it!" Erica snatched the ring back. "I should have known better than to come to you in the first place. There are plenty of people who will be glad to collect a bundle for one lousy night's work."

"Don't go ballistic on me. I didn't say I wouldn't do it. I was just looking at all the angles."

"Fine! Try spending those angles on your next Armani suit." She started for the door.

He caught her arm. "Don't be that way, Caroline. You need me. Where are you going to find somebody else who knows the Hardwicks well enough to ask them out to dinner?"

She pretended to hesitate. "You have a point there."

"You bet I do! Come on, let's have a drink to celebrate our new partnership."

"Are you sure?" she insisted, because it might look suspicious if she gave in too easily. "I don't want somebody who's going to wimp out on me at the last minute. There's too much money involved."

"You just said the magic word. I'm an entirely different man when money is involved."

"I know." He looked at her sharply, but she was smiling. "How about that drink? I really need one."

"I must tell you I'm surprised at the way this meeting turned out," Derek remarked as he poured Scotch into two glasses and added ice cubes. "I was braced for a lot of angry recriminations. Frankly, I was dreading it."

"I've learned not to dwell on the past," she said lightly. "There's only one thing that's nagged at me all these years. What the devil did you put in my drink that night in your apartment? I had the grandfather of all headaches the next day."

He laughed. "Sorry about that."

"What was it?" she persisted. "I know a few people I'd like to give it to."

"I don't know the name. They were knockout drops. A bartender friend of mind gave them to me. He said just a couple would do the trick, but I might have overdone it."

"I'll say! I looked really stupid in those photographs you took of me when I was out cold."

"I thought you looked fantastic." Derek's expression changed as his eyes traveled over her, starting at her firm breasts and continuing down her long legs. "I always knew you had a great body, but I didn't realize *how* great until I saw you nude."

She gave him a sultry look from under lowered lashes. "You're a very experienced man. A lot of men are good at *un*dressing a woman, but I'll bet not a lot of them know how to put her clothes back on. Thanks for dressing me before you took me home."

"It wasn't easy." He chuckled. "Getting your panty hose off was a snap. Putting them back on again was the hard part."

"I'm sure the Hardwicks wouldn't have cared if you'd brought me home naked. I've always wondered which one of them thought up that little scheme to discredit me. Was it Joe or Miriam?"

"It was Joe's idea." Derek laughed coarsely. "He might act like a prude, but deep down he's a dirty old man. You should have seen his face when I showed him those pictures of you. I'll bet he kept some copies for himself—and not for evidence."

"You both must have gotten a big laugh out of it," Eric said evenly.

Derek's eyes shifted. "Yes, well, like you say, that's all in the past. We're partners now. Drink up and I'll make you another drink. This is a celebration."

"I wouldn't buy any paper hats and noisemakers yet." She set her drink down and started for the door.

He was instantly on the alert. "What do you mean?"

"It's payback time, Derek. You just admitted to several different crimes. If there's any justice in this world, you're going to spend some time in jail."

"You can't prove anything! It's my word against yours and a judge has already ruled against you."

"That was because he didn't have all the evidence. This time it's going to be different."

His eyes narrowed to mere slits. "You're wired, aren't you?" He swore obscenely. "I should have known."

As he moved in front of the door, Erica regretted indulging herself. The desire to confront him had been overwhelming, but Derek mustn't get his hands on the tape.

Thinking quickly, she ran to the window and knocked on the pane to get Mike's attention. Derek grabbed her arm and jerked her back before she could tell if Mike had seen her.

Derek's face was red with fury as he tore at her clothes while calling her every foul name he could think of. Erica fought back fiercely, praying that someone would come before it was too late.

Her prayers were answered by Mike, pounding furiously on the door. When he broke it open, Derek turned like a cornered animal. "Who the hell are *you?*" he snarled.

Mike didn't bother to answer. He decked Derek with one mighty punch. But after Derek went down in a heap, Mike hauled him to his feet and prepared to pound him to a pulp. It took the combined efforts of Erica and Nancy to stop him.

"Did you get everything on tape?" Nancy asked Erica.

"Every disgusting detail," Erica answered with satisfaction.

"Nice going! Now let's get out of here before somebody sends for the police. We'll let the judge do that after he hears the evidence."

When they got outside, Nancy urged Mike to take Erica back to the hotel. "She's been through enough today. Take care of her."

"I'm okay," Erica said. "Aren't you coming with us?"

"You two don't need me around." Nancy laughed. "I thought I'd get in touch with somebody I knew in law school."

Mike was instantly alert. "Are you anticipating trouble getting the charges against Erica dismissed?"

"Don't worry, I wish all of my cases were this rock solid." Nancy got into a cab that had pulled up to the curb. Mike hailed a second taxi.

As Mike and Erica drove through the crowded streets, Erica said, "I can't believe I'm finally free."

Mike squeezed her hand tightly. "I'll never forgive them for putting you in a cell."

"That part was over quickly. I meant free after all the years of hiding and being afraid they'd find me and take Nicky away."

"Nobody's ever going to hurt you again," he vowed.

"Oh, Mike, what would I have done without you?"

"I'm grateful I was there for you, but you'd have thought of something, my love." He kissed her tenderly, heedless of the cabbie watching in the rearview mirror. "You're a very resourceful woman."

Erica smiled mistily. "A mother will do anything for love of her child."

"You never gave me an answer when we talked about it, but I hope you'll let me adopt Nicky after we're married. I couldn't love him any more if he was my real son."

"He'll be so happy. Nicky knew you'd make a perfect father the first night you two met."

"He showed keener perception than his mother," Mike teased. "You put me through hell before I could convince you."

"It wasn't by choice." Erica gazed at him with pure love in her eyes. "But I'll spend the rest of my life making it up to you."

"It won't take that long. All you have to do is marry me, sweetheart."

The wedding was beautiful. All the society columnists commented on how gorgeous the bridal gown was, how happy the loving couple looked, how adorable the bride's son was as he walked down the aisle carrying the ring on a satin cushion. All the columnists except Sally Coleman. She wasn't invited to the most important social event of the year.

When the festivities were finally over, Erica and Mike spent their wedding night at his house—technically, her house. Mike gave it to her for a wedding present. Erica didn't want to go away on a honeymoon. As she explained to him, everything she'd ever wanted was right here in Honolulu.

It was quiet in the den after the noise and gaiety at the Smith estate. They drank a final toast and talked contentedly about the wedding.

"I don't know how your mother managed to put on such a glorious affair in so short a time," Erica marveled.

Mike chuckled. "I told her that's all the time she had. After the cliff-hanger we went through in New York, I wasn't taking any chances on something else delaying us."

"Nancy was wonderful. When she played that tape, the Hardwicks knew it was all over. I wonder if the judge will prosecute them and Derek."

"It wasn't worth waiting around to find out." Mike's hard expression softened. "Did I tell you how exquisite you look tonight?"

Erica gently smoothed the skirt of her pale pink satin-and-lace wedding gown. "It's so beautiful, I hate to take it off."

He linked his arms around her waist and dipped his head to kiss the valley between her breasts. "Then I guess we can't go to bed," he murmured.

She smiled radiantly. "I said I was reluctant, I didn't say I was unreasonable."

He framed her face in his palms and gazed at her in a kind of wonder. "Do you know how much I love you?"

"You can mention it now and then during the next fifty years," she whispered.

"I intend to show you—starting right now."

Mike gathered Erica into his arms for a stirring kiss that expressed more than words, their deep and lasting love for each other.

* * * * *

Silhouette®

SPECIAL EDITION™

COMING NEXT MONTH

#1021 MOLLY DARLING—Laurie Paige
That's My Baby!
Rancher Sam Frazier needed a mommy for his little Lass—and a wife in the bargain. He proposed a marriage of convenience to Molly Clelland—but he never dreamed he'd long to call the instant mother his Molly darling....

#1022 THE FALL OF SHANE MACKADE—Nora Roberts
The MacKade Brothers
Footloose and fancy-free, Shane MacKade had a reputation as a ladies' man to uphold, and he took his job seriously. Who would have thought a brainy beauty like Dr. Rebecca Knight would cause this irrepressible bachelor to take the fall...?

#1023 EXPECTING: BABY—Jennifer Mikels
An urgent knock at the door introduced Rick Sloan to his neighbor—Mara Vincetti, who was about to give birth. Next thing Rick Sloan knew he was a father figure for the new single mom and her baby!

#1024 A BRIDE FOR LUKE—Trisha Alexander
Three Brides and a Baby
When sister-of-the-bride Clem Bennelli met brother-of-the-groom Luke Taylor, it was a case of opposites attract. They agreed theirs would be a passionate, no-strings-attached relationship—but neither one expected to want much, much more....

#1025 THE FATHER OF HER CHILD—Joan Elliott Pickart
The Baby Bet
Honorary MacAllister family member Ted Sharpe was carefree and single. But secretly he yearned to be a husband and a father. And when the very pregnant divorcée Hannah Johnson moved in next door—he lost his heart, but found his dreams.

#1026 A WILL AND A WEDDING—Judith Yates
Commitment and marriage were two words Amy Riordan never believed would apply to her. After meeting similarly minded Paul Hanley, however, she began to think otherwise—and now the word "wedding" was definitely in her future!

This April, find out how three unsuspecting couples find themselves caught in the

The Parent Trap

Sometimes love is a package deal....

Three complete stories by some of your favorite authors—all in one special collection!

DONOVAN'S PROMISE by Dallas Schulze
MILLION DOLLAR BABY by Lisa Jackson
HIS CHARIOT AWAITS by Kasey Michaels

Available this April wherever books are sold.

SREQ496

Silhouette

SPECIAL EDITION™

That's My Baby!

"I've been baby-sitting sweet little Lass,

but I'd never let on that I loved her rugged rancher daddy as much as I do her. Imagine my surprise when Sam Frazier proposed! Perhaps this is a marriage of convenience for now, but I can be a real mother to Lass—and maybe one day soon, my dream will come true and I'll hear my husband lovingly whisper my name...."

MOLLY DARLING
by
Laurie Paige
(SE #1021)

In April, Silhouette Special Edition brings you

THAT'S MY BABY!

Sometimes bringing up baby can bring surprises... and showers of love.

TMB496

Yo amo novelas con corazón!

Starting this March, Harlequin opens up to a whole new world of readers with two new romance lines in SPANISH!

Harlequin Deseo
* passionate, sensual and exciting stories

Harlequin Bianca
* romances that are fun, fresh and very contemporary

With four titles a month, each line will offer the same wonderfully romantic stories that you've come to love—now available in Spanish.

Look for them at selected retail outlets.

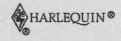

HARLEQUIN®